MW01714138

The Housetrap Chronicles Omnibus: Volume 4

R. J. Hore

CHAMPAGNE BOOK GROUP

The Housetrap Chronicles Omnibus: Volume 4

This is a work of fiction. The characters, incidents and dialogues in this book are of the author's imagination and are not to be construed as real. Any resemblance to actual events or persons, living or dead, is completely coincidental.

Published by Champagne Book Group
4736 Royal Avenue PMB 109155, Eugene OR 97402
U.S.A.

~ * ~

First Edition

ISBN: 978-1-77155-367-4

© 2022 R. J. Hore All rights reserved.

Cover Art by Robyn Hart

Champagne Book Group supports copyright which encourages creativity and diverse voices, creates a rich culture, and promotes free speech. Thank you for complying by not distributing this book via any means without the permission of the publisher. Your purchase or use of an authorized edition supports the author's rights and hard work and allows Champagne Book Group to continue to bring readers fiction at its finest.

www.champagnebooks.com

Index

Page #	Title
7	*The Road to Hell is Paved with Parsnips*
87	*'Twas the Week Before the Night*

The Housetrap Chronicles
Book 10

Chapter One

I scowled at the brown paper bag balanced on my desk with some suspicion. "Bertha, come in here immediately. What is the meaning of this?"

I had a noon appointment scheduled with an important prospective client and asked my secretary to send out for a smoked meat sandwich lunch from the Dwarf Deli down the street to hold me until after the meeting. The neatly-lettered bag before me was labeled Merry Mary's Contrarian Comforts.

Bertha Wildwater, large gold hoop earrings dangling, swept in through the inner office door and began to unfasten the bag. "I thought it was time to expand your narrow culinary horizons."

Neatly folded napkins appeared followed by two containers. With a flourish she opened the first. It revealed a suspicious-looking salad highlighted by what appeared to be yellowish-brown carrots covered in a dark ebony sauce. The second, small container held a greenish paste. She handed me a gold-colored plastic fork.

"Before I consign this mess to the waste basket, what is it? I'm just curious. Not that I plan to eat any of this slop. I think I've suddenly lost my appetite."

"*That* is Mary's world-famous parsnip avec burnt gravy salad accompanied by a side of mushy peas." Bertha's hands rested on her narrow hips. The floor-length rainbow skirt swirled restlessly. Brown eyes narrowed. A sandaled foot tapped. Colorful toes flexed. "Oh, good Gilgamesh, try it Randy. It won't kill you. The line-up where I had to stand in front of her Shoppe was half a block long."

The door to the outer office swung wide, and a scruffy character in a floor length beige trench coat and large floppy hat entered.

"I believe my next appointment is here."

"Oh, I'll get that, will I?" she snapped and stormed out with a flourish. Bertha's been taking drama lessons at night school again.

I swept the mess off my desk and into the waiting maw of the waste basket shaped like a starving bulldog. I'd won this prized possession between innings at a Central City Carp game. The plastic bulldog gulped the mess down without complaint, and the jaws snapped shut with a burp.

For some reason Bertha frequently suggested I donate my prize to charity, but I demurred.

"Mister Able Bowdee to see you, Mr. Aloysius. Go right in, he has nothing else on his desk this morning."

You could have carved her words with a dull knife. She closed the door behind him with a nasty click.

Able Bowdee, a wizened goblin of indeterminate age, weather-worn, and with a reputation as shabby as his coat, slid into the chair opposite me and removed his battle-beaten fedora. He was also the unofficial big boss of the vegetable market down at the junction of the two main rivers that meet at the Garden Forks in the middle of Central City.

Rumor had it he could be exceedingly generous, or deadly, depending on results and his mood.

I folded my hands into a replica of a Buddhist temple. "How may I be of service?"

He looked around my office with eyes that reminded me of the famous bleeding statue of The Virgin Harry, a noted unsuccessful practitioner of fisticuffs. The red glow settled on me. "I have a serious problem."

His voice sounded like a gravel truck accidentally dumping its load.

"Then you've come to the right place. Serious are the only kinds of problems we solve."

He leaned across the desk. I bent forward. "Some dirty lowlife has been hijacking wagon loads of vegetables before they can reach the market. It's costing me a fortune. I want them caught, wrapped up, and turned over to me—for re-education."

"Do you know where the heist is taking place? Is it inside the city at the market or before they get here?" I'm not much for enjoying the country life. Would really prefer to avoid, if possible. Had enough of that as a tad.

"Happens on the way down to the city. The parsnip fields are from somewhere near the back of nowhere, up north of the town of Grimtun, that beachy place on the lake. Never been there. To the fields. No need. Trip of several hours, I hear, which is why the bloody things are so expensive. And I have a serious demand. The Annual Parsnip Festival takes place in less than a week. I need to have several shipments in my warehouse within the next four days. Those veg have to be properly prepared."

A long boney finger wagged beneath my nose.

"I'll pay you well to catch the rascals and see at least five wagonloads delivered safely through to the Forks. I don't want any of the nosey Committees involved. I have competition. If a word of this gets out I lose the contract to supply the Festival."

I hesitated. I'm a city boy now. The thought of grubbing around in the fertilizer on someone's plowed field did not really appeal. Who would ever imagine they had a parsnip festival? "Well, I don't know…"

He snatched up his cap and stood. "Good. We have a deal."

A leather pouch landed on the desk with a subtle clink.

He paused in the doorway. "I expect results. Don't disappoint me. I don't handle disappointment very well. You have three days."

Able Bowdee was gone. I looked at the pouch, picked it up and weighed it in my hand. "Oh well, I suppose I could use some fresh country air."

Before I could inform Bertha I was taking a saunter into the country, the door to the outer office opened again, and an oversized hobgoblin in a well-worn postal uniform pushed through balancing a rather large cardboard box.

"Are these the offices of Aloysius, Wildwater, and Associates, Private Eyeballs?" he bellowed. The box balanced precariously in his oversized hands.

"That's what it says on the front door." This from Bertha. "If you can read."

"When did this happen?" I stood. "Have the door repainted immediately."

"That week when you were too busy reading the ball scores to notice. We're leaving things just the way it stands. Makes the place sound upmarket."

"You are not an associate. We don't have associates. You are my secretary." Who never does what she's told.

"This carton is heavy." He set it down on a corner of Bertha's desk. The box wobbled.

I noticed the air holes in the side. There was a slight odor of stale cigar.

"Remove that thing immediately from my desk!" Bertha pointed a long reddish-brown finger toward the floor. Emerald nails sparkled.

"That will be a half Argentum. Delivery fee." The messenger

leaned on the box. He didn't make an effort to move the parcel.

The hobgoblin was even taller than my secretary, and heavier, although I suspected after all the night classes she takes, Bertha could disassemble and plant him into the floor faster than you can say Mrs. Robinson. I folded my arms and yawned.

Bertha whirled on me, still standing innocently in the doorway of my inner office. "Did you order this without completing a requisition?"

She passed bookkeeping last month, and the formerly gentle paper flow has become a tsunami.

"Wasn't me. Pay the poor fellow from petty cash and let's see what we have inherited." I was curious but had to get going on the hunt for what was rotten in the vegetable bin.

"Oh all right." She paid then slammed the desk door closed as the messenger quickly departed. The box shuddered precariously. "Let's see what we have here." She flourished a long sharp implement, the first-place prize from her knife-throwing classes of two years ago. "Knowing your usual clientele, should I check for explosives first?"

"Gently," I warned. The box shuddered.

"I know what I'm doing, which is more than I can say for some of my partners some days."

"You don't have any partners," I pointed out. "You are not a partner."

She sliced the tape holding the lid in place and whirled around preparing to give me a verbal broadside.

The top of the box flew open, and a familiar voice said, "Did you miss me, gorgeous?" and the beaming round face of Captain Charlie of the Committee of Public Safety popped out, arms flung wide. The stub of a cigar went flying across the room into an old coffee cup.

Bertha jumped back.

I admit I took a step back too. Charlie, my former friend and professional cherub and I were not on speaking terms. As a matter of fact, I believe our last conversation ended with him telling me in short plain language he never wanted to see or hear from me again.

He hopped out, perched on the edge of her desk and leered at Bertha. "Are you free for a quiet romantic dinner tonight, kid?"

"I'll check my calendar. No, wait, I just remembered. I have to put out the other garbage." She glanced at me, one eyebrow raised.

Well at least she didn't threaten to flatten him, which is her usual response. Charlie, back in the day when I knew him, held a reputation around the department as a bit of a womanizer. A bit of work for someone who barely reaches even to my waist.

Still perched on the corner of her desk he sighed, rolled his eyes, and turned the famous smile on me. "Hi Randy, how you been?"

"What's the problem? Remember, Shorty, the CPS and I are through. We have a signed agreement." A benefit from the ill-fated trip on the *Sarah Madder*. Although agreements never stopped the powers before.

Charlie turned paler than usual, hopped down from the desk and checked the outer door to make certain it was closed. He locked it.

"You got to help me Randy, old friend, ol' buddy. We go a long way back. I'm in deep, deep doo-doo. I'm being framed for murder. They're all after me. You have to hide me somewhere safe and find out who really did it." He glanced up at Bertha and winked. "I bet you have somewhere you could hide me, like in your bedroom closet."

"Oh, your mother would really love him," I said.

"Not if he was at death's door and there was a knocking," she said.

I frowned. "Besides, Charlie, you are an officer of the Com PS. Surely they're already investigating the crime. They won't convict you without some solid evidence."

He snorted. "You used to work with them. You know what they're like when the wizards get a suspect in their sights. Make steel bear traps look like pin cushions. They have something, and they think they have me. Besides, there's a certain extremely attractive pixie, name of Bessie. Remember her from Frozen Files?"

"Afraid I never had the pleasure." I suspected I knew where this was going.

"Well, Bessie is ambitious to the ultimate. Got herself promoted. Fast. Became my assistant, then my deputy. Now she wants *my* job. Well, anyway, Bessie got her delicate little hands on something that led her right to me, and now the whole pack of hungry wolves are howling for my blood. So to speak."

"Who is it you are supposed to have murdered?" Bertha had a pad out and a pencil poised.

"We're not taking the case," I said. "I'm busy and booked solid for the next week. I don't have time."

"I'll handle it then," she said. "Full retainer up front."

"For you babe, anything." He glanced my way. "But I think you should bring the old man along. This is going to be a tricky one."

"We're not taking the case," I repeated. "I'm too busy, and if he's come here that means serious trouble's close behind."

"If anyone can solve this case it's Aloysius and Wildwater."

Charlie gave us one of his patented smiles.

"This firm is Randolf Aloysius, period." I glared at Bertha. "Or it will be when my secretary gets around to correcting the multiple errors gilded on the front door glass."

"I don't care if you call yourselves Randy and Bertha Comma, I'm begging for your help."

He actually dropped to his knees and wrung his hands together. I hadn't seen that move in a long time.

"Let's get back to business." She stabbed her pencil in his direction. "Who did you say you are supposed to have killed?"

"He didn't."

They ignored me.

"Some run-down wagon driver with a string of bad luck."

"Does he have a name?" Bertha persisted.

I shook my head and went back into my office. I'd probably eventually agree to take the case, but only after I solved the parsnip heist. Good to let him percolate in a vegetable stew of his own making for a while.

After all, Charlie was the one who loudly refused to take my calls or allow me to poach on the vast resources of the Committee of Public Safety on those rare occasions when I needed some technical help or inside dope.

"What is the name of the deceased?" Bertha was still at it.

"I think it was Edward, or Eddard, or maybe Edwin."

Reaching into my desk drawer, I frowned. It wasn't like Charlie to forget a name, or a phone number. I checked the clip and slipped Bess, my favorite pistol, into her shoulder holster.

"Why would they connect you to the murder of a wagon driver? What was he, another cherub?"

"Goblin."

"And the connection to you?"

I turned out the light and paused in my doorway. At least Bertha had learned persistence.

"His wife."

Ah hah. Of course. That figures.

"But don't get the wrong idea, sweet cheeks. It wasn't serious. I may have taken her to a private club or two, and a shady restaurant, but it wasn't serious. He didn't even know about us."

"I've heard that one before."

"It speaks." She turned to me. "Any other questions before I start the investigation?"

"Yeah, where are you clowns planning to hide me?" Charlie

kept looking at the door. "I don't think Bessie knows about my connection to you, but if she looks in the files…"

"Which she will even if she studied under you." I sighed. "Where did this deceased character work? Sometimes the fellow workers know a lot more about what's going on than you think they do. Always a good place to start."

"He drove a wagon for old Able Bowdee down at the Garden Forks Market. You know, that pile of rotten vegetables. Was out of town a lot. That's why his Mrs. got so lonesome."

"Ah," I said. "We'll take your case at double our usual fee, because of the complications with the Com PS."

Chapter Two

"So, what's our next move?" Bertha leaned in, pencil still poised. "Should I go check out the Market?"

"Absolutely not! Leave that mixed bag of groceries to the pro. I want you in charge of keeping our client safe. Stash him somewhere this Bessie person and the other cloaked minions of the Com PS will never think to look."

"I've died and gone to heaven." Charlie beamed up at her. "We get to spend some quality time together. I hear violins and choirs already. I know a little place…"

"Where you are going to ultimately end up will probably include heated charcoal and bongo drums," I said, interrupting his swoon.

I noticed Bertha had taken her pearl-handled splatter gun out of her desk drawer and slipped it into her woven shoulder bag. The colorful purse with the beadwork and flowers. This could get out of hand very quickly. I had to take charge.

"Bertha, there is a cloistered religious order located just north of the city limits. They have a vow of silence during months beginning with sunshine. Hire a horse cab and take Charlie up there. Better find a suitable disguise for him. I suggest as a blind, old lady. While on the way, pump him for details of his affair with the wagon driver's widow and whatever info you can get on his deputy, Bessie. Like why she might dislike him more than most normal people would."

I took a page from Bertha's notepad. "I'll write you an introduction to the Head Mistress. He owes me one." I did him a big favor many years ago by going over the garden wall and finishing my education elsewhere. "See Charlie safely inside, then head back to the office."

Bertha took a shabby gray coat out of the closet and held it up. The garment was one I'd used on occasion. The thing has the habit of taking on the appearance of whatever you want it to look like, from shapeless dress, to neat black suit. But only from a distance.

"This should do the trick," she said. Bertha tossed the coat at Charlie and began rummaging in the closet. "I have a large wig in the back here somewhere. Why a horse cab? Steam would be faster."

"The Vegan Order of the Great Green Mother Earth is a touch retro. Arriving by a horse-drawn vehicle will get you through the main gates. And a unicorn is too expensive. I'll meet you tonight at the Bear and Gill, and we can compare notes. Give me time to have a quiet supper first."

"What about me? I want in on this." Charlie struggled into the coat as Bertha draped the wig over his head. He had to part the straggly white hair to peer out.

"Later. Maybe. Where would I find this latest conquest of yours?"

"Which one?"

"The grieving goblin widow with the deceased husband. She is a goblin, isn't she?" They are notoriously catholic in their choices of partners, unlike elves and some stuffy others I could think of.

"She has a penthouse just off Main Street. Comfy little place. Overlooks the river. But this time of day you will probably find her in the Central City Library."

"She reads a lot while grieving for her husband?" Bertha straightened the wig and wrapped the effect in a shawl that left a bit of hair and two blue eyes showing. She added a pair of dark glasses from her desk drawer.

Among her other minor arts, she majored in serious disguises. I don't know what she'd do with herself after hours if not for night school.

"No, she has an office there. Third floor. By the exotic cook books."

I frowned. "What does she do for a living?"

Charlie shrugged. "I'm not really sure."

"Does she have a name?"

"Of course. Ask for Garbella Sieve. Everyone there knows her."

"How did her husband Edward, Eddard, or maybe Edwin, die?" I pretended to write. Don't really need to. I have a memory like a steely trap. Once something gets in there it seldom leaves. Another wayward thought struck me between the eyes. "Did he live with his wife?"

"I think a heavy wagonload of some root vegetables overturned on him. Parsnips, I think." Charlie examined himself in the mirror Bertha held up.

"Don't you know for certain? Weren't you on the case? Why do they think it was murder instead of an accident?"

"I was focused on the large hole in his head probably caused by a garden pickaxe. He lived with his mother someplace way up north where they grow parsnips. How did you pick up on the fact he didn't live with Garbella? He did stay with her on the nights after he made his weekly delivery."

"Just another lucky guess." And a sneaky suspicion. Charlie used to like playing things pretty safe, romance-wise. He's a lover, not a fighter. Well, not outside of work, anyway. "What do they have on you that makes them think you did the deed? Other than the fact you were amusing his bored wife?"

"They found the pickaxe near the scene of the accident. Apparently it had my fingerprints on it."

"Could they use trace dust to review the crime scene? That would clear you." Therefore, too obvious. "Any witnesses?"

"The event took place on a deserted stretch of road late at night in the middle of a summer storm. One of those sudden things blows up by the lake. Wiped the air clean."

"But not the fingerprints?"

"The pickaxe was carefully laid underneath the overturned wagon."

"Is that all they have on you?" This query from Bertha.

"Well, no. Garbella had a letter from her husband she turned over to Bessie at the CPS. I haven't seen it. Apparently he says in it he was aware of our—harmless, causal luncheons and was coming to the city to beat my head in."

"With a pickaxe?" She examined her handiwork.

He looked like someone's ancient grandmother after a long hard night of stomping grapes and chugging the end result. "Yes."

"I think you two had better leave now. By our new emergency exit." One of the wards I placed on the front stairs had just tripped. It's supposed to go off only if hostile intent is noticed.

Bertha dragged Charlie toward the storeroom and shoved him inside.

His usually smooth tones came out through the closing door as a squeak. "Not that I'd normally mind, but if trouble is coming do we have time?"

We had the emergency exit installed after a number of annoying incidents. There is a back stair that runs from the building's upstairs hall down to an alley in the rear, but any serious visitor would have that covered. There is a hidden window in the storeroom that leads to a fire escape and up onto the roof of the adjacent building. Then it's a simple hop, skip, and jump like Jack and Jillian across the rooftops to safety. That's the theory, anyway.

The locked office front door rattled. "Open up in there, this is the Committee of Public Safety. We have a warrant to search the premises."

"Just a minute. Be right there." I took my time drifting over to the door and fumbling with the lock. The Com PS must be turning over a dead leaf if they were actually worrying about warrants. They were probably sticking closely to the big black book, seeing as how Charlie was one of their own.

I stepped back as the door was flung open. A glaring pixie in a floor-length duster burst through. She pushed me aside and stood in the middle of the floor. "All right, where is he?"

A squad of four large hobgoblins followed her inside. "Search every crack and corner. He's a sneaky little beggar. Don't leave a desk drawer unopened or a chair unturned."

"How may I help you?" I pasted on my best smile.

Ice-blue eyes peered up from beneath a short, sharp blonde haircut. As pixies go, and they usually do, she had a trim, wiry figure and wore a dress red uniform jacket with a floor-length blue cape over the duster. The weather isn't that bad for a fall day. The high black boots were a bit too much, though.

"Well, where is that no-good friend of yours? Harboring a wanted fugitive can lead to a quick revocation of the so-called immunity agreement you signed." The words were launched into the air along with a minor spray of spittle.

The document in question wasn't really an immunity agreement—more like a truce signed with the Committee of Public Safety after I survived the *Sarah Madder* affair.

"I have a lot of no-good friends. Which particular one are you referring to?" I kept the smile in place.

A tall, thin elf in a brown trench coat came through the door. He nodded to me. A bored grin flickered. "No sign of anyone in the back alley, Bessie."

"That is, *Senior* Deputy Captain Bessie. You know the proper protocol. I've warned you about that before, *Junior* Inspector Columns."

"Yes, ma'am." He arched a delicate eyebrow in my direction. He had the look of a recent graduate from the CPS Academy.

"Did you use trace dust in the alley?"

"No, ma'am." He peered around the room. "No need to. There

was a thick layer of dust on the back stairs."

"I'll have a serious word with the cleaning service," I said. We don't have a cleaning service.

"Stop calling me ma'am," she snapped. "I'm no older than you are."

"Climbing up the ladder of success quite rapidly, I suspect." I nodded. "Congratulations are due."

Bessie glared at Junior Inspector Columns. "Let's do this by the scroll so there are no screw-ups. Read him his rights."

He cleared his throat, took out a card then ignored it. "You have the right to request an advocate to be at your side during your trial. You have the right to have half of the judges chosen from civilians. You have the right to object to torture and drugs—but only if you surrender voluntarily."

I smiled. "But that only applies if you charge me with something."

"I'm working on that." She glared poisoned daggers at me. "Where is he? This will go hard on you if you hold anything back."

"You still haven't told me who you are looking for. Would you like some coffee? I have fresh chicory and a half bottle of genuine Irish around here somewhere if you'd like a cup? Just give me a minute. I'll have to do some washing up. It's the maid's day off."

"I wouldn't mind a drop of the Irish," Inspector Columns said.

"Yes you would!" She rounded on me. "You know very well who we are looking for. That rascal, *former* Captain Charlie of the Sixth Precinct. He is wanted for murder."

I suspect she'd spent far too long working in Frozen Files. Her sharp voice reminded me of chipped ice.

"Don't you mean for questioning in regard to a murder?" I shook my head. "Sorry, but I haven't seen him or spoken to him in ages. We had a bit of a falling out. This would be the last place he'd come."

"We have ways of making you talk."

"Yes, and I know most of them. I'm also acquainted with a certain Miss Vickky, probably better known to you in the ranks as Queen Victoria. She and I go a long way back. I could give her a call if you would like someone to vouch for me. I'd hate to have to bother her, though…"

Old Vickky has quite the reputation among the CPS agents. Besides, I doubted the pixie would have the croquet balls to actually contact her. Inspector Columns was carefully studying the ceiling. The four hobgoblins gathered round.

Bessie's face turned an interesting shade of crimson. Lips moved but nothing came out but a wisp of steam.

Blue-black eyes went to red and back to black again. She really was quite attractive, if you fall for the delicate as fine bone china, sharp-toothed, narrow faced type who probably packs a dagger and a set of ladies' double-barreled revolvers somewhere beneath the latest high fashion for height-challenged little devils.

You could have heard a pint drop.

"We've looked everywhere, boss. No sign of the suspect anywhere." One of the hobgoblins finally spoke up.

"Looks like a dead end," Columns said.

"Fine." Senior Deputy Captain Bessie glared around the room looking everywhere but at me. Finally those dark eyeballs settled on my finely chiseled face (I've often been taken for granite). "Don't leave town."

"I have nothing planned." I stayed well clear of her as she prepared to retreat. No need to encourage the Com PS to slip a bug, dead or alive, on my person.

"And let Junior Inspector Columns know if you hear anything about the fugitive. Anything at all. Columns, give him your card."

The inspector handed me a gold engraved piece of cardboard. "Call me anytime."

I nodded and noted he worked out of the Sixth Precinct. He had my complete sympathy. I used to work there.

The pixie was staring at the empty desk in the outer office. "Who sits here?"

"That belongs to my secretary. Today is her regular day off. She usually visits her sick mother." Or tries to uncover and investigate who Meaghan Wildwater is dating now.

"I guess we're done here." She headed toward the door.

"Just out of curiosity, who is Charlie supposed to have murdered?"

"A goblin heavy wagon driver, name of Eddard Eddardson." Columns shrugged.

Bessie stopped in the doorway. "Do not, under any circumstances, give the witness any information on the case."

"But I thought…"

"You are not paid to think. That is what I'm for." Senior Deputy Captain Bessie stormed out through the door followed closely by the hobgoblins trotting along behind single file like a pack of well-trained cave bears.

"You have my deepest sympathy," I whispered as Junior

Inspector Columns fell in at the end of the parade. Even if he was one of those intolerable elves.

"Thanks," he said.

Chapter Three

I lost my appetite and couldn't be bothered looking for it. I decided to head straight for the Central City Library and the grieving widow.

The CCL is a notorious three-story stone building located near the center of downtown. I took a steam trolley the six cobblestone blocks as the gray sky threatened rain. The library's imposing front steps rose past a marble tableau depicting the Fall of Humpty Dumpty. There were a few serious errors in the representation. The sculptor never did receive his final payment and retired to Icedland with egg on his face.

The building's front doors were polished brass and heavy as the stale atmosphere inside the place with its high ceilings shrouded in mist. To ensure the properly respectful air, the tarnished gas lamps lining the dark paneled walls were turned down to their minimum flame. Of course that made it difficult to read anything in the main hall. I suspect that was the whole idea. Readers are discouraged from loitering. Research tomes and dusty scrolls littered rows of scratch-gouged wooden tables. Monitors in floor-length black robes patrolled between the heavy tables carrying long willow wands. The wands were used to prod any patron who drifted off and threatened to drool on the materials.

Under the watchful eye of the matron-in-charge of the first floor, I ascended the creaking wooden steps to the second level. This was the lighter reading section. The windows were larger too. A rheumy-eyed wizard in a faded cap, with inch-thick glasses perched on the tip of his nose, sat at a cluttered desk by the top of the stairs.

He held up his hand for me to stop, fumbled through papers and books, and fished out a tired sign that he set at the edge of his desk in front of me. The sign proclaimed, "Committee of Public Knowledge and Enlightenment, Information."

"Do you have any information for me?" he asked in a dry

voice. “Any books needing banning? Anything untoward on the shelves?”

The CPKE review parenting and morals and run the Dead Letter Institution that holds banned and obsolete books. I guess today was a quiet day and the gatekeeper was bored.

He peered at me over his glasses. “Well? Have you found anything disgusting? Anything that needs banning or,” and he leaned forward across the desk, as his voice dropped to hushed tones, “Anything that warrants—*burning?*”

“Sorry. I’m not one of your literary agents. I’m looking for a Garbella Sieve. I understand she has an office on the third floor.”

He sighed and leaned back. “There are no offices on this floor.”

“What about the third floor?”

“There is no third floor.”

“Where do those stairs lead?” I pointed toward an open door across the room and the beginning of a set of steps with a definite upward slant.

“To the next floor. But you don’t want to go up there. Are you certain you haven’t noticed a magazine downstairs with a cover in poor taste or an article with an improper point of view? I understand the latest issue of *Thyme* has a disgusting illustrated rutabaga recipe we should investigate.”

I know the head honcho at *Thyme*. She was a stickler for the facts. As a matter of useless information, we used to be quite a hot item before she saw the light of fame and fortune and moved to the big city. Seldom been back here since. Muddy Hogland Town has that effect on some. Attracts them like flies to dirty money. My loss, I guess.

“Nothing to worry about there. I can vouch it’s clean as a councilman’s conscience.”

He looked disappointed.

“Well, I guess I’ll head on up to the thir—next floor.” I made to slip around him.

He grabbed at my sleeve. “You can’t go up there. It’s haunted. I told you there’s no third floor.”

I gestured. “Where do those stairs lead, then?”

“To the fourth floor. Three floors in this building would be unlucky.”

I shook my head. “I’ll take my chances.”

“I warned you.”

These stairs were narrow, steep, and creaked loudly like my knees after a hard day. Whoever might be up there would be well aware I was coming long before I reached the landing. The windows were narrow slits, the curtains black and dusty, and the walls crammed with rows of shelves half-filled with books and scrolls and loose piles of paper. The feeble light illuminated the ceiling and the faded scene painted there. The images of studious wizards and distracted witches wandering in a barren garden looked like something painted by failed art students depicting the last day before the first snowfall.

There was a single, pale yellow light glowing from a brass lantern in a shadowy back corner of the room. I headed that way.

"You must be lost. The information desk is one floor down." The voice was pleasant, almost musical.

I wound my way between heaps of paper, following a well-worn trail of footprints in the dust. A goblin sat at a large wooden desk. She looked up and frowned. Like most goblins, it was hard to tell her age. She wore a shoulder-length blonde wig and eyelashes that could have tickled her sharp nose. The ruby lipstick caught the lamplight; it was luminous and framed pointed, white teeth. The black-outlined red eyes contrasted with pale green skin that had seen more than some weathering in its day.

Had Captain Charlie come to this? Not his usual taste in escorts.

"Miz Garbella Sieve, I presume?" I leaned over the desk and flashed a brilliant smile. Her desk held a stack of well-thumbed books. The one on top proclaimed: *The Restorative Powers of Root Vegetables*. The subtitle was: *Cooking with Magic*.

"Who wants to know?" She had slipped something out of the desk drawer and into her lap.

Probably a small cannon.

I carefully flashed a square of laminated cardboard. "Randolf Aloysius, Private Eyeball, at your service. I'm investigating the murder of your husband, Eddard Eddardson."

"We all know who did it, that cheating, no good, low-life from the sixth precinct, Captain Charlie." The musical voice descended into something from a damp basement. "Now he'll get what's coming to him."

"I just have some questions. If you don't mind."

"I do mind." She managed to squeeze out a single tear. "Eddard was such a sweet boy. Snatched away from me while still in the early springtime of his youth."

Garbella reminded me more of a late summer algae bloom. I wondered what Eddard saw in her. "Do you have a picture or an image of your late husband?"

"No, and I'll ask you to leave me now to my grieving."

The other papers on her desk looked like bills of lading. For bulk vegetables? I had to give her that she was well-spoken for someone hiding in the top floor of a library and connected somehow to the parsnip trade. No pictures of the departed? So much for fond memories.

"One last question. Do you work for Able Bowdee, the vegetable king down at the Forks Garden Market?"

She snorted. "None of your bloody business."

I took that as a yes and also lied about the number of questions. "What was your husband doing driving with a load of parsnips out in the country so late at night?

"That is where they are grown. How do you think they get to market—walk on their own?"

"But late at night, in a storm? Why the rush?"

"We like our vegetables fresh." She smiled, displaying those sharp teeth. "I've politely asked you to leave. There is no need to investigate. I have faith in the righteous long arm of the Com PS. Justice will be served. Now, I have work to do. If you do not remove yourself from my presence immediately, I will have you removed."

She raised her arm in the air and snapped her fingers. "You have been warned. The stairs behind you are rather steep. Fatal accidents can happen."

I noticed a shadow detach itself from the wall behind her. Yellow eyes glowed. I backed up. "See you later," I said.

"I don't think so."

I caught the shimmer of green scales in the faint light from her lamp. The shadow became the short, stocky figure of a demon. My retreat was not graceful, but effective. I may have missed a step or two in the way back down. Thankfully, he did not follow. Demons were swift and shifty. I had no desire to see if Bess could stop him before he reached me with his claws.

"Told you not to go up there." The wizard at the information desk didn't look up.

"Thanks for the warning."

I paused for breath inside the foyer by the front doors. Interesting, Garbella Sieve was nothing like I would have expected from Charlie. She certainly didn't seem to be in mourning over her recent loss. Who requires a demon bodyguard? I decided I needed to snoop around the Forks Garden Market.

I stepped outside. Of course, it was raining. The wizards of the Committee of Planetary Surface Probabilities had erred again in their standard optimistic forecast. I haled a steam cab.

The Forks Garden Market was a commercial area close to downtown squeezed into the junction between the Big Muddy and the Little Muddy rivers. The area holds a collection of mismatched but artistically unusual buildings and random statuary of local dignitaries, some realistic, a few impressionistic. To see an illuminated and towering warped stone impression of an aged gremlin city councilor was a sight best left to after a bout of late-night libations.

The tiny, crowded market shops along the Little Muddy shore held a variety of predominately homemade goods and unusual gifts. Wooden stalls advertised local woven baskets, genuine rare antiques, secondhand books and self-published authors, and unused clothing guaranteed not to have been stolen. A small mixed crowd of the best and worst Central City has to offer browsed the offerings. Further on, a narrow booth proclaimed, "Teacup Translations," another weathered one beside it displayed a sign announcing, "Palms Purged of Bad Luck."

There was probably a very good reason I seldom came down here.

The Big Muddy shore held the Forks Garden Market, a long row of stalls set inside a building that once served as a stable back in the day before the country was completely civilized and we spread smoke, oxen, and unicorn droppings across the plains. The stalls were arranged alphabetically, with Parsnips located beside Rutabagas. The parsnip stall looked suspiciously bare, with only a few sad and withered remnants huddled in the bottom of the bins. Must have been one heck of a good recipe to sell out of the stuff.

A tattered poster above the display advertised the Annual Parsnip Festival. A slightly blurred image that reminded me of a certain Miz Sieve wrapped in a large towel proclaimed, "Don't Forget to Vote for Miss Root Vegetable" in large, lurid red lettering.

"You looking for choice parsnips, buddy?" A scrawny goblin in a tattered coat shuffled from the shadows behind me.

"No, just browsing."

He looked disappointed. I tossed him a coin. "Just out of curiosity, where would you get your supply from? It looks to me like the local vendor has run out. Maybe he's saving them all for the big festival next week."

He bit the coin and snorted. "Listen, buddy, there won't be no festival. The supply has all dried up. But I has my sources. You'll have to pay up front for prime veg if you want them."

"Someone cornered the market?"

He looked around and backed up. "I don't know you. I don't

want to know you." The words, "You ask too many questions," faded away as he disappeared back into the cracks and crannies of the woodwork.

Back outside, a large area was marked off on the grounds with yellow tape and a sign proclaimed, "The Site of the Annual Parsnip Festival. See the latest issue of the *Daily Mooned* for a list of attractions."

I headed toward the Market Administration building. Located right at the junction of the two rivers it was the newest and fanciest structure on the property and clad in sparkling white granite. The roof held an observation tower that reminded me of a middle finger thrust toward the sky. The tower was topped by a skeletal metal antenna. The business offices were on the second level. The ground floor was taken up by two businesses. The entrance to upstairs lay between them.

Mia Cuppa was a fancy coffee and cake shoppe. A slender elf in a clinging elegant silver gown stood inside the door staring out through the full-length glass. Mouth-watering smells of fresh baking and cinnamon greeted me when she opened the door hopefully as I passed by.

The other establishment was labeled The Malt Fall Coon Club. The door looked to be solid oak planks. The painted image on the door was of a raccoon wearing a peaked cap pulled down over his masked eyes and carrying a billy club. The narrow windows on either side of the entrance were blacked out. A stony-faced troll in a tight-fitting dark suit stood outside leaning against the wall with his bulging arms crossed over his chest. Even with the door closed I caught a whiff of stale brew and heady smoke.

"You coming in?" the troll grunted out.

"Just passing through." It didn't look like the sort of establishment I'd frequent, even on a bad day. At least not without a heavily armed escort, but duty demands and must obey. I headed inside and up the circular marble staircase. There must be a lot of money, good or bad, in vegetables.

I knocked on the door indicating, A. Bowdee and Associates, Management Consultants.

"Come in," a nasal voice invited.

So I did.

Chapter Four

"Well, have you found my missing parsnips?" Able Bowdee looked up from a large oak desk littered with various sizes of brass trophies, all shaped like vegetables.

I helped myself to a chair. "What can you tell me about a goblin, name of Eddard Eddardson?"

"Never heard of him. Did he do it?" He stuffed a thick black cigar between his lips and snapped his fingers.

"I think he worked for you as a wagon driver." I watched his eyes.

A wizened brownie straightened up from a desk in the corner, hobbled over with the use of a gnarled wooden cane, and flicked her fingers. The cigar flamed into a column of blue smoke that sent a dribble of ash toward the floor.

"Miss Gadeby, do we have an employee name of Ed Edwards?" He blew a solid ring of smoke across the desk.

I ducked. She flicked the noxious cloud aside with her paw.

Miss Gadeby looked as though she had come across the ocean with the first colonists to the New World. With brownies it was always hard to tell age. Her whiskers were streaked with gray and her eyes watery. The glasses balanced on the tip of her nose appeared thick enough to support a highway bridge. Her shapeless black gown featured several neatly sewn patches.

"Edward Eddardson worked as a contracted driver for a farming commune way up north. He passed on last week." She had a voice like sandpapered marbles.

"Quit and moved away, did he?" Able chewed on his cigar. "What has this to do with recovering my missing parsnips?"

"I believe there is a loose connection. Have you ever heard of a Garbella Sieve?" I resisted the urge to hold my nose as he exhaled.

He spat a gob into a nearby wastebasket. "She used to be the firm's bookkeeper until I fired her and hired old Prudence, here." He gestured toward the brownie.

She eyeballed me and growled. "At half her wages."

"You're older. Don't need as much." Able's eyes narrowed on me. "You're wasting time. You should be out digging in the dirt."

"I'd like to go and talk to some of your workers. Root around and see what I can turn up."

"Prudence will show you where you can find them." Able pointed a boney finger at me. "And don't come back here until you've recovered my parsnips. Don't screw up. I can find out where you live." He waved us away, took out a stained handkerchief then began to polish a brass carrot.

I followed Prudence Gadeby out the door and assisted her down the stairs to the main floor. She seemed a bit shaky. "Can you take me to where the veg are unloaded?" I said loudly. Her furry ears seemed a bit droopy.

"No need to shout, sonny. I may be wobbly, but I can hear a pin drop before it hits the floor." Balancing on her cane, she led me on a zig-zag course across the yard and toward the rear of the Forks Garden Market.

"How did Garbella leave the firm?"

"The usual way. Through the front door." Watery eyes peered at me through fogged glasses.

"No, I mean were there any hard feelings when she was fired?"

Prudence paused and took hold of my sleeve. She motioned for me to bend down so she could whisper in my ear. "Hard feelings weren't the description. From what I heard, it was more like the Fall of Troy, you know what I mean? Screaming and throwing and breaking things. Able used to have several pictures on the walls of his office. She broke a half dozen before the bodyguards arrived and carted her away."

She peered around. Her voice dropped. "Garbella got battered something good. Spent the next day or three in Gracie's Hospital getting patched up."

"Do you know why Able fired her?"

"Sure thing, sonny, she had very sticky fingers and more than parsnips stuck to them. According to Sonja over at the Mia Cuppa, Garbella figured she had Able Bowdee wrapped around her little ring pinkie and was planning to marry the old goat. When he didn't come across with the offer, she decided to help herself. Got her fingers caught and broken in the cookie jar."

"Thanks for the info." I straightened and frowned. "I thought Garbella was already married to Eddardson? Or did that come after she left Able?"

"Don't think Garbella would care if she had two or three husbands, from what I hear. But I do think young Eddard happened shortly after she left Able. She scooped the kid up right quick, she did." Prudence Gadeby tugged on my sleeve again. "My turn, sonny. Do you like to dance?"

"What?"

"Dance. You know, trip the lite phantasmal, chew up the rug, dare the dawn, jiggle the bug. I may be shaky, but you should see me shake. I have rhinestone covered hoppers, and I know how to use them. There's the big Ella's Ball at the Parsnip Festival, and I need a partner who can keep up." She twirled around leaning forward and balancing on her cane. "Well, do you want to come over to my flat tonight after work for a bite of supper and practice? I'll make fish cakes, and you can bring your choice of poison."

"I'd love to," I said, "but it just so happens I have to be out of town the night of the festival." Which might even be true if I don't locate the missing parsnips by then.

"Pretty weak. You can do better than that, sonny, but come on." She led me around to the rear of the market building.

A swarm of gremlins were unloading a wagonload of turnips. I hoped they didn't bruise easily. The turnips, not the gremlins. I know how resilient gremlins are.

"Who's the foreman here?" I called out. "I have a couple of questions. And I can pay. I also have Able Bowdee's permission to ask them."

A gremlin with a red plaid bandanna around his scrawny neck and large sunglasses tied against his flat nose with an old shoelace, hopped down from his perch on a barrel and sauntered over to us. "I'm in charge here. Captain Slowse is the name. Let's see the color of your coin."

I held one up. "What can you tell me about…?"

"Hold on bud, that's a copper piece. I'm allergic to everything except silver."

I sighed and handed him an argentum. The smallest denomination. "This had better be worth it or I'll take the loose change back in blood."

That got me a snort. "That I'd like to see. What's the question?"

"Questions. Do you know a wagon driver name of Eddard Eddardson?"

"Yeah. Nice kid if a bit slow. Hear he had a bad accident in a thunderstorm. Rolled the wagon, lost the load, and then ran headfirst into a pickaxe."

"I understand he was married to a Garbella Sieve. What can you tell me about that?

"What am I, a marriage counselor? It was a whirlwind romance."

"I hear she kidnapped Eddard and held him hostage until he said yes." This from a wiry old gremlin taking a breather from pitching turnips underhand.

"Otherwise known as the Wicked Witch of the West Bank," a youngster with bulging eyes chipped in. "Or so I hear the older fellas say after they had a run-in with her one night at the Malt Fall Coon."

"Eddard was a regular guy. Always on time with his loads. The least bruised veg of anyone on that route." Captain Slowse scratched one floppy ear. "What's your interest in this? You really working for old Able or someone else?" He glanced at Prudence.

"He's working for Able," she said. "Trying to find those missing parsnips."

I figured by his tone, Slowse might have liked Eddard. "I'm also investigating the driver's murder. An acquaintance of mine's been wrongly accused of it. I think the whole mess may be connected."

"Follow me." The gremlin headed off without a backward glance.

We went through the rear market doors, around a pile of turnips, then through a door marked Broom Closet. "Step into my office," Slowse said. He perched on an overturned pail. "Have a seat." He kicked an apple bucket in my direction.

To say the space was crowded would be an insult. We couldn't even close the door. I decided to stand. Prudence Gadeby took the bucket, flipped it over and used it as a seat perched between my knees.

"I think the kid had a raw deal," Slowse began.

"You mean besides his bad choice of a missus?" This from Prudence.

Slowse ignored her. He popped a floppy string of black licorice into his mouth, offered a piece to Prudence and me. I declined.

"The kid got all the late-night drives down on the road from Hades." Slowse looked thoughtful.

"Where's Hades?" That was a new on me except for the obvious, and I didn't think even parsnips came from there.

He shook his head. "City folk. The things they fail to teach in school these days. Hades is a small farming and fishing community on an island way up north of Grimtun. The land thereabouts is ideal for growing parsnips. The trip down to Central City takes two or three days even when the weather is good. So when parsnips are in season, the wagon drivers run the road day and night. Eddard always got stuck on the night runs; usually the last leg from Grimtun to Central. His fatal trip was on the first leg for some reason."

"Why does it take them so long? The world has turned over and now it's modern. What are they using?" That's when I remembered they said wagons.

"No steam trucks for this company." He gave a grunt. "Too expensive."

"No unicorns either," said Prudence Gadeby. "Able's far too cheap and besides, those wagons loaded with veg are heavy. We use teams of oxen. Gets you walking speed at best."

"Tell me about the hijackings. Who would want to steal a wagon load of parsnips? Was there only one theft?"

Prudence counted on her gnarled fingers. "There's been six, no seven, parsnip wagons stopped and stolen. Everything gone: cargo, wagons, and the beasts what were pulling."

"Eight if you count Eddard's load. Most of the wagons disappeared before the local constables arrived on the scene." Captain Slowse frowned. "Strange, now when you think about it. Young Eddard usually drove the last leg; yet the night the kid died he was coming down from Hades."

"Who changed his schedule?" I tapped Prudence on the shoulder.

She swiveled around to look up at me. "Garbella did that the day before they fired her. Able didn't bother to change it after he threw her out."

"I have to either find out where the thieves have cached the stolen parsnips or get five new wagonloads down here, all in the next four days."

"Good luck with that." Slowse scratched behind one ear and examined the tip of his finger. "We're running short of teams and wagons. We've got lots of other veg need delivering here."

"Running short of drivers, now too," Prudence said.

Slowse looked me up and down. "Ever ride shotgun?"

"Once or twice." Maybe more than that, besides my years in the service, I've ridden a steam coach to Basalt Ville and a dirigible to the tropics. Both cases required some duties including protection. "What exactly did you have in mind?"

Captain Slowse gave me a gremlin version of a cross-eyed grin. "I have an empty wagon going north tomorrow morning. Can get you on it. Going all the way to Hades. You can ride back down with the next shipment of parsnips."

I could come up with several objections to that scheme. Riding an ox cart for a day or two and then back again was not my idea of amusement. And I didn't have the time. If I went to Hades, it should be on a one-day round trip. Why go? What would I find in Hades? I gave Slowse my most penetrating stare. "Who do you think is behind these hijackings?"

"Well." The captain glanced at me, gazed at Prudence, then looked around. We were definitely alone in the broom closet. He got up and peered out into the warehouse. A group of gremlins were playing catch with turnips near the loading doors and too far away to overhear our conversation. "Well, there is a troll consortium over on the East Bank. They would love to see the Parsnip Festival fail. It overlaps with the Pumpkin Carving Competition they're trying to start."

"The trolls don't have the collective brains to pull this off." Prudence took a clay pipe out of a patch pocket then said, "Do you mind?" and then lit up without waiting for answer.

I could think of at least one troll who could have pulled this off with one slippery hand tied behind her back, but this vegetable crime was probably far beneath her notice. I asked the next obvious question. "Could Garbella be involved in this? Did the hijackings start before or after she was fired?"

"After," Prudence said between puffs.

I decided my next course of action was a visit to the town of Hades as much as I dislike that idea. The hijackings happened on the road between there and the port of Grimtun. If the missing parsnips were anywhere, they should be hidden in that neighborhood. My head was starting to ache. My stomach mentioned it skipped breakfast and missed lunch. The time had come for me to retreat to the Bear and Gill for refreshment and then start north bright and early tomorrow.

"It has been a pleasure meeting you two. I'll let you get back to work now."

"Just do me one favor," Captain Slowse said. "Catch the bastard who did Eddard in. You don't have to be gentle when you met up with him, either."

"Or her, as the case may be." Prudence blew a smoke ring.

She was much better at it than her boss.

Chapter Five

The Bear and Gill is a neighborhood establishment run by an old acquaintance of mine, Griz. In fact, it was his eldest daughter, Charity, who I used to squire around back in the day when she was an up-and-coming cub reporter on one of the local rags. Now she was the chief editor at *Thyme* down in Muddy Hogland Town and a very big thing in high fashion print circles. My bar tab was finally clear so there was little pressure on me from her father to make an honest wife out of her. Charity and I were still good friends, I think. The lack of harassment suits both of us just fine, although perhaps me a bit more than her. Griz weighs over three hundred pounds and has a temper.

Faith, Griz's youngest daughter, met me inside the door. "What'll it be tonight, Uncle Randy, the usual?" She tilted her head toward my favorite booth. "You have company."

Bertha waved. There was a tall empty glass on the table in front of her.

I leaned in. "What are you doing here? I said to meet me *after* I had a quiet supper."

"I need to give you the latest report. Also, it's about time the firm sprang for a meal. What are you having?"

"Probably heartburn and a headache." I glared at Bertha without effect and turned to Faith. "I'll have the usual: a watercress sandwich, a platter of potato chippings, and a thick chocolate and cinnamon with a dollop of Irish."

"Sounds about right. What about a pitcher of La Bat's Breath for later?" Faith grinned.

"Oh, all right." I'll probably regret it in the morning.

"And for you, miss? What will his partner-in-crime be having?"

"This is Bertha, as you very well know. And she is my secretary, not my partner."

"Isn't he just the kidder." Bertha smiled. "I'll have tonight's special, the puree of parsnip in creamed rhubarb sauce and lemon. And another Granny's Iced Tea."

"Sounds disgusting," I said, and then looked up at Faith. "Where do you buy your parsnips?"

"Dunno, I'll check with Pops. Be back in a jiff."

I glared at Bertha. "Well, what did you learn today?"

She consulted her notes. "Let me see, The Vegan Order of the Great Green Mother Earth is certainly something. I don't know why I'd never heard of them before."

"They like to lie low. What did you learn on your ride up there from Charlie that will be of any use in our investigation?"

"Well, the head mistress of the place isn't really a mistress. He's a half-sized elf with a long gray beard and a severe overbite. Parents must have gotten crossed up with an undersized ogre somewhere in his family's dimmed past. He did remember you, though."

"Probably for my academic achievements. Just remember, we mongrels are the best people. Did he agree to take Charlie in and hide him there until we finish our investigation?"

"He did mention having to lock you in a clothes closet a few times for misbehaving in class and illegal use of disguises. And yes, he secured your buddy in one of the meditation cells there. Said he would be safe as in his mother's arms."

"I met his mother a few times. Safe is not how I would have described her." I think Charlie learned all his bad habits from her. "Did you get anything else useful out of the captain on your drive up there?"

"Well, I got the impression his girlfriend, this Garbella character, made the first move. Showed up at the precinct one day begging for a private meeting away from his office. They ended up in a bar next door, and it went downhill from there."

"What did she want with him?"

Faith re-appeared beside our booth and set our drinks on the table. "Pops says he gets his veg right from the Forks Garden Market. They deliver. He says lately the parsnips come separately, and there's a new driver. Prices on produce deliveries have doubled in the last week, though."

"Interesting." I looked at the tall glass clutched in Bertha's hands. "Granny's Iced Tea. Looks pretty tame. Must have been a quiet day after all for some people."

"I'll have you know that this comes from an old family recipe. Faith claims it originated with Griz's grandmother. A Kodiak from some place up north." Bertha licked her lips. "It's guaranteed to keep you fluid and mobile to forty below."

I shook my head. It didn't rattle so I continued, "What did Garbella want from the good Captain Charlie?"

"You mean, according to him, besides his warm little body? When he escaped from her clutches back at her apartment he returned to the precinct. She had asked for a copy of a file on a retired gang of horse and unicorn thieves out of some place near Grimtun. Said she wanted to help rehabilitating them. Apparently they were just released from Granite Mountain."

"Ah hah." Granite Mountain was a hulking, imitation castle built on a great lump of rock by the Committee of Public Safety. They use it to hold those evil-doers they don't feel are worthy of their wizard's personal and often painful private attention. "I think I see the light."

"Well don't shine it in my eyes. Here comes supper." Bertha licked her lips. "Looks delish as usual."

"Here we go." I began to tick off points on my fingers. "One. Garbella Sieve wants a gang of thieves for some reason. She needs the contact details and backgrounds. Two. To do this the easy way she contacts the captain of the 6th Precinct. Someone well-known around town when it comes to tumbling for the fairer sex."

"From what I've heard, calling Garbella fair could be mistaken for a serious exaggeration," Bertha said through a large mouthful of dripping parsnip and sauce.

"Three. She latches onto one of the favorite veg wagon drivers, and she controls their schedule. Four, she has to get rid of Charlie because he can connect her to the gang she's after. And for some reason, Garbella decides she also has to get rid of her new husband. Bingo, two dodos with one turnip. But why him? Why young Eddard?"

"It was a pickaxe." Bertha mopped at the cream sauce on her plate with a chunk of Griz's famous black bread. The bread was renowned for its rib-sticking properties and often used to patch shoes and leaking water tanks. "Maybe she was turning her subtle charms on the leader of the gang of thieves and her apartment was getting overcrowded with foolish and drooling males."

"A good a theory as any, I suppose." I frowned and sipped my chocolate.

"So, what's our next step? Where do you want me to go tomorrow?"

"I want you back in the office, answering phones and amusing any prospective clients foolish enough to pass through our infamous portals."

Bertha snorted. “What will you be doing while I’m baby-sitting the filing cabinets?”

“I think I’ll make a quick trip up north. I want to check out these parsnip fields and see what I can learn about the lay of the land up there. You are going to see what you can find out about this gang of thieves. Since you can’t pinch another copy of their file from the CPS, contact your buddy, Pippy Gazette over at the Central City Liberty One newspaper and see what she can dig out of their files on a gang of horse and unicorn thieves recently released from Granite Mountain.”

“She’ll want in on the case,” Bertha warned.

“Stall her. Lie. Tell her we’ll give her an exclusive.”

“Pippy will be on this tight like wool on a sheep. She’ll want to go up there with you.”

“Which is why you won’t call her until after I leave tomorrow morning.” I pointed at her with my spoon. “When you get home tonight call a rental company and arrange for a car to be delivered to the office. I’ll pick it up, and you can call Pippy after I’m safely on the road.”

We could afford to travel first class with double fees for this caper. But who knew what the roads would be like up there? “See if you can rent me a UHRV from the Murrican Steam Gold office. Make it a three-day rental, just in case.”

“That will cost us a small fortune.” She frowned. “What is a UHRV?”

“An Unnecessary High-Riding Vehicle. Who knows what the roads will be like once I leave Grimtun.” I pushed my plate back. If I allowed Pippy to accompany me I could probably get the newspaper to pay for our transportation, but the thought of being cooped up in a small space with an inquisitive brownie reporter tossed that thought back over my shoulder. “Finish up your meal, and I’ll walk you home.”

Bertha gave me a familiar look from her greater height. “I am quite capable of taking care of myself, Randy. I’ll walk you to that hovel you call a home to make certain you get there and are in any shape for tomorrow.”

“Put this all on my tab,” I said to Faith, hovering in the background.

Faith nodded. “Have you heard from Charity lately?”

“No. I think she’s forgotten little ol’ me.” I stood, and she helped me into my coat.

“Well, in that case, you’ll be excited to learn she will be in town tomorrow night. She will be staying here with us. Pops said he expects you will join us for supper. He said to tell you that is not a request.”

I glanced toward the bar. Griz was leaning on the woodwork polishing a hole in the gleaming finish. He glared at me like he was fresh from hibernation. I waved.

"Tell your father I will try my best, but it could be difficult. I'm on the road out of town tonight and not certain if I will be back tomorrow before dark."

"We'll keep a candle in the window, although knowing you, I'll tell them not to keep dinner hot." Faith shook her head. "I don't know why Charity puts up with you.'

"Because I'm cute and a witty conversationalist?" Behind Faith I noticed Bertha looking very much like she would like to enter into this chat. Probably with suggestions on how I could make it to the Griz family dinner. I give her a severe glance, and for once she settled back and remained silent.

"Come on, Miss Wildwater. You were going to walk me home. I mean to my car." There was no way I was leaving her behind to stir things up.

Chapter Six

I headed north behind the tiller of a Murrican Steam Gold UHRV wondering if I may have over-estimated the need for such a huge beast. A stagecoach with wooden wheels would have provided a more comfortable ride. The thing had large rubber tires that came to my chin and a full-bore Jurassic steam engine with a polished brass boiler and gleaming twin stacks in the rear as high as a hobgoblin. Even the almost useless dials ranged in front of me giving wind speed and fuel load were gleaming brass and glass. The hood ornament was a shiny bronze cupid with a bow and arrow that according to the warning label on the dashboard actually worked.

A miniature chandelier hung just behind my head and a silver vase on the dash beside the door held a half dozen red roses. A little bit too much for my taste at this hour of the morning. I was careful not to drop breakfast crumbs on the oriental carpet. Gold wire circles held my morning cup of chocolate. At least there was a gilt garbage can near the foot pedals.

The classy brownie in charge of the Murrican Steam Gold Shoppe had warned Bertha about the fuel range. The wood bin was full of neatly split and seasoned birch and the tank of fish oil topped up. These containers took all of the space where a rear seat would normally be found. Luggage, if one deigned to bring any, belonged up top lashed down between brass rails. Fortunately I was traveling light, with just a change of socks and underwear. At least the red velvet front bench seat was wide and well-padded. I soon discovered the top speed of the vehicle hovered somewhere between a fast walk and a slow wagon.

"So much for traveling first class," I muttered. The UHRV also came equipped with a telephone hanging on the wall beside my head. I decided to call Bertha and discover how she made out with Pippy. Balancing the receiver on my shoulder I spun the dial. It buzzed in my ear.

"World-Wide Elves. Insert your gold card for service."

The voice, low and throaty, stood the hair on the back of my neck. “I don’t have a gold card. I just want to place a local call.”

“Oh. Apologies. Please insert your platinum card for service.”

I could almost feel the speaker’s heavy breathing in my ear. My toes curled. “I don’t have a platinum card. As a matter of interest, I don’t have any card. I do have coin or script if they are of any interest.”

“A silver card?” Someone sounded disappointed.

“Sorry, no. Can’t help you there. Now, how can I use this contraption to make a call?”

“Is this vehicle stolen? I am placing a call to the Committee of Groundside Transportation. You will be intercepted at the next intersection. Please have your documentation ready and do not resist.”

I detected a definite threatening tone. “I’m not in the city. I have rented this vehicle, and I have the papers to prove it.” At least I think I did. I recalled Bertha handing me a bundle of stuff when she gave me the ring of gold and silver keys.

“I will be contacting the Committee of Inter-City Travel and Touring. They will be instructed to intercept you. Please…” That was a pretty good imitation of an ogre’s growl.

I hung up. Given what I knew about dealing with some of the committees, I had a couple of years before the request would filter to the proper department. Let the renter then beware. We pressed on north.

By the time I got to Grimtun the fish oil tank registered empty. Fortunately, fish oil was not in short supply in Grimtun. Half the fishing fleet were already out of the water for the season and stored in their cradles along the shore. I pulled up beside the docks and a battered wooden shed with a faded tin roof and a sign that used to advertise fresh fish. At least that’s what I think the remaining row of yellow letters announced.

A goblin garbed in a yellow slicker and red rubber boots eventually stepped into the sunshine, took a corncob pipe from his mouth as he studied me carefully. “Going to a wedding?”

“No, just taking a little drive in the country before winter. Can you fill me up?”

“Do you have a committee member in there?” He leaned forward and squinted at the heavily orange-tinted windows.

“No politicians. Only me. Do you have any fish oil?”

“Yep. Loads of it. Prime. Fresh this season.” These words came out mumbled around the stem of his pipe.

Fresh was not how I would have normally described the aroma drifting across the docks. “Can you fill my tank with fish oil?” I rolled each word out slowly so as not to confuse him."

"Nope." He spat on the weathered boards.

I held a fleeting image of me stopping every fifteen minutes to throw another log into the burner. "I can pay you for the fish oil."

"That's not the problem." The goblin scratched behind his ear.

I hung out the window and stared at him. "What is the problem then, my fine fellow?"

"You have to unlock the filler cap."

"Oh." I fumbled with the ring of gold and silver keys, got out then went around to the rear of my vehicle.

He pointed to a bright silver-plated circle protruding from the vehicle's side. I uncovered the cleverly hidden keyhole and studied my ring of keys.

"Try one of the silver ones, sonny."

It worked, and the lid popped open.

"How much oil do you want?"

"Fill her up," came out through clenched teeth.

The goblin brought out several battered cans and a funnel and poured the oil in. The Murrican swallowed six cans. "That will be six argentums." He held out a stained paw.

"I don't want to buy the whole town," I grumbled, fishing through my purse for the silver coins.

"Whole town would have cost you ten."

I sighed and pointed north along the beach. "Is this the road to Hades?"

"Why you going there?"

"I'm not. Just curious."

"Then that's the road."

I fired up my transport and drove away. We soon cleared Grimtun and were on a sand and gravel road winding through hayfields and swampland. The aroma of dead fish lingered for several leagues. Scattered views of the gray and rolling lake flashed through the trees on my right. To the west, hayfields turned to ploughed fields that obviously had been planted and harvested. The road became a two-track rollercoaster through the marsh. The Murrican complained loudly, snorting and bucking, and the balloon tires did little to smooth things out. I've been in storms on ships that rolled less than this expensive thing.

At last we linked up with a relatively smooth two lane road of crushed gravel. I held a sinking suspicion that this was the main road from Grimtun, not the narrow winding trail I'd been wrestling with for the past hour. This road led through cultivated fields to a narrow causeway jutting out into the lake. At the end of the causeway a treed island sprawled along the horizon. I cranked down my window. A chipped and weather-pitted sign shaped like a hand pointed one finger at the causeway. The letters spelled out "ades."

"I think we've arrived," I said to the last of my cold chocolate.

So, now what do I do? Linger around the fields waiting for someone to show up with a wagon loaded with parsnips? Press on to Hades and question the locals? The wind off the lake attempted to shake my vehicle.

My stomach rumbled for attention. That affected my decision. There was probably an inn or stage stop for travelers if anyone ever came this way. The inhabitants must refresh themselves somewhere. I pushed the long lever into gear and rolled toward the causeway.

With open water on both sides of the road, one side calm, the other shrieking with wind and waves, we crept out into the stretch of road leading into the lake. We looked to be only about the height of a gremlin above the level of the water. Waves pounded onto the gravel. Fortunately, the way was relatively straight.

Once or twice the Murrican's tires even slipped on the slick track. I wondered what the crossing would be like once the sun went down. The Murrican boasted an impressive collection of brass lamps mounted on the hood and across the roof. I idly imagined how much oil they'd consume on a dark and stormy night.

Halfway across to the island was a slight rise and a single lane bridge constructed of heavy wooden planks. I figured if the bridge was safe enough for loads of vegetables it should hold the weight of my precious UHRV. The structure shook and thundered as we crept across.

For one moment the hair on my neck tingled as though I passed through a set of magic wards, and I shivered. Then the sensation passed. I could have sworn the planks shifted beneath our wheels and breathed a sigh once we were back on solid roadway.

"The stupid things I do for clients and their coin," I mumbled.

I wasn't even sure what I was looking for up here. I was going to cross-examine a bunch of farmers and fishermen. I wasn't even certain what kind of folk I was going to be meeting up with.

"Must be slipping in my advancing years. Next time, Randy my old friend, please do some serious research before you hit the road instead of leaving things to chance and your nimble brain."

We rumbled off the far end of the causeway and on to relatively solid ground. The road led off the causeway, through a broad marsh on either side and into a forest.

"Well, we have arrived. Now what?" The way to Hades lay

ahead. “Next stop, lunch.” The Murrican belched smoke and gave off a strong whiff of fish. I suspected I would be well into the woodpile before we got back home.

I briefly wondered how Bertha was doing and then shrugged. She could take care of herself.

“Onward in search of lunch,” I said and urged my trusty steed forward in among the overhanging trees. “Hades, here we come, ready or not.”

Chapter Seven

After chugging through a forest for a few minutes we rumbled out into the open and a winding stretch of road running along a cliff that edged the shore. A large wooden sign in serious danger of slipping over the brink advised, "Welcome to Hades." At least, that's how I translated the weather-faded "Wel t Had." The land on the side of the road away from the lake was taken up with overgrown empty fields fading into forest. Where were all the houses?

I continued driving. It took me a few minutes of staring out the window at the deserted fields to become suspicious about the rounded grassy mounds half-buried in the long foliage. Some had smoking chimneys of stone or metal pipe, at least one boasted an opaque glass window, and a few had obvious hints of brightly colored wooden doors sunken into the grass. If most of the leaves hadn't already fallen the huts would be almost impossible to spot. I began to have serious doubts about finding a decent restaurant but carried on regardless.

Coming around a bend in the road I sighted a two-story wooden building squatting on the shore. The establishment was complete with wooden docks and a stone breakwater running out into a bay. A large storage shed leaned into the wind near the water. A row of fishing dories painted with multicolored stripes lined the shore beside the docks.

"Civilization at last." So far I hadn't seen any sign of life, other than the odd curl of pale smoke from a chimney. "This must be downtown Hades." I parked in front of the main building. The Murrican sighed, burped, and creaked to rest. The oil tank dial registered less than half full.

A large sign above the double doors announced "Alfholl" in fairly visible lettering. I pushed through and stepped inside. The room was dim, and it took a minute or two for my eyes to adjust. Oil lamps hung on the walls, the shades thick and allowing only a faint glimmer through. There were several round tables set with candles. At the far end was a bar running the full width of the room. Someone in an apron stood there illuminated by a stone fireplace.

"What can I do for you?" came out in a deep male voice. "Are you lost?"

I strode through the room toward the bar. "Any chance of getting lunch?" I said in my friendliest tone, adding a smile. I studied the barkeep. He was on the shortish side, maybe my height, but wider with messy red hair that completely covered his ears. I found difficulty in focusing on him. His face kept shifting in the poor light.

Yellow eyes reflected the candles on the bar. "Sorry friend, we're all full up."

I turned around, the room was empty, except now I noticed there were plates and mugs on almost every table. Most plates held food.

"I can pay," I said.

"Lunch is finished for the day. Why don't you try in Grimtun?"

"I just came from there." I glanced behind me, positive I heard the sound of chairs scraping on a wooden floor. The plates were empty. The front doors opened and closed, banging together several times.

"Neat trick. Let's try this again." I slapped a silver argentum on the bar. "I'll have a plate of what they were having. What's on tap?"

He shook his head. "Sorry, we're closed now."

"Oh Erik, give up and feed him so he can be on his way." The speaker from the far end of the bar was definitely female.

I turned in the direction of the voice. A shadow flickered in front of a lamp.

"Won't you join me?" I said.

"You stay out of this, Freydis, he was just leaving." The barkeep crushed his cloth into a tight ball.

"I can recommend the deep-fried parsnip chips with battered whitefish." The shadow moved toward me and flickered into the form of a thin creature my height with red hair cascading past her shoulders and large glowing orbs that turned into yellow eyes as she approached.

She smiled. "I battered the fish only this morning with a wooden maul so I can guaranty its tenderness. I'm Freydis, as you may have guessed by now. And you are…?" She extended a delicate, pale hand and long white fingers, most covered by elaborate silver and gold rings covered in curls and swirls.

"Randy Aloysius." I accepted her hand. The flesh felt cool.

"You just work here, Freydis," the barkeep mumbled.

"True Erik, but I also own the place. We'll have a mixed platter, the chips and fish with the Maltese vinegar sauce, and two mugs of the local. Chilled." She turned those big yellow eyes on me. "If you don't mind?"

"Of course not." Even if I did, I wouldn't. I followed her to a nearby table.

"Give me a minute while I clear this mess off." Freydis scooped up plates and spoons and mugs with one hand while whipping a cloth over the damp surface with the other. "The lunch crowd is often in too much of a hurry."

I tried to nonchalantly study Freydis as she swirled around the table and headed to the bar. Difficult to follow her movements, because of her speed and she did not always appear too solid. Even the floor length brown gown she wore flickered in and out. Erik had disappeared.

I thought I knew and could identify most creatures by sight or sound. These folk were not to be found on my mental chart, even after some quick prodding.

"So, what brings you all the way to Hades, Randy? Are you lost?" Freydis settled into a chair opposite me.

Lamplight shined through from somewhere behind her right shoulder. "Interesting establishment you have here."

"We're proud of it. Been in my family for years. And you are in Hades because…?" Those eyes fixed on mine. Freydis reached out across the table and took my hand in hers.

"I'll bet you can tell if I'm lying."

"Quite easily." She squeezed my fingers.

"What happens if I don't tell the truth?" I smiled.

"We have large barrels on the dock we use to store fish oil. They would easily hold a body. We've discovered if you toss in a few rocks, close the lid and roll the barrel into the bay, it quickly sinks to the bottom. May take years before it surfaces again."

I couldn't tell if she was joking. "I'm a private investigator from Central City." I dug in my jacket pocket with my free hand and slipped a business card across the table.

"I'm here on business investigating a murder that an old friend of mine is accused of." I decided to leave out the part about the missing parsnips. For all I knew, the villagers were the vegetable thieves.

"Did he do it?" She had quite the musical voice.

"Probably not."

"Why come way out here? We haven't had any recent murders that I know of." Those yellow eyes scanned my face.

"The murder occurred on the road from Hades to Grimtun."

"Ah, yes. There, that wasn't too difficult at all, now was it?

And here comes our lunch." Freydis released me.

Erik stomped from behind the bar carrying a tray with a steaming platter of food and two mugs carved from severely stained solid wood. The mugs held a dark colored liquid that sloshed over the lip, reminding me of the waves outside.

I picked at the parsnips and nibbled on the fish. Freydis was correct. The fish was melt-in-the-mouth tender. The parsnips I could cheerfully ignore, but I had to be polite. There were questions in need of answers.

I held up a piece of parsnip on my fork. "I understand these beauties are grown in Hades and you are famous for them."

"Not really grown in town. The fields are at the far end of the causeway, on the mainland."

"Do your people handle all the shipping too?" I accidently dropped a large chunk of parsnip on the floor and kicked it under our table.

"No. The city folk come up and take over once the wagons are loaded. What has your murder to do with the vegetable wagons?"

I found it disconcerting carrying on a conversation with her. She kept flickering and shifting allowing the lamps and candles to shine through her body. "I didn't say it did."

"Listen very carefully to me, Randy. You could quickly get way in over your head—up here—all alone. Right now I'm the only one standing between you returning to your office in one piece or you rolling down to the beach inside of a fish oil barrel. Erik is just scratching his armpit in glee at the thought of setting out a new anchor, with you attached to it. I'm a very good listener." The yellow eyes made a mild attempt at burning holes in my brain. "You are going to tell me the whole story, from beginning to end, right now. Aren't you, Randy?"

I blinked and shook to clear my head. "Nice try, Freydis, but that trick won't work on me." I resisted fingering the amulet Bertha gave me for my last birthday. "I'll tell you everything I know, but first I have a question."

"Can't blame a lady for trying. Don't get many opportunities to practice way up here. What's your question?" She grinned, and for a moment her lips were the only solid feature imprinted on her face.

"What kind of folk are the people living in Hades?" I had an itch in the back of my skull that I should actually know the answer. That itch was driving me mad. Hopefully, I hadn't upset her. I don't think I wanted to see Freydis angry. I launched a quick prayer toward the Trickster Coyote and his buddy, the Raven.

"Why Randy, I thought you would have guessed by now. You being a famous private eyeball and all."

She leaned forward across the table and took both my hands in hers. The better to judge my reaction, I suspected. I held my breath.

"Hades is the home of the Huldufolk." She smiled sweetly. "And I'm the village elder. In the olden days you would have called me the queen."

That figures! The early refugees from Icedland. They were said to be related to the high elves. I should have known. Back in the day, when I was a young pup in the Service, my platoon commander was a reckless little runt name of Dreki. He was always boasting he was from royalty. He often got kidded about his height, but he claimed his people were reduced in size from the snooty, overbearing, far-too-tall elves who infest the civilized south. The shrinking came about from living on a small, overcrowded island, according to him. At least Dreki got kidded until he pulled that shimmering, disappearing trick and leveled the kidder from behind. Tricky rascal.

"Do you happen to know someone name of Dreki?" I ventured. There was a slight family resemblance in the delicate contours of her face.

"He was my younger brother!" Freydis released her grip on me and leaned back in her chair, obviously startled. "He ran away from home in search of adventure. Last we heard he died in a brothel on Titan." She frowned and almost faded completely away.

"Yes he did. It was a burning brothel we were liberating from a band of slavers. There was a children's orphanage on the third floor. He was the first one up the stairs. Got most out before the roof collapsed."

Younger brother? That was a long time ago. Freydis still didn't look any more than just past being a teenager, herself.

We emptied our mugs, asked for refills, and I told her the whole parsnip and murder story, up until now. When I finished she sighed, stood up and glanced toward Erik, still hovering behind the bar. "Give him the bridal suite for tonight. He's leaving early tomorrow."

"The town won't like that." Erik glared at me.

"Tough peas and carrots," she said, then rose to her feet and handed me a napkin. "You will pick up all those parsnips you've dumped on the floor and wipe up, leaving things spotless."

"Yes ma'am." Discretion was a virtue when you have no idea how powerful the individual who was giving you instructions is.

"Don't you yes mam me, I'm not your mother. You can leave that monstrosity you drove here in parked out front. The thing will be safe enough there. The children will get a giggle out of it." Freydis whirled and almost melted into a cloud of light, then paused. "I will ask around and see what I can discover about these missing parsnips and the murder, although since they both happened between here and Grimtun I doubt I will find anything of value. You don't leave the area around the Alfholl or the docks and beach. Of course, you may go up to your room."

Freydis hesitated in the doorway, then turned again and smiled at me. "There will be a dance in the hall this evening. You will be expected to attend as my guest. If I have anything to report by then, I will tell you."

"Just to let you know, I don't dance," I said. I can of course, I just don't. It's one of those stubborn things Charity likes/liked about me.

"Tonight you will." Freydis disappeared through the doors. They vibrated slightly allowing a brief flash of sunlight, but did not open.

I turned to Erik and held out my wooden mug. "Any chance of getting a refill? What is this stuff, anyway?"

He took the mug from me. "On the house." Erik tilted his head in the direction of the now-motionless front doors. "Old Freydis can be a real pain in the hind quarters when she gets a bit between her teeth. Fortunately doesn't happen too often these days. Your room is up those stairs, last door on the right."

An elaborate staircase slowly came into view. I hadn't noticed it before. The stairs rose beside the far wall and disappeared through a gap in the ceiling. I could have sworn there was nothing there but large square plaster panels before.

I sat back alone at the table and sipped from my mug. "This stuff is quite tasty. What is it I'm drinking? If I had to guess, I'd say it was a mixture of old Irish and something local." Not that I'm an expert, just curious.

Erik yawned. "Last call before tonight's affair. That is a local blend all right. Made right here in Hades. You'll never find the like down south. We don't export it. We call it Jotun Juice."

"But what's in it?" I licked my lips.

"Oh the usual. Burnt parsnip puree, some local herbs and spices including leaf of parsnip picked beneath a full moon, and boiled fish roe. Sturgeon is the best. There are several secret recipes around Hades."

I set my mug carefully on the table. "I should probably head up to my room." In truth, I wasn't certain my feet would obey my commands.

“Yes, you’d better get some rest, my friend. There will be some dancing tonight. And old Freydis, she does like to dance. There will be more drink too.”

“I don’t dance,” I said. My legs had somehow turned to liquid. “I may give up on anything stronger than water,” came out as a mumble. My chin slowly descended until it rested on the table top. “I can’t seem to move.” The table took this opportunity to begin a slow spin.

“So Erik will carry you upstairs, he will. You’ll need those legs tonight.”

I caught a glimpse of Erik coming around the end of the bar, and then the few remaining lights in the room and the candles on the tables flickered and faded away into darkness.

Chapter Eight

"Wake up, my sleeping beastie. Wake up! Time to get Prince Charmed dressed for the ball."

I opened one eye and waited for my vison to clear. Freydis stood at the foot of a large four-poster bed holding up a clothes hanger with what appeared to be a jacket and trousers. They were both fluorescent green. I blinked and tried to sit. Instead I flopped backwards deep into a soft mattress. I tried to focus on Freydis.

She wore a shimmering aquamarine gown with a full ballroom skirt and an off-the-shoulder look enhanced by a narrow gold torq twisted around her throat. Red hair piled high around a diamond tiara. Freydis was semi-transparent. I could just make out the shape of the open door behind her.

"I don't feel well," I said. "I think I should just stay here until morning."

"Not on your little nelly, sonny, the music is about to start. Get yourself dressed. I will wait outside your door for five minutes. Any longer than that, and I will come in and dress you myself." Freydis seemed to grow taller, leaned over the bed as she smiled. The yellow eyes opened wide. Her voice sank to a subterranean level. "And there is no guaranty I will be gentle."

"I'll get up but I told you, I don't, I can't, dance."

"Leave that to me." She draped the clothes over the foot of my bed, pirouetted, then swept out of the room.

I decided it would probably be best if I didn't annoy her and stepped out into the hall a few minutes later. The jacket was long, the puffy shirt ruffled, the pants my size. The whole ensemble came in varied shades of green. Even the buckled shoes fit. I left the top hat balanced on a bedpost.

Freydis looked me over.

"I feel like a right willy-nilly," I said.

She wore bright red, high-buttoned boots that clashed with the ankle-length gown. "You'll do nicely."

"No I won't," remained under my breath.

She held out her hand. Rings dazzled while gold serpent bracelets circled both bare arms. "Come, they won't start the music until we arrive."

"I still don't dance." I'd heard the bedtime stories about the bad old days when lonely travelers were lured into underground palaces by the little people with wild and forever promises of gold, and romance, and dancing. Their queens were said to be especially adept at the practice. Those sad silly tales were a relic of the old county. But that didn't happen in today's modern world. The committees certainly wouldn't allow such carryings-on.

"Just follow me." She led me down the sweeping stairway.

I almost said, "Anywhere," before I got a firm grip on my rebellious tongue.

The crowded Alfholl was lit by a thousand candles floating from the ceiling in brightly polished wooden wagon wheels. At one end of the hall, on a dais decorated with emerald bunting, stood five musicians wearing floppy, tasseled caps and holding sparkling fiddles. A crowd of couples filled the main floor. Complete with top hat and short jacket, Erik leaned behind the bar. A row of mugs lined the gleaming surface from one side of the room to the other. Everyone was heavily bejeweled and all garbed in a shade of green, be it aquamarine, jade, emerald, olive, or some ancient forgotten forest or grassy knoll. Slightly unsettling, everyone but me was also semi-transparent.

I blinked. The effect on the hall floor below us was dazzling.

At the foot of the stairs she gave a wave of her hand. "Come, let the dancing begin." The crowd screamed and parted, and Freydis led me onto the floor.

"I can't dance," I said, and then was swept up and swirled away to the sound of wild fiddling and a laughing, unruly crowd.

I think she carried me, off my feet, as we hurtled around the room. Her skin was red and flushed, bright eyes fixed on my face. I know now how one might feel if they fell into a churning washing machine suddenly caught up in a tornado. Elbows flew in all direction, boots narrowly skimmed my toes, and red hair spun like laundry hung in a windstorm. The room blurred, the music howled, and countless transparent feet sounded like a herd of bison on a stampeding rampage. Then the musicians exchanged fiddles for pipes and the dancing sped up.

It must have been after several hours, with me flying like a spinning rag around the room, when we whirled past the bar, Freydis swept up a mug, and we whirled out an open rear door and into the chill night. I don't think my feet had touched the floor since we first stepped onto the polished floorboards.

I also didn't believe I'd ever catch my breath again. Freydis linked her arm with mine and led me down to the pebbly beach. There was a full moon balanced on the waves and an onshore breeze just strong enough to whip the water into rolling waves and breaking foam. Behind us the door to the hall swung closed, cutting off a path of escaping golden light and dampening the wild music down to an itch that threatened to start my toes tapping. My tired feet resisted.

Freydis wasn't even breathing hard, although a sparkle of perspiration graced her forehead when she turned to face me.

"'Tis a magic night," she whispered. Freydis held out the mug. It held an all-too familiar dark liquid filled to the brim. "Would you like to share a sip?"

I was panting like a long-haired hound crossing the Gone Bye-Bye Desert in mid-summer. "How, how did you manage to liberate a mug without spilling half the contents?"

"*Long* experience." She gazed at me, took a sip, then licked her lips. "Well?"

Memories of earlier today flashed through my fevered brain. "Ah, if you don't mind, I think I'll pass on that kind offer."

She patted my cheek. "You've sampled our famous Jotun Juice and suffered the after-effects. The second sip won't be nearly so—forceful."

"I'll still pass, thank you."

"To the old gods." Freydis leaned her head back and downed the contents of the mug in one long gulp. She flung the wooden mug high over the waves. "Take my offering and be satisfied."

She stared out over the lake. "Do you find it peaceful here?"

I could see the moonlight shining right through her body and gown and sparkling on the foam. "It might well be, except for the dancing and the selection of beverages."

She smiled. "I know of a pleasant vacant home close to mine. The rent would be free and the nearest neighbor an excellent cook. Do you like fishing?"

"The only fishing I do is in the stew pot or the frying pan." A small voice deep inside was whispering, "Run, Randy, run!"

"Well, we can always find use in Hades for a chief forester or a farm supervisor." Those yellow eyes turned from examining the lake to stare at me.

Someone must have opened the door behind us a crack. A

bright ray of light haloed the edges of her red hair. Notes belonging to a drunken jig that even I recognized as *The Wild Icedlander Buoy* stumbled toward the lake.

Erik's voice followed the beam of light. "Just checking. Would anyone down there like a refill?"

"Not me," I said.

"We're good," she said. "As can be expected."

The band chose that moment to slow to a rendition of *When Ice-cold Eyes are Smitten.* I've traveled a fair bit on this world and a few others. That brought back a sad flash of memory of a sunset on Venus when I was young and stupid. But that is also another story.

"All right, then," Eric said, closed the door, and the music faded and died away.

"I've really enjoyed my visit to Hades." I spoke to the back of her head. Freydis was studying the waves again. "But I'm on a case, and I have a business back in Central City. I should call it a night, turn in early, and get on with my work tomorrow."

She looked over her bare shoulder and studied my face. "Well, I did say I would see what I could find out about your missing parsnips and the murder, and my word is good. Alfgeir, here to me, now."

A moment later the hall door opened, and a youth appeared from inside. "Yes, Mother?"

"Fetch me a parsnip. A raw one just collected from the fields no more than a day ago."

He disappeared into the shadows.

She rubbed her hands together. "We have to make a circle. Give me a hand and collect round stones that were washed by the waves tonight. Only those visible to the moon's light."

I collected the stones where the waves wetted the sand, and she arranged them in a ring and then squatted cross-legged in the center. The buttoned red boots had been replaced by green glass, high-heeled slippers.

"You'll get your gown dirty."

Freydis smiled and winked. "It wouldn't be the first time." She cracked her knuckles.

Alfgeir appeared from around the corner of the hall. He wore a top hat and long jacket, both in the obligatory green. Shorter than me, he had a trim red beard and carried the largest parsnip I'd ever seen.

Freydis held out her hand. "Good choice. Now give it to me and go back to your dancing before Cathinca finds another partner."

"Aww, can't I watch?"

"No, you are too young."

"That's what you always say, Mother."

"Then it must be true. Go! Before I..."

He fled.

Freydis waited, eyes closed, until he vanished back inside the hall and the door banged closed leaving us with only the moonlight. She picked up the parsnip, dirt still clinging, and sniffed at it. Next, she ran her tongue slowly around the vegetable, and took a small bite.

"Parsnip, reveal your secrets to me," she whispered, eyes shut, a slight smile playing around the edges of her mouth.

We must have waited at least ten minutes on the beach, me standing and Freydis rocking gently back and forth with the wind rustling her hair like it was a waking nest of long, thin red snakes.

At last her eyes opened, and she smiled. "Ah hah, I have it now."

"Good. What is it you've found?"

"What's it worth to you?" She stood up and shook the sand from her ball gown. She stepped across the circle of stones and stood nose-to-nose with me. "What is my information worth to you, Randy?"

"Well, I could pay..." My throat went dry. Was she angry? Insulted? Would anyone ever find my body? "I... Ah..."

"Poor helpless mortal," she said, flung her arms around my neck and kissed me soundly on the mouth. "That will have to do for now, I suppose," came out when she paused for breath.

I didn't move. She took my hand. "Walk with me along the beach while I tell you what I know and think about what happens next."

I caught a glimpse of the large fish oil barrels lined up on the dock. My spine tingled. I would easily fit into one with room to spare.

"Poor dear, your fingers are ice cold. Let me warm them." She breathed on my hand.

"What have you learned?" I croaked. Might as well learn my fate. The night was clearing my fuddled brain though.

"Your precious parsnips are hidden inside a large barn outside of Grimtun. You need to deliver how many wagons to the Forks Garden Market?"

"Five wagon loads." I sighed. "And I'm running out of days." Did I have time to get back to Central City, find enough help, return to Grimtun, rescue the parsnips, and deliver them in good condition to Able Bowdee before the Annual Parsnip Festival? A groan escaped me.

"I may be able to assist you with that. But I do have a price," was whispered in my ear.

I winced. Maybe I should just book a one-way ticket to Europa.

"If I help you, and you ultimately deliver the parsnips on time, you will agree to return and spend a weekend in Hades. I will take you fishing. Is it a deal? Yes or no."

I must have looked confused. My, "Yes," was a mumble. I nodded. Was that voluntary or…?

"Agreed, then. Unfortunately, I cannot see anything which will help you to solve your murder. The wagon was waylaid, the parsnips spilled when the driver tried to escape, and someone struck him as he lay beside the wagon. I couldn't see who did the deed." She smiled. "No parsnips were involved in the sudden death of the driver."

Yellow eyes bored into me. She took my hand. "We have a deal, correct?"

We shook on it. At least I think I did.

Freydis wrinkled her brow. "It would be better to rescue the parsnips after dark, and I need some time to prepare. You may sleep in late tomorrow morning, and we will meet at your ridiculous machine by noon." She took a firm grip on my arm and spun me back around in the direction of the Hades's Alfholl. "So, we have plenty of time. The music is still playing. The bar is open until dawn. Listen! They're starting up the *Ragna Rock*. One of my favorites. Shall we dance?"

My feet left the ground, and I found myself dragged back toward the steady sound of screeching fiddles and heavy stomping. Resistance was futile.

Chapter Nine

I woke with the sun streaming through the open window. It was almost noon. I stared at the ceiling. The lace curtains fluttered in a breeze.

To say I'm not fond of elves was no wild exaggeration, although I'm forced to admit that I have come across a few in my lengthy career, very few, mind you, who are *almost* decent. My developing opinion of these vertically challenged throwback inhabitants of Hades was confused at best. Like their taller brethren they were pushy and overly confident they were always right. I threw off the covers and sat up. I was dressed in the same clothes I arrived at Hades in.

I tried to recall the events of the previous night or more accurately, sometime earlier this morning. I vaguely remember dancing with Freydis. I may have accepted a mug handed to me by Erik. What was I doing walking along the beach at sunrise? Without shoes!

I tapped my skull. Amazing, it did not vibrate or pound. I wiggled my toes. My feet were bare. No sounds drifted up from below. Had someone stolen my favorite socks?

"Best if I just grab my stuff and get out of here ASAP. No sense waiting around to find out what evil scheme Queen Freydis has in mind for me." I gathered my things, checked my weapons, then headed downstairs into the main hall.

Thc placc was ncat as my Aunt Ccrisc's spccial high-class parlour where she entertained the wealthy gentleman before they went upstairs. I paused at the foot of the staircase and gazed around. The hall looked as though nothing had taken place in there the night before. The tables and chairs were all neatly set out. The locals should be getting ready for the luncheon crowd. I think the room was empty, although with these shifty Huldufolk it was difficult to tell. I went out through the double doors and into the sunlight.

"About time you got up." Freydis, dressed in a heavy plaid

shirt and weathered denim jeans, stood leaning against the Murrican. Glass slippers had been traded in for scuffed, brown work boots. She was not alone.

A half-dozen or more of the Huldufolk waited there with her surrounding my vehicle. Their garb caught my eye. In quite a departure from the finery of the previous night, they were all dressed in a variety of work clothes and headgear. Most wore bowler or top hats. A few had what I took for plain metal helmets fashioned from worn-out pots and pans. But it was the large collection of axes that made me nervous. Most clutched weapons taller than themselves. Of course, the whole crowd tended to flicker and shift, giving glimpses of sunlight on the road and the Murrican behind them.

The only way I could tell the young males jostling in front of me from the females was the ragged fringe of red beard, although I was not certain that was a fool-proof method.

"I think we're all here." Freydis looked around. She smiled at me. "I'll give them their marching orders and then you may take over and assume command."

"Marching orders?" came out as a dying frog's feeble croak.

"Yes. Rally around everyone. Alfgeir, step forward."

The youth I vaguely remembered from some dim event I participated in last night stepped out of the crowd. He wore a green bowler hat that clashed with his red beard, and a leather jacket with a hint of gleaming mail peeking out from beneath. The axe in his hand towered overhead. If that sight wasn't frightening enough, his belt contained a large array of tools, including a shorter axe, and a heavy hammer suitable for breaking rocks.

"Yes, Mother." He saluted.

She leaned forward and wiped his nose. "Now, I'm naming you as second-in-command. You will keep the troop in line and do everything Randy tells you. Promise?"

"Yes, Mother."

"Now wait just a minute here," I said. "What are you planning to do?"

She winked. "We are planning a raid on the villainous horse and unicorn thieves who waylaid several shipments of parsnips legally sent south from here."

"Hooray for the queen!" went up from the crowd around the Murrican. Weapons rattled and feet stomped in the dirt.

"We cannot allow any interruptions to our main source of income. We will not permit it." Freydis rose to her full height and looked me in the eye.

If it wasn't for her backwoods outfit, I would have easily taken her for some ancient Royalty.

"A nice speech, but someone might get hurt."

"*That* is the whole idea!" Alfgeir shouted.

"Hoo-rah!" More foot-stomping and axe-rattling followed.

Freydis beckoned to one of the folk in the pounded metal helmets. Long red braids poked out from beneath. "Cathinca has the maps I drew with the location of the barn and the stolen wagons. She will act as your guide."

"You're sending women and little girls into this mess?" I rolled my eyes. "That is…"

"That is *what,* Randy?" cut into my unprepared speech. Yellow eyes narrowed into thin slits. Pointed eyebrows twitched. "Do you have an objection to my plans you would dare like to voice? Have I missed something?"

Silence fell heavily on the street.

"Just getting clarification," I said.

"We should have a battle flag," Alfgeir said. "To terrify the enemy."

"I think you are frightening enough as you are." I sighed. "Besides, a flag would only get in our way. We are going to rely on stealth for this venture, not overwhelming brute force."

"No grand charges?" Alfgeir sounded disappointed. "With horns and banners and blood-curdling yells?"

"Absolutely none."

"Listen to your commander," Freydis said. "Pay close attention to him."

"We could make a banner out of a fierce fish-head and an old boat hook," Cathinca suggested.

"I think not." The image that brought to mind was something less than terrifying.

Freydis glanced at the sky. "If you leave now, and drive very slow, you can launch the attack at dusk. They won't be expecting you."

"I'll take your word for that." I sounded bolder than I felt.

"You had better." The smile returned, and she winked at me again.

I examined my small army. "There's no room inside for all of these fine fellows and fair damsels. At best I can take two with me on the front seat."

"No problem. We've emptied the woodpile. That can hold three or four. The rest can ride up top on the roof." Freydis surveyed us. "I think that's everything. Domhildur is in charge of the picnic lunch."

I rolled my eyes. "First of all, without my chopped wood I don't have enough fuel on board to get us to Grimtun, let alone me back to Central City."

"Don't worry, we've topped the fuel tank." Alfgeir flashed a broad grin.

I looked the Murrican over. "And what are those casks lashed up top?"

"More fuel," Cathinca said. "Spares." She held rolls of what appeared to be several maps stuffed under each arm.

"In case of emergency, like if we get thirsty." Domhildur, a round young damsel with a green top hat decorated with dead flowers and two braids tied over the entire arrangement, nodded eagerly. She wore a suspiciously long leather coat that brushed the ground and carried two covered wicker picnic baskets, one in each fist. A pair of short axes were suspended across her back.

I shook my head. Even if this mad scheme was successful, how would I get the parsnips safely back to Central City?

"Allow me give you a proper farewell," was whispered in my ear. "Won't you join me in a dark corner of the Alfholl for an until-we-meet–again little something?" Two red eyebrows danced on a mischievous forehead.

"I don't think that's a good idea."

"Probably not, but…?"

"We should be going." I inspected my force. "First of all, please leave all the long-handled axes behind. I suspect we would do more damage to ourselves by accident with those than to the opposition." I pictured a tangle of Huldufolk swinging wildly with large sharp blades. "Besides, we don't have the room. Your short ones will have to do."

That announcement caused a collective groan.

"Behave and listen to your commander." Freydis crossed her arms and furrowed her brow.

She looked fierce enough to back off a rabid dragon. Must practice that in a mirror.

"Aww." At least the troops were paying attention.

Another ten minutes passed as Huldufolk chose favorite short axes, argued about seating, and eventually I ended up with Alfgeir and Cathinca perched on the Murrican's front bench. Domhildur and her baskets took up residence in the wood box, along with two drooling youths in top hats. Four more Huldufolk climbed up top and pushed and shoved until a glare from Freydis settled them down.

I leaned against the Murrican's door and examined the interior.

A headache threatened. "I think we're all ready."

Freydis wrapped both arms around my waist. "Now, don't forget your promise to me. Things will go seriously wrong for you if you don't live up to your word."

Did I make a reckless promise last night? "Can I have something in writing so I don't forget the exact wording?"

"The notarized document is already waiting for you on your desk back in the office."

"Oh."

She kissed me. I couldn't resist. Elven queens and seriously nasty witches were like that. Even short, reclusive ones. Besides, it wouldn't have been polite, considering everything she was doing to aid me.

Freydis released me. "You will send my troop directly back to me as soon as you are finished at the barn. Promise me that."

"Yes, ma'am." So much for me borrowing a few spare wagon drivers to get me safely home with my parsnips.

"I told you not to call me mam. Do so again and I may become extremely cross. You wouldn't like that." She wagged her finger in my direction.

"I expect not." I climbed up into the driver's seat and closed the door.

"If they march all night they should be back here by dawn. I will expect them then. All of them." Freydis blew me a kiss.

"I'll send the recruits straight home." I put the Murrican into reverse gear, and we backed into the street. Glancing behind us I caught a glimpse of Freydis and Erik standing in front of the Alfholl waving in the middle of a crowd that flickered and shifted like thin lace in the wind.

We chugged toward the causeway leading back to the mainland.

Alfgeir was bouncing in his seat with excitement. "Mother would never let me go farther than the parsnip fields. I could help load the wagons, then always had to return straight home. What an adventure."

Cathinca pulled out a parchment map and spread it over her lap. "Stay on the main road."

"Keep your grubby fingers away from the picnic basket or I will chop them off." Domhildur's voice drifted from the rear.

"Mother is very strict."

I glanced over at Alfgeir. "Don't play with your axe while we're moving."

We reached the causeway.

"I've never been across here before," Cathinca said. "Never been this far."

"It's ever so dangerous," Alfgeir contributed. "What with sea dragons, and tsunamis, and a volcano at the far end. It's a good thing I'm here to protect you."

There was the sound of slapping from the direction of the wood box. "I warned you," Domhildur said.

We rumbled and bounced across the loose squared timber that made up the bridge in the center of the causeway. I felt the twinge as we passed through the guardian wards.

There was a loud cheer from the gang clinging to the roof. "We made it!" Hob-nailed shod feet stamped on the ceiling. Someone up there with an excellent voice started up a chorus of *It's a Long Way to Tipsy Mary's*. Someone had brought a set of pipes for accompaniment.

The appearance of a fiddler wouldn't have surprised me, although the Murrican was rocking in all directions like a leaf in a thunderstorm. Hanging on upstairs would be excitement enough.

"Stay on the main road," Cathinca announced. "And slow down. We want it to be dark by the time we get there."

"All righty." I groaned.

"She reminds me of my mother sometimes," Alfgeir said.

"How fortunate for you."

For some strange reason, Cathinca gave me a sharp poke in my ribs with the butt end of her axe handle. "Concentrate on the road."

"Yes, ma'am."

We rumbled off the causeway and found the main highway. Alfgeir and I both sighed and stared straight ahead. The chorus upstairs started another round. Someone in the wood box squealed, "Ouch!"

We had several leagues to go before dark.

Chapter Ten

Cathinca unrolled a second map as we neared Grimtun. "Take the first road to the right."

We turned along a wide gravel track. The windscreen on the Murrican automatically darkened. The sun, now in our face and looking like a large Humpty-Dumpty on fire, was settling on the treetops converting the sky to blood-red. The crowd on the roof fell into silence, although the piper was still murdering a soft version of *Take Me to Hades, Again, Elfur.*

"There should be a place to pull off and reconnoiter up ahead after the next bridge." Cathinca tossed the map over her shoulder and shook out a third version.

I slowed the vehicle. "How many maps did Freydis draw?"

"Do you want plenty of detail or not? I have two more. The last one shows the inside of the barn."

"Mother always was a stickler for detail." Alfgeir wiped his nose on his sleeve.

"That's what I'm afraid of." There was a patch of open grass beside the creek, and I pulled over.

"Are we there yet?" came from one of the passengers on the roof.

"I hope so," Domhildur added. "We should eat now. These dried fish and ground parsnip sandwiches will get stale if we wait until after the battle."

Alfgeir leaned around Cathinca and peered at me. "Do you always eat before a battle? That sounds much better than waiting until after."

"But if we wait until after, there will be more to go around. You know, because of all the deaths and serious wounds." Cathinca unfolded a large diagram on a dried square of animal skin.

"Good point." He nodded.

"But I'm hungry now," called one of Domhildur's companions

from inside the wood box.

"We will eat now," I announced, shutting off the Murrican's engine with accompanying pops and groans from the boiler. "This will not be a battle, at worst, more like a brief skirmish." I hoped.

"Aww."

Domhildur ordered everyone to sit in a circle and passed out the sandwiches, rationing them to one per combatant. I declined her offer on principle. Mainly the conviction that if the ingredients didn't kill me the after-effects would. Everyone also received a paper napkin.

"I am not going to wipe your faces. You will take care of your own." She set the picnic baskets down in the center of the group. "You may each take one more sandwich. When you are finished, garbage goes in the baskets. We do not leave a mess."

She pointed to one of the smaller top hats from the wood box. "Yes, Gunnbor, you may start a fire if you keep it small. Coals only. No flames higher than a mouse's backside."

Alfgeir leaned over and whispered in my ear. "Domhildur tends to be bossy at times. She is going to be a teacher when she grows up. Beginner's class."

She seemed all grown-up to me and quite fierce. "Probably a natural."

Darkness crept overhead except along the western horizon and the edges of the clouds. They were still touched with crimson and orange. The forest was black. I was beginning to have more serious misgivings about this expedition. Even if it succeeded, how was I going to get enough parsnips to Central City in time to save the festival? Then there was the slight matter of the murder. I still had to find out who dun it and save Charlie's worthless skin.

I gazed around our camp. Why did this feel more like a Samhain Night school picnic than a forward military base? Of course the Huldufolk were difficult enough to spot in the daylight. In the gathering dark, around a tiny fire, they were almost invisible.

"Everyone who has to relieve themselves, go now," Domhildur announced. "There may not be time later. In the trees, not here!"

Alfgeir busied himself examining the edge of his short axe. He drew blood and stuffed his thumb in his mouth. "Good. The edge, I mean."

Cathinca pushed in on my other side, squatted on the ground then unfolded a parchment. "Here is the diagram of the barn. You will note the six wagons lined up along the west wall. They are full of parsnips. There are four guards playing Young Milkmaid. There are two more sleeping in the loft. There is one outside, um, studying the stars."

She waved a second scrap of parchment under my nose, opening the map with a flick of her wrist and laying it alongside the first. "This shows our route to the barn. Past this little woodlot is a field. Beyond, the barn is over a snake fence. The barn door faces west and toward the farmhouse."

"How many are in the farmhouse?"

"No worries. They've just had a big meal and will sleep till morning."

"Excuse me," I said. "I don't mean to be rude, and I'm certainly not questioning your veracity, but just how do you know all this?" As I watched over her shoulder, one of the figures on the map of the barn stood up, stretched, and went outside.

"You were there." Alfgeir put away his axe. "You were there when Mother checked with a parsnip." He stood up. "I'm all ready to go."

"We are too." The others filtered and flickered back into the clearing adjusting helms and clothing. A red beard was holding hands with a set of long braids dangling from beneath a battered pot helmet. After a glare from Domhildur, fingers were released.

"We go on foot from here," Cathinca announced.

Weapons came out. I decided I'd better take command before serious wounds occurred. "Okay, everyone pay close attention. You will stay close to me. We will use stealth."

"We can be pretty stealthy," Alfgeir said.

"Good. I do not want to see any bloodshed. We will overpower and tie them up." I wondered if I could bribe any of our prisoners to help me get the parsnips back south to market.

I drew Bess from my shoulder holster and checked the clip. There were eight penetrol shells in there. The hollow, red dye-filled shells will paralyze a living target, although the definition of *living* was broad enough to include such like vampires and zombies. With some creatures the effect takes longer. Most average folk go down within seconds. Normal clothing doesn't slow the paralysis. How long the freezing lasts depends on the nature and size of the target.

I turned to Cathinca. "I don't suppose you can tell from your maps what kind of villains we are up against?"

"Of course. Goblins."

"There are at about seven of them, more or less." Based on past experiences, I don't put all my faith in the accuracy of magic maps.

"Correct."

So, I should be able to bring down at least two or three before complete chaos ensues. Goblins were speedy little devils and tended to swarm when attacked. "Here is the plan. I will go first. The rest follow single file. Do we have any rope?"

"We brought several lengths, just in case. They are stashed in the wood box." Domhildur clapped her hands. "Finnboga, fetch the rope."

A short, red-headed rascal wearing an oversized black bowler fitted with tiny horns scrambled into the back of the Murrican and returned with arms filled with hemp.

My army was jumping up and down, stretching muscles and flexing axes, hammers, and other assorted hardware including at least two baseball bats.

"We will shed no unnecessary blood." I frowned around the troop, trusting they could see my face in the gloom. I was having difficulty seeing them.

"Aww."

"We will rely on stealth."

Domhildur reached into the large purse slung at her side and shook out some pieces of loosely woven brown cloth. "I brought some empty parsnip sacks." She handed them around. "They will be useful in bagging the enemy."

"Use the flat side of your axes. I want unconsciousness, not decapitated." I figured if these rascals about to face us really were famous horse and unicorn rustlers they probably had loose connections with the minions of the law in Grimtun. I wanted no delays in getting back to Central City once I figured out how to go about it.

We crept up the road along the trees, then into the stubble of the cornfield single file. Ahead, across our path, stretched the outline of the wooden snake fence. Beyond, the bulk of the barn loomed like a black castle. In the distance, the house stood dark. I felt Alfgeir's breath on my neck.

"Let me go first," he whispered.

"First, you have to be a gentleman and help me over the fence," Cathinca said. Her arms were full of maps.

"Oh just put those silly things down. We don't need them now." Alfgeir flourished his axe.

"Your mother wants them back and in good condition. *She* insisted."

"Oh." He fastened the handle of his axe to his belt and lent Cathinca a hand, boosting her over the rails with a heave and a grunt.

Domhildur paused and looked around at the line of warriors fading into the night and strung out behind her. "Well? Who is going to assist me?"

Silence.

"I'm waiting."

I've heard many ominous voices in my lengthy days. This was definitely a danger-filled tone.

At last Falgeir stepped forward, straightened his bowler, then bravely put his hands on her waist.

"Watch where those fingers are going!"

"Yes, mam." He moved his hands higher.

"Not too much higher, young man."

He heaved, and Domhildur cleared the fence, dusting herself off on the other side.

"Brave lad," Alfgeir whispered.

We crept from the rear of the barn, along the side trying not to stumble over hidden things, until Cathinca grabbed at my arm. "There's one just around the corner," she hissed in my ear, pointing to the map.

I drew Bess and chambered a round.

Alfgeir chuckled, shook out a parsnip sack, and slipped around me before I could say, "Whoa." He moved without any noise, impressive, given all the metal attachments adorning his body. His axe balanced in his other hand.

There was a thump, a groan, and the sound of fabric meeting flesh. A minute later he returned, grinning, and held up his sack. "Bagged one."

Six more to go, maybe.

"The rest are all in the barn now." Cathinca flourished her map. "They're playing cards, except for the sleepers in the loft."

"Should be easy enough to sneak up on them," Alfgeir grunted. "Let's go."

I was going to point out that my Huldufolk army were still fairly visible in the light, given all the attachments hanging from their outfits. There was no sense in delaying. I could feel the pressure of eager bodies pressing up against my back. I have been in a few serious military engagements before and in some not quite so serious. I suspected in order to keep Freydis from flaying my hide I had to return this squad to her in reasonably good condition.

"Advance, but no noise." I clenched my jaw and followed Alfgeir toward the open double doors and lantern glow, all the while wincing at the sound of much pushing and shoving behind me.

We peered inside. "There are six playing with face cards."

One of the players glanced up.

"Charge!" Alfgeir yelled then dashed inside, waving his axe.

"Long live Queen Freydis!"

The others swept by me on either side, almost knocking me over.

"Hades forever!"

"Loki and Luck!"

"Fish on Friday!"

"Free the Parsnips!"

The goblins scattered to meet the charge. There were too many combatants in front of me to allow for a clear shot. The scene reminded me of playing rugby on Mars, when I was much younger, of course. The goblins had no time to go for their weapons, but they still had their teeth and claws. The noise was enough to wake the dead if they were nearby. I shook my head. One goblin made it all the way to the row of wagons parked against one wall. He began hurling parsnips into the fray.

Then I noticed the activity in the loft. Half a dozen ropes were uncoiling and dropping. Goblins appeared over the edge. They were armed. They were climbing down or sliding.

I shot the first one in mid-air, and he dropped like a dead pigeon. The second one tried to make it difficult for me by swinging on the rope. My shot loosened his grip, and he disappeared into a stack of hay bales. The third one was leaning over the edge of the loft peering down when I hit him square in the chest. He teetered back and forth before performing a wounded swan dive and a satisfactory plop on the barn floor.

By this time most of the card players were hog-tied and bagged, and a swarm of Huldufolk were heading up the ropes, axes and other utensils clamped in their jaws. The loft surrendered.

Alfgeir saluted, grinning like a Cheshire cat with gas. "The enemy has been defeated, sir! All present, accounted for, bagged, and tagged like a load of whitefish. Or parsnips. Mother will be pleased."

Someone tugged on my sleeve. Cathinca looked worried. "I was afraid of this. There are no horses, unicorns, oxen in here. I didn't see any on the maps. No livestock at all." She shook her head. "How will you ever get the parsnips down to the city?"

I turned to a goblin, his head sticking out of a parsnip sack. He had one blackened eye and a large lump rising from the top of his green skull. "Where are the animals that were used to pull these wagons?"

He spat blood and grinned. "Gone, all gone. We sold them. You're out of luck, bud. You'll have to walk the parsnips out of here."

Chapter Eleven

We rallied the troops.

"We could fill the Murrican with parsnips," Alfgeir suggested. "With our help it won't take long, and we can still get home to Hades before Mother throws a fit."

"The Murrican won't even hold half of what's on one wagon" I frowned. "And I'm almost out of fuel. I probably don't have enough fish oil to make it to Grimtun."

"I could show you the shortest route." Cathinca waved a map.

"No use." I was tired, hungry, and starting to feel the effects of a couple of very long days. Maybe I could fill the back of the Murrican with wood and have enough to juice to get across the nearest border. I sighed and shook my aching head. No, I couldn't abandon Bertha to face the wrath of Able Bowdee on her own.

"Check your fuel gage," Domhildur said.

"Probably reads empty." I hadn't glanced at it on the way down. I knew I should have the range to get us to the parsnips before we ran out. Although, we did have a heavy load.

"I'll go get it and bring it here for you." Alfgeir tied his axe back onto his belt. "Give me the keys."

"Do you know how to drive?" Sleep threatened.

"Of course."

"Do you have a license?" That was the law. I suspected he was still a minor too.

"Don't need one. My mother's the queen." He grinned.

"Oh, here." I tossed him the ring of keys. He grabbed Cathinca's hand, and they fled.

"No loitering!" I yelled after them. With a groan I settled on top of a nearby hay bale. I was almost asleep when I heard the purr of the Murrican's twin stacks. The big machine backed through the open barn doors, shook, and coughed to a rest. Water dripped from the bottom.

"Check your fuel gage," Domhildur said.

"Are all Huldufolk females bullies?" I muttered as I creaked to my feet.

"What's that?" She leaned toward me. Her green top hat tilted at a dangerous angle. The twin short axes, now slung again across her back, clanked together.

"Nothing."

I opened the cab door and peered inside. The gold-plated gauge claimed it was full. I turned to Alfgeir. "Where did you find the fish oil to top it up?" My gaze settled on the barrels lashed to the roof.

"I didn't." He shrugged. "I didn't fill it up. Just drove it here. Might have detoured through the creek. Cathinca wanted to see how deep it could go."

"Don't blame me," the sturdy young lady announced. "That was all your idea."

I frowned and scratched my head. "Well, if you filled it up with fish oil in Hades, and we drove all the way here, something doesn't add up. And we didn't burn any wood."

"We didn't fill the tank with fish oil in Hades," Domhildur said.

"We used Jotun Juice. Thought it would be better." Alfgeir gave a broad grin. "Useful to have around if we gets thirsty after all this battling and traveling adventure stuff."

"That's what is in the barrels on the roof." She licked her lips.

"But the gauge still says the tank is full." I stared at the prospective schoolmarm. "How do you explain that?"

"Simple thermal dynamics. Burns better, provides more power too. A lot more power."

"How much more power?" I stared at the row of wagons.

"A lot more power. Bet you could probably pull several wagons behind that oversized thing of yours. Full wagons." A pair of large yellow eyes batted at me. "I've never been to the big city. You should probably take me along. In case you have any mechanical problems. After, you could show me around the town." She did an imitation of a pouty face. "Freydis doesn't have to know. I won't tell. I bet they even have dancing down there."

"But I'd tell," said Alfgeir.

"So would I," added Cathinca.

"And Queen Freydis would definitely notice if she was one small, young lady short." I shook my head. "Let's hook this thing up and see how many wagons it can pull. There's a hidden hitch at the back. All we need is some chain."

"Thank you for the compliment." Domhildur curtsied.

"Compliment?"

"For calling me small." Her face turned red, and she ran off calling, "Chains! Find us some chains."

Chains were rounded up and secured to the trailer hitch. We fastened the Murrican to a loaded wagon and moved forward. No problem. The second wagon was connected to the first, and we rolled forward again. Still no problem. The Murrican chugged and hissed and puffed odiferous blasts from both stacks, and rumbled ahead.

We had five wagons hitched up when Domhildur called a halt. "I think that is at the limits of safety. Your car is heavy, but any more of a load and you'll rip the rear right off."

"How do you know this?"

"Domhildur's my name, math and physics my game." She blushed again. "We'd better be going before the queen sends out a search party."

"What should we do with these?" Alfgeir pointed at the pile of bound and gagged goblins. He fingered the handle of his axe.

I smiled. I licked my lips. Those unfortunates in the stack looked worried. "Someone is going to sing." I removed the gag from the prisoner on the top of the heap.

"Never!" choked the goblin. "You will get nothing from us."

"Do you realize who you have been stealing parsnips from?" I took out my billy club and slapped it against the palm of my hand.

The Huldufolk crowded around. Weapons rattled.

"Old Able Bowdee." The goblin snorted. "We're not afraid of him. He never leaves the city."

"They're not his parsnips until after they reach the city," I lied.

"That's right! Do you know who you're stealing from?" Alfgeir leaned over until his red whiskers tickled the goblin's nose.

The others shuffled closer looking fierce, or trying to.

"Not Able Bowdee?" Red eyes opened wide.

I winked at Domhildur.

She leaned in close. "Oh, you poor wee beastie. You have been stealing from the Queen of the Huldufolk, the Ruler of the Lake, the Mistress of Mayhem, Fierce Freydis herself. When she learns it was you folk, she'll come storming down here with thunderbolts and tornadoes in each hand and skin the bunch of you alive. Probably turn you right inside out."

"And waterspouts too," Alfgeir added.

Cathinca rolled her eyes.

"We didn't know the parsnips belonged to her, honest. It was just another a contract sent from the city. Don't know who signed the order. Mostly we only steal horses and unicorns on request."

I gave my best sorrowful sigh. "Well, I may be able to intercede with the queen on your behalf if you can tell me anything about the recent murder of a local lad name of Eddard."

The goblin shook his head so violently I thought his floppy ears would fall off. "That wasn't us. We were told to stay away from the road that night. Was just a single wagon coming down from the North." He ran his long tongue over a row of sharp teeth. "No goblins involved in that caper. I'd know." He booted the bundled prisoner next to him. "Rufus would know more. He spied on the jacking."

I freed Rufus's mouth. "Speak up, wretch."

"Just like Dorfus said, one wagon. One wagon on the road. Tree lying in the way. Wagon flipped, pickaxe popped, game over."

Ah, the moment I'd been waiting for. "So, tell me my little friend, who did the dirty deed that ended young Eddard's life?"

"A demon. Didn't see me 'cause I hid in the ditch. Flipped the wagon and then took the axe. It was hidden under the wagon. Got him good. Didn't see it coming. Hit his head and sound asleep, he was. Demon left the pick beside the lad and went his way. So did I, only stealthy like a fox. Demon didn't care, not him."

Now where have I encountered a demon recently? Ah, yes, the library, with a nasty, name of Garbella.

Alfgeir kicked at the pile of prisoners. "What about them?"

Domhildur frowned. "We should be going soon if we want to be back to Hades before dawn."

I figured with luck I could haul the five wagons south without any help from these little villains. On the other hand, if we just left them there they might get loose and come after me or pursue the youngsters from Hades. At the worst they'd be freed tomorrow morning when the ones in the farmhouse woke up.

"Take three hostages with you to make certain the rest keep the peace. Present them to Queen Freydis as gifts and let her figure out what she wants to do with them."

She'd probably just frighten the jeepers out of them and send them home with a severe scolding, lashings of tongue, and promises not to hijack any more shipments of vegetables. But then, I didn't know Freydis all that well. We'd just met. I suspected she had a temper.

Someone tugged on my sleeve. It was Cathinca. "Queen Freydis said you can keep the casks of Jotun Juice that are tied to the roof. You shouldn't need them to get yourself home, but you aren't allowed to open them."

"Not just yet," muttered Alfgeir.

"Maybe at the wedding dance," came from someone in the crowd hoisting a goblin on her back.

That sent an icy finger dancing down my spine.

With bundled goblins slung across shoulders, the expedition from Hades started north up the road. I shoved my Unnecessary High Riding Vehicle into gear and gently crept out of the yard. The farmhouse remained dark. Last night must have been quite a party.

Miraculously, the train of one Murrican and five vegetable wagons held together without any serious damage, and I made it safely to Central City and through the darkened streets before the sun cleared the horizon. The eastern sky was just showing shades of pink as I swung into the Forks Garden Market and flattened the decorative fencing outlining the site of the official Annual Parsnip Festival. I disconnected the UHRV and drove over to the entrance to the Malt Fall Coon. The troll in charge of bouncing was just chaining the door shut.

"You work for Able Bowdee?" I called.

"Who wants to know?" He nodded.

"I just left five wagon loads of parsnips on the field. I think, to keep your boss happy, you should post a guard on the parsnips. Mr. Bowdee would not be pleased if they got stolen again."

"Gotcha." He unlocked the chain securing the club door, stuck his head inside then bellowed.

I figured whatever he had in there for security would find watching over parsnips a piece of carrot cake. I tried the front doors to the main office building. They were open. I went upstairs. The door to Bowdee's office stood closed but unlatched. Miss Prudence Gadeby was at her desk going through some papers.

She peered over her glasses and frowned. "You're up early, or is it late?"

"What are you doing in here at this hour?"

"Work. What does it look like? Do you think I'm here at this hour for pleasure? Come here to admit utter failure and plead for your life, eh? I can tell you right now it won't work. Bowdee has no time for losers. Best start running." She actually smiled. "You might be safe if you can get off-world before breakfast."

"Can you take a message for Mr. Bowdee? Tell him he has five wagonloads of parsnips sitting in the middle of the festival grounds. Don't worry. I have the thugs from the Malt Fall Coon keeping an eye on things, and I'll leave word with the gremlins at the vegetable sheds. We wouldn't want anything to happen to the parsnips, would we?" I smiled back. "I'll drop in later to make a full report to Able, but right now I'm heading for bed."

"Oh." She blinked.

After I shook a flock of gremlins loose from their dormitory located in the attic of the veg warehouse, I fired up the Murrican again. The needle on the golden fuel gage still read half full. That was plenty enough for the next little trip I had to make.

Once I got this mess straightened out I'd have to see what could be done about Huldufolk queens and rusty-chain clad contracts. Maybe pay a visit to a member of Committee for Obfuscation and Procrastination and see what can be arranged to save me short of exile or suicide.

Chapter Twelve

After stopping at the office to pick up a couple of full clips for Bess I headed north out of the city again, this time in the bright light of early dawn. It was breakfast time when I pulled into the parking lot at The Vegan Order of the Great Green Mother Earth. The high stone walls gleamed golden in the morning sun. The wrought iron outer gates opened after I gave the latch the secret handshake. Maneuvering the Murrican into a stall, I strode across the lot and knocked at the tiny wooden gate set in the entrance to the pyramid. This building was one of the step kinds, with five layers of sandstone ending in a small, flat top.

I used to tell Gabriel the whole thing reminded me of an oversized, pink birthday cake.

The entrance to the interior was just wide enough to allow one medium-sized local inhabitant to enter once the heavy planked door was opened. Minutes passed before a slot opened in the center of the portal, and two eyes peered out. “We don’t want any.”

“I’m here to see Grand Mistress Gabriel. I want to relieve him of an annoying package.”

“He’s too busy to see anyone.”

“He’ll want to see me. I’ll be taking a load off his mind.”

“The Grand Mistress does not wish to be disturbed. He is even now in the card room trying to discern his future.”

“You’d better let me in then. I can warn him Charlie will have him, bets taken, and a sucker stripped down to his underwear, if we don’t undertake an intervention and rescue right now.” I gave the secret hand sign, the bull’s horns over easy, just to show I knew something of which I spoke.

The acolyte, in a hooded, brown threadbare robe that barely reached his boney knees, unlocked the door and passed me through. “Just as well. I been worried about the boss. He’s been having a bit of a hard time ever since—your package arrived.” The goblin stepped aside.

"Thanks, I'll see my way through." I paused. "Not that I'm interested, you understand, but what's for breakfast?" What I really needed was forty-eight hours of uninterrupted sleep, but the scent of something tasty was creeping through the darkened corridors.

"The usual. Steak and eggs." The doorkeeper blinked. "I can get you a pot of hot chocolate and Irish if it would help."

"Send it to the Divination Room. With cups." I found the pair of them, eyes down, cards in hand, and a large stack of gold-painted chips piled in front of Captain Charlie. Mistress Gabriel looked to be in distress. The table in front of him was bare of anything resembling chips.

"I've come to rescue you," I said. "Both of you."

"About time." Old Gabriel, a mongrel like me, although heavy on the elf-blood, sighed and laid his squares of pasteboard down, face up. "If I didn't know any better, I'd say this unworthy little novitiate was holding back important face cards up his large loose sleeves."

"I'll say it's about time you got here." Charlie flung his cards in the air. "I'm bored out of my skull. Have you solved the murder and got me off the rusty hook yet?"

"No, but I have some ideas." The hot chocolate arrived, and I poured. "I'm going to pay your friend Garbella a visit. Preferably at home to catch her off-guard." I glared at Charlie. "How would you like to show me where she lives?"

"Why not, I could use the excitement. I'm about ready to stick my head in the noose out of boredom." The cherub struggled out of the granny garment he'd been wearing since we sent him into hiding and tossed the magic wig into the air.

I recovered the wig. You never can tell when it might come in handy again.

We headed out to the parking lot. Junior Inspector Columns was leaning against the Murrican chewing on a cigar. He looked up. "Good. I was afraid I'd have to come into the fruitcake farm after you." He aimed the cigar at Charlie. "Captain, you are formally under arrest. Will you come with me quietly?"

The inspector didn't look particularly fierce, and both hands remained clearly in our sight.

"Can't, I'm too busy," the cherub said. "Maybe tomorrow."

"Why don't you join us? We're off to rattle a suspect." I smiled. "By the way, how did you find us?"

"Simple. We've had a CPS bulletin out on that monster transport truck you're driving. You've been under aerial surveillance via stealth blimp ever since you left Grimtun last night." He winked at

Charlie. "If you promise not to run away without my permission, I'll follow on my morepedal."

"Cross my heart," Charlie said. He climbed up into the high passenger seat on the Murrican and groaned. "Next time bring a ladder, will you?"

"You must be out of shape." I wheeled us out through the gates.

"Too busy in the office." He leaned back and closed his eyes.

I glanced in the enormous rear-view mirror assembly. Columns was trailing us on one of those new-fangled morepedals. They were like a bicycle, sort of, only much lower, with tiny fat rubber wheels. There were pedals, but they were seldom used as whole thing runs on inertia. Big flywheel gets spinning, propels the thing along at city-legal speeds. I shook my head. You'd certainly never get me on one of those things.

I glanced at Charlie. He looked asleep, chin resting on his chest. "Is Columns one of yours?"

A sly grin crept across the cherub's lips. His eyes remained closed. "You might say that."

"To balance off your other more toxic protégé, the pixie, and Deputy Captain, name of Bessie?"

"Yes."

"How did your fingerprints end up on the pickaxe handle?" I swerved to avoid an early morning delivery wagon drawn by a team of retired unicorns. "And how do I find Garbella's lair?"

"I have no idea about the axe." Charlie frowned, and his eyes opened. He chewed his lower lip. "Head for Crossing Avenue. Just off Main Street. Down near the river. She lives in that co-op tower. The one they call the Buckhamster."

"Have you handled a pickaxe in the recent days?" The neighbourhood in question we were heading toward was not the greatest.

"Not since I had to substitute for the boss several weeks ago when they broke ground for the new grandstand at the Parsnip Festival Grounds." He turned to look at me.

I rolled my eyes. "When you were finished playing in the dirt, who did you hand the pick to?"

"That assistant of old Able Bowdee's, I think."

"Which one, the elderly bookkeeper or your old girlfriend?" I had the feeling we were getting warmer. We pulled up in front of the Buckhamster. Inspector Columns chugged up behind us and dismounted.

Jeeves collapsed at my feet with a sigh like hot escaping steam.

Garbella made it to the room at the end of the hall and slammed the door in Charlie's face.

"Open up. This is the law. You are under arrest," he hollered into the keyhole.

"Stuff it, junior. You'll never take me alive."

Followed by a loud scream, a thud, and the door opened.

Junior Inspector Columns appeared with a struggling Garbella Sieve under his arm.

"There was a strange person at my bedroom window. I demand you arrest him." Garbella tried a wild kick and failed to connect.

"He's not that strange," Charlie said. "Give him a few more years at the precinct, and then we'll see. Columns, do you have your standard issue handcuffs?"

"Yes, Captain. Oh, and the reason I came in through the bedroom window was because there are no back stairs, just an outside fire escape."

"Good lad."

I scratched my head and shot Jeeves in the chest again for good measure. "I wish we had something to secure this beast. Even after three shots of penetrol I have no idea how long the demon will be out. Regulation handcuffs won't do us any good with him."

"Don't worry about that." Charlie went into the bedroom, rummaged through a top dresser drawer, and came up with what looked at first glance to be gleaming gold wire.

"Magic handcuffs. Suitable to hold anything up to a class two wizard. What have you been up to?"

"Never mind."

He tossed them to me, and I wrapped the demon's hands securely behind his back. "This will definitely make him behave."

Columns sat Garbella on top of the largest suitcase. Charlie took up a prosecutor's stance. "You had better talk if you know what's good for you."

"Are you going to read Miss Sieve her rights?" The inspector leaned against the wall.

"She has no rights. Not when she gets me deep into the doo-doo." Charlie paced in front of her, waving my billy like a conductor's baton.

I checked a tag on the luggage. "You were planning to leave today, at noon?"

"You figure it out."

"The gang up north of Grimtun has been broken, the parsnips

recovered, the festival will go on. What have you accomplished?"

"This isn't the end."

"It is for you." Charlie glared at her. Sitting, she was almost the same height. "The CPS dungeons await."

"The boss will…" and she clamped her mouth shut.

"What will the boss do?" I voiced a suspicion. "I think we should head on over to the Forks Garden Market."

"You'll be too late!" she shrieked.

Confirming my suspicion. "Can Inspector Columns handle transporting the prisoners?" I looked at Charlie.

"If you lend him the Murrican."

The elf nodded. "Leave them to me."

"That means, we have to take the morepedal. I've always wanted to try one of those things." Charlie grinned. "Let's go." He turned back to Columns. "Try not to bruise the prisoners too much getting them down thirteen floors."

"I won't drop them."

I did hear a bump, bump, ouch, ouch, sound as we reached the landing and stared out the front door at the tiny contraption parked at the curb. "Maybe I should walk."

"Nonsense. This will be fun. Just like the good old days. I'll drive. We're in a hurry, hop on." Charlie had a wild gleam.

I didn't remember any good old days. I climbed on behind the captain and closed my eyes.

Chapter Thirteen

We swung onto the Forks Market Garden property and bounced to a stop. There was an ogre perched on a pile of parsnips in the middle of the festival grounds. I staggered off the morepedal and waited until my teeth stopped chattering.

"Everything under control?" I kept a firm hold on a fencepost to keep from swaying.

"Peachy keen," the ogre grunted. "Place is crawling with gremlins checking on me. I get no sleep."

"Good." I pulled out the clip in Bess's handle and added a few more cartridges for good measure. Charlie was still patting our transport. "I can put in a good word to Miss Vickky. Maybe she'll buy you one for a patrol car when she busts you down to street duty."

"Enough chatter. I have an arrest to make and then forty-eight hours sleep." Charlie stretched. "Lead on."

We went into the main office building complex and up the stairs. The door to Able Bowdee's office was closed but not locked. We didn't bother to knock.

Able was sitting in his chair, rigid as a choirboy on a holy day. He didn't rise to greet us. Probably had something to do with the amount of cord wrapped around him securing him in the chair. A paisley gag covered his mouth.

"Good morning," I said.

Able shook his head so vigorously I was afraid his bulging eyeballs would fall out. He nodded back toward the entrance to the room and moaned.

Miss Prudence Gadeby stepped out from behind the door. She balanced on her cane. "I found him like this."

"Of course you did." I smiled.

Able shook his head again, hard.

"I believe Mr. Bowdee wants to tell us something. Would you be so kind?" I nodded to Captain Charlie.

"I'll remove the gag, will I?" he said.

"I'll get help." Miss Gadeby turned to go. "I'll send up one of his gangsters from the club downstairs."

"Stay here. I have a few questions for you." I wagged a finger at her. My other hand slipped inside my jacket.

"She did it! She tied me up! The old biddy was going to kill me," came flooding out between Able Bowdee's lips. "Me! After all I've done for her."

"You must send me a list of those," Prudence Gadeby said. "Excuse me, but I must be off." The tip of her cane left the floor.

"Watch out!" Bowdee sputtered.

"I am. Drop the cane." I gave her my best official ex-CPS agent stare.

"Sorry, I need it to escape." The cane swung up to the horizontal.

I shot her in the shoulder. The time it took the penetrol to soak through the heavy sweater allowed her a reflex action to pull the trigger. I ducked. The projectile parted my hair, took out an expensive hanging lamp, and shattered the picture of a frowning dignitary in judge's robes hanging on the wall behind Able's head.

"You have ruined my grandfather," Able Bowdee cried, struggling in his bindings.

"As I recall from the historical records, your grandfather was ruined from an early age." Charlie wrestled with the ropes holding Able to his chair. "Hold still. They elected Bowdee senior to the judge's chair because he spent so much time behind bars he was the local expert. Stop wiggling, or I'll leave you here in this condition."

He glanced at me as I bent over Prudence Gadeby. "Is she down for a while? I'd hate to get exploded by that artillery while I'm freeing this villain."

"Sleeping like a baby." I kicked the cane across the room and did a preliminary search of her outer pockets for other weapons. I straightened. "Speaking of which, I could use some of that sleep myself. Can you handle things around here if I take off early?"

"I'm not a villain. There's the real villain." Able raised a shaking hand and pointed. "That creature! She boasted of how she arranged to intercept the parsnip shipments. How she and Garbella had been skimming from the company for years. They were about to leave the country. Had plans to move to the Moon and retire there." He gulped. "She tied me up and was going to empty the safe. Threatened to pull off my toes one-by-one if I didn't give her the magic combination. I knew what would happen if I did."

"Yes. She couldn't leave you around after that to squeal. I will expect box seats for the Annual Parsnip Festival. Maybe you could also see your way fit to appointing me as one of the judges for the Miss Root Vegetable contest. As a courtesy for the forces of law and order." Charlie perched on top of the desk beside Able.

"Isn't that law and disorder?" I muttered.

"Do you mind if I call the precinct and have the office send over a carriage for the prisoner? And, by chance, do you have any expensive cigars?" Charlie beamed at Able.

"Yes. Of course. Top drawer. Help yourself."

Charlie winked at me and lit up, blowing a wreath. "I think I'll order one of the special black ones drawn by Night Mares. It always shakes up the locals and makes for an impressive entrance, don't you think? Clears the streets of unnecessary traffic too."

"Whatever makes you happy." I glanced around the office. "Well, if you don't need me for anything, I'll head home."

"Do you mind taking the morepedal with you? You can drop it off at the precinct later. Just don't take too long to turn it in." He frowned. "Or maybe leave it at my apartment instead."

I recalled why working with Charlie used to annoy me on occasion.

~ * ~

The next morning I was sitting at my desk flipping through a thick Central City registry when Bertha came in. She took one look at me and pulled up a chair. "Spill it, boss. What happened? Everything." She held up her hand. "Wait. I'll get you a hot chocolate."

Both my eyebrows went up as I watched her whip over to our little unit, pour and mix two cups. She set them down on the desk and made herself comfortable.

"What's the catch?" I'm naturally suspicious.

"There's no catch. I was worried about you, of course. Oh, there is one minor thing."

I studied the ceiling. Yes, it did need painting and some repairs to cover those old water spots. "What have you done now?"

"Nothing. Really. Well, Pippy Gazette did make me promise that I would allow her to accompany you on your next case. Sort of as a ride-along and do a special inside article on the typical day of Central City's most prominent private eyeball." She took a quick breath. "It was the payment I had to make in order to get the inside dope on the gang of horse and unicorn thieves. So spill the parsnips. What's the story?"

I sighed. "Miss Prudence Gadeby and Garbella Sieve were the

brains behind the parsnip thefts. According to Charlie last night, they planned to raise the price of parsnips and take over the Annual Parsnip Festival. Everyone is singing like a flock of hungry starlings trying to reduce the punishment coming down from the CPS. They were going to take the proceeds from the festival and run instead of donating the funds to the city charity."

Bertha frowned. "I always heard the donation was less than expected due to high overhead."

"Or someone skimming. Charlie assures me that Able Bowdee will donate all the promised funds this year. Inspector Columns has been assigned to accounting for the duration of the festival."

"But what about the murder? How did you get your little buddy off the hook? Who killed Garbella's husband?"

I leaned back in my chair. "Garbella did it. Well, she had her pet demon do the deed. They got Charlie's fingerprints from the pick he used to break ground at the festival grounds. Kept it in case they'd need it for anything, like blackmail. Garbella's husband Eddard found out what was going on and threatened to spill the greens so they did him in."

Bertha shook her head. "A nasty business. Oh," she hurried to her desk and returned, dropping a thick brown envelope in front of me. "This came for you while you were away. Personal and Private was written in blood on the cover so I didn't want to open it."

I prodded the package with my finger. "That is thoughtful and unusual for you."

She shuddered. "Gave me a real weird feeling when I handled it. Couldn't read the return address. It was smudged. Looked like *Ha* or something like that." Bertha examined my face. "So, what's up? The flap was also sealed with red wax. Looks like the image of crossed parsnips." She giggled. "That's silly, right?"

"Right. Can you do me a big favor? There's one of those new-fangled creations parked out back in the alley. Think they call it a morepedal. Can you deliver it to the sixth precinct for me? I'd do it, but I have an appointment to make."

"I'd love to. Always wanted to try one of those cute little things." She hesitated. "Do I have to see Charlie at the precinct?"

"No, just leave it on the street out front." I went back to flipping through the pages of the city directory.

"What are you going to do today?"

"I'll be making an appointment to see a prominent representative of the Committee for Obfuscation and Procrastination. I need someone who is an expert at breaking magical contracts signed under duress or unconsciousness." Which should clean me out of any profit from this latest venture, or failing success of that, perhaps I could transfer ownership of Miss Prudence Gadesby's one-way ticket to the Moon.

"I could pick up lunch for you on my way back." Bertha paused in the doorway.

"Fine, but absolutely no parsnips!"

The Housetrap Chronicles

Book 11

Chapter One

It was the week before Crispness and Bertha and I were discussing our plans for the up-coming festival. At least Bertha was doing all the talking and as usual, I was only half listening. Bertha Wildwater is my part-banshee assistant, executive secretary, and according to her, Full Partner in our modest operation. I'm a pure-blooded mongrel myself, not that this information is all that important to the story.

Our latest gilt door lettering fairly shouted out: *Aloysius and Wildwater, Private Investigators*. I'd given up on changing the sign back to something closer to what I still believe is more accurate. It's not that good help is too difficult to find in Central City, but we'd both grown used to each other's many quirks as well as could be expected after this length of time. I trusted her enough not to poison me when she made the coffee which, come to think of it, wasn't all that frequently. She doesn't do windows either. That's fine as there is seldom anything worth gazing at through our grime-coated second story panes. You could barely make out the swirling snow or the street below.

But I digress. As most of you know, the Festival of Crispness falls once a year on the shortest and usually darkest day of the year at the end of the week announcing winter's arrival. Central City is famous for its lengthy bitter cold season and snow drifting up to the red eyeballs. Crispness gives the locals a reason to celebrate for a full week before they give up on shoveling and hibernate for two or three months or flee south.

"I think we should decorate the office." Bertha, frowning, stared around the reception room as though seeing it for the first time.

"We've never decorated the office," I commented from the relative sanctuary of my inner sanctum.

Open in front of me on my desk was this morning's copy of the

Central City Liberty One. The paper was the full-color special Festival Edition listing all of the simply marvelous coming events for the entire week. I was diligently reading the advertisements and ads in order to make certain I found myself safely elsewhere and avoiding the crowds and the unnecessary holiday expense.

"You're an old stuck in the mudbath. Just because we've never decorated this place is no excuse. I took an entire week of Inferior Decorating for Unnecessary Holidays at night school last year. I have a million suggestions."

"Sounds expensive. Afraid not. Maybe next year."

Bertha picked up a pencil and pad from her desk. "I'll just jot down a few colorful festive ideas."

"Jot all you like. Connect the jots! Color them in. The answer is still a firm no. Besides, it would upset our clients if they couldn't see our regular décor when they came through the door."

"That's another topic I plan to address. There should be lots of bargains in the stores after Crispness." She scribbled madly. "This old furniture has to go."

"Go where?" I dragged my gaze away from the full-page photo of Miss Lea A. Toe who was giving a recital tomorrow night.

The shapely young goblin was wearing a few strategically placed and colorful ribbons. If her voice was anything like her dangerous curves I might break with tradition and drop in at the Committee of Wealth and Healthfare Members' Hall for a peek.

"There is nothing wrong with our office furniture," I sputtered. "It's quite serviceable."

"Two desks that look like they were center field during the cannon fire in old Waterloo, swivel chairs that need safety belts, and some wobbly client seating that threaten to fold up whenever sat upon. Then there is a waiting room couch with lumpy cushions that are resting on the floor, not to mention our kitchen needs serious updating, and our hole-filled carpet has lost its magic." Bertha snorted. "You'll just have to pry a few moss-covered coins loose from your threadbare pockets. I'm an expert shopper. I'll work wonders, you'll see."

Before I had a chance to mount a protest, she continued, "Do you even buy Crispness presents? I don't recall if you gave me anything last year."

"Didn't I give you a pair of fine wool socks?"

"I had to darn the thumb-holes before I wore them home. You had been using them as mittens."

"All right, you can decorate the office. Just don't fall overboard. And we don't have a kitchen in here, just an ancient coffee pot and an argumentative hot plate."

"I plan to. Speaking of plans, what are you doing for Crispness dinner? Mother would be glad to see you for some unfathomable reason. She whips up a mean fattening feast." Bertha turned her smoldering stare on me.

"I don't like crowds. Won't all thirteen of your brothers be there? Besides, I already have plans." I've never met Meaghan Wildwater but have heard some pretty strange tales from Bertha about her mother, her wayward wanderings, the many skimpy outfits, and even once threatening a hot stove with violence or worse. Apparently, she wouldn't even need to turn on the burners to heat them up.

I couldn't help myself. I had to ask. "Does your mother still wear a bikini in the kitchen while she cooks?"

She gazed down her narrow nose at me, brown eyes lidded, thin lips pursed.

I could feel myself shrinking into the depths of the chair.

"Only during the summer months," came out in a flat, deadly voice. "I could speak to her if you like. I'm sure she would make an exception for you this year and find a blue and gold one to be festive. She's always in the mood. I can even ask her not to include parsnips on the menu."

Ouch. Another unpleasant memory raised. "That won't be necessary. I have my own plans." Bertha's tales of the infamous Meaghan Wildwater and her legendary dalliances danced through my head; then these were shoved aside by a playing piece from my own checkered past.

Anytime I thought of Freydis, Queen of the Huldufolk, and stern mistress of the parsnip cartel, my enfeebled mind wandered north. But that was a tangled legal brief from another distant time and place.

"Why don't you leave the office early today and see what decorating bargains you can uncover. Better yet, take the rest of the day off, you deserve it." *And leave me alone.* I'm not a big fan of the holiday season. Too many bad memories as a young child.

"I think I will." Bertha smiled, then she paused and tilted her head to one side, as though listening. "Someone's coming. I feel the wards on the front stairs tingling." She peered out into the dim hall. "There's no one here. Well, I'm off."

"Have fun shopping." *And don't spend all of our coin.*

Chapter Two

The door flung open wide, banging hard against the frame and echoing all through the office. A thin layer of dust drifted down from the imitation crystal chandelier.

A squeaky voice broke into my reverie. "Are these the premises of Wildwater and Associates?"

"Sorry, never heard of them," I called out, folding the newspaper with a sigh. "Read the sign on the door if the glass is still in one piece."

Looking up I stared into the main office. A short, rather rumpled elf stood there, stocking cap in hand. He stared around, big-eyed, like a lost soul on the edge of a steep precipice. Sighing again, I stood and went to the door. "How may I help you?"

At best, I clench my jaw and tolerate elves. Usually they are tall, know-everything, sly do-gooders always dressed for an official meeting with magic royalty who don't consort with us lessor mortals without good and usually expensive reasons. This character was little taller than me, garbed in coveralls like a workman whose job involved some serious dirt. His pointy ears stood straight out on the sides of his head, jutting from beneath an unruly nest of black hair like a pair of poised radar antennae. The cap was decorated in the official festive colors of deep blue and skinflint gold.

He fidgeted. "I need help."

"As do we all, sir. What is it you want? How may I be of assistance?" I must have been feeling mellow. Probably had something to do with the season. Besides, elves always had surplus coin, or a clear way to access some.

"I was told you, this firm, could help me."

Whoever they are, they probably lied. "Well, what seems to be the problem?" I led him into my sanctuary and pointed toward a seat. Bertha had sensed something as she was leaving. "Was that you on the front stairs a few minutes ago?"

The cap came off again to be twisted in his hands. "Yes. I changed my mind. Too obvious and exposed. Came up the back way from the alley. Are we really safe in here?" He glanced around the small space carefully. "Are we alone?"

I leaned down and peered under my desk. "Yes. I believe so." *Stop wasting my time.* "Well?"

"I need a spaceship and a pilot."

Some days we get the strangest requests. "Is that all? I'm afraid you've come to the wrong place. I suggest you try the civic aerodrome and bring a large sack of coin." I leaned back in my chair, pleased to share my wisdom.

"I don't have any coin, but I do have a spaceship. I need a pilot and a crew for a desperate rescue mission." He leaned forward, whispering. "*This* is a serious emergency."

Isn't it always? I resisted a sudden urge to count the fingerprints on my door glass. Maybe the reception room out there could use some upgrading. I suppose I should also stop hanging my wool socks from the bookcase shelves to dry. They made for a colorful row but added nothing to the decor. The dryer in the laundry room at my apartment building had a curse on it. Two socks went in, one came out—been that way for a month now.

"We don't have a lot of time." He glanced at the gurgling water clock on the shelf behind me and pointed. "It's running slow."

"I know." The device, a globe filled with artificial snow, was a present from an admirer. Since it failed to detonate I kept the timer going as a useful reminder that the days, and life in general, were fleeting. I didn't need to look. The information provided was always a day behind.

"We have to hurry." He chewed on his cap.

"Then I suggest you hire a steam cab."

He stared at me blankly. "Why?"

"To get to the aerodrome quickly." I had the feeling we were starting to wander in endless circles. I stood. "Well, if there is nothing else…"

He licked his lips. "Are you Master Wildwater?"

"No." I gestured toward the outer office door.

"When will he be back?"

"*She*. I believe you are looking for Bertha Wildwater. She's out of the office right now. Won't be back at all today. You'll have to return tomorrow." I smiled. Might be better to drive her mad instead of me. Will serve her right for all this treacherous talk of holiday decorating. “Would you like me to make you an appointment to see her?”

He winced. “That doesn’t leave us a lot of time.”

“Can’t be helped.”

He stood. “First thing in the morning. I’ll be back.”

I look forward to it. “Do you have a name?”

He hesitated in the doorway and glanced around again. “Everyone calls me Mouse, but my real name is Nicholas. Or just plain Nick. That’s what they say my mother called me.”

“Well, just plain Nick, come back tomorrow at eight bells sharp. I’m sure Bertha Wildwater will be deliriously happy to see you.”

She usually comes in early; most days by seven-thirty. Tomorrow I might actually be in on time so I won’t miss out on any of the fun.

Chapter Three

The stirring of the noisy multitude on the sidewalk below my open window woke me. I glanced down. Already the usual assortments of creatures scurrying to work were jostling each other, pointed elbows raised. If I didn't hurry I'd be late getting to the office. I didn't want to miss the meeting between Mouse and Wildwater.

A light snow fell as I headed to the office. Bertha was already in and sitting at her desk thumbing through a Crispness catalogue.

"I'll make the coffee," I said.

"Don't let me stop you." She arched an eyebrow.

I was just adding slightly used grounds to the pot when there came a light tapping at the front door. "Come in," I called.

She glanced up.

Mouse tip-toed inside and quietly closed the door. He peered around and then at Bertha. "Are we alone?"

She frowned. "No, Randy is standing right over there."

He dragged a rickety chair over to beside her desk and perched on the edge of the seat. "I have an appointment."

"To see Randy? Your name?"

"No, to see you. You are Wildwater, aren't you?"

"Last time I looked." She turned to stare at me, eyebrows topping her forehead.

"I was told to come and see you. I need a pilot and a crew for a desperate rescue mission. I already have the spaceship."

I smiled and added the water to the pot and stirred in the grounds. The hotplate would require some fancy finger-wrestling moves. I used a spell I'd learned in kindergarten.

"We're running out of time." Mouse was fairly bouncing on his chair. "We have to leave today."

Bertha glared in my direction, then turned, smiled sweetly, and took out a pad and paper. "First, we should begin at the beginning. Do you have a name?"

"Everyone calls me Mouse, but my real name is Nicholas. Or just plain Nick. That's what they say my mother called me."

"Very good. And who suggested that you come and see us, Nicholas?"

Clever girl. Find out who the joker is who sent this character in our direction so we can return the favor someday, complete with past due interest.

He twisted his stocking cap into a rope and rocked back and forth on the edge of the chair. I could hear it creaking from across the room. "Her name is Mae. She told me to come and see you. She said you could help me. We really have to leave today if we're going to get there on time."

I almost dropped my coffee cup. "Mae?" I whispered. "Where did you meet this person called Mae?" I only knew of one individual with that moniker who came immediately to mind, and she was not someone to be toyed with. If *she* sent him to us…

He turned to stare at me. "You know, the Mae who runs the High Dive. I know Tootsie there. Told her my story. She took me in to see Mae."

Mae, the sleek, high-powered goblin who runs almost everything illegal and otherwise in Central City. "And then she, *Mae*, told you to come and see us?"

"Yes."

"I think we'd better go into my office." I gestured toward the door. "You can tell me everything you told Mae."

Bertha was already on her feet, notebook in hand. She smiled at the confused elf. "It's much more private in there. Randy is my senior partner. I'll be right beside you."

"Best if you begin at the very beginning, so there's no confusion," I said.

"Well, I know Tootsie way back from…"

I held up my hand. "Since you're in a hurry, to speed things up why don't we skip straight through to the story you told to Mae. Begin there." I also know Tootsie, aka Toots.

She's a young goblin and current main entrance hostess at the High Dive and understudy to Mae on how to use the art of sweet and slinky to get just about anything you want. She also doubles as the nasty muscle on some unmentionable jobs that might involve odd things like the occasional broken bone or serious dislocation.

"Well, you see, I work at the Chimneys in the yard. The place is shut down this week for the holiday. Not much going on. Everyone else heading home. No new loads coming in or going out for the next week." He paused for a breath.

I nodded. I'd heard of the Chimneys. Berth looked at me, the expression on her face blank. "It's a staging area for heavy equipment and supplies going up to faraway places, like the Moon or mining operations on asteroids."

"Right. I usually work in the yard, cleaning the sleds." Nick bobbed his head then continued, "Like I said, everyone else had supposedly gone home for the holidays, and the boss left me to lock up. I was in the back office when a message came through. I heard the foreman, Rooge, play it back. He didn't know I was in there. He set the printout to destruct and left. I can repeat it word for word."

He closed his eyes. What came out of his mouth was complete, right down to the occasional static crack and pop. "It's all set for Crispness Day. The employees will be distracted by the celebrations, and our agent there will see they stay that way. Most of the fleet will be in port for the Crispness Daze. No one is going to miss a bunch of goblin and gremlin kids or look too hard for them once they're gone. We'll be in and out of Calypso before you can shout Plum's Pudding. Capt'n Rinch says you'll get your cut as soon as we can sell them off to the mines. We'll be using the new access code you sent us so remember to change it again the day after Crispness before you leave. See you at Titan on New Seers Day."

Nick stopped for breath. His face, which had glowed red as he talked, returned to a more normal greenish cast. "After the foreman went home I checked the waste basket. He wrote the code down." The elf pulled a crumpled scrap of paper out of his pocket and passed it over to Bertha.

She slid it across the desk to me.

I shook my head and flattened the paper out. The single word written there was SUGARPLUMS.

"This is all very interesting," I said. "What's on Calypso that's important enough for a pirate raid?" I'd been out of the service too long. I wasn't up on the latest installations.

"Pirate raid?" Bertha stared at me. "What are you talking about?"

I hadn't been out of circulation *that* long. "Captain Rinch was a famous pirate leader. Ran a gang of villains who have a hideout somewhere in the outer system. Rumor had him running some kind of a slavery operation. I thought the old devil was still in jail. Must have skipped out."

I turned to Nick. "Do you know what's so important on

Calypso? What's this stuff about children? Why don't you go to the authorities? This sounds more like a job for the Committee of Public Safety."

"Been to see the Com P.S.," he said. "Spoke to some high mucky-muck name of Charlie. Said it was out of their jurisdiction. Said I had no solid proof. Showed me the door." His head bobbed. "That's when I told Toots my story over a cup of hot chocolate and marshmallows."

Nick licked his lips. "There's an orphanage located on Calypso run by a company, name of Spacefaring League of Elementary Decorum. Always short of funds. They run an orphanage for the children of space-faring employees. Because the kids are goblin and gremlin no one important will care what happens to them. They'll be sold to an illegal mining company working deep on some asteroid and will never see the stars again."

"That's terrible," Bertha said.

She gave me *that* look, the one that silently screamed, *Randy, you must do something!*

"How do you know so much about this?" I stared into his eyes.

"I used to be a stoker on a condemned freighter doing the Mars to Titan run. You hear things."

I frowned, fingers tapping on the desktop. So, now what? Mae obviously expected me to do something. Would therefore be unhealthy not to. Bertha would probably poison my coffee if I didn't act. I could go throttle Captain Charlie. That would give me some brief satisfaction but accomplish little else. Then there was Mae…

I turned to the elf, staring at me like a worshipper at the foot of the Mountain of Knowledge and Ancient Wisdom. "Well, what do you," *and Mae,* "expect me to do?"

He bobbed his head eagerly. "I've found a spaceship and gathered enough supplies. Mae said you were a pilot. We have to leave today or we'll never make it to Calypso before Crispness Day. We have to mount a rescue expedition."

Chapter Four

All this nonsense coming from a character with the moniker of Mouse. "Seriously, what is in this for you? Why do you care?" When you have no idea what you are going to do, stall and ask questions.

Nick was twisting his cap into the shape of a pretzel. "Look, since I found the job at the Chimneys I haven't stirred from Central City, but I do know what is going on out there. I was no saint. Time to make up for that, and we're running out of it. I was an orphan too. Are you coming with me? If not, I'll go on my own."

"Are you a pilot?"

"No."

"Wherever did you get a spaceship?" This was all complete nonsense.

"I told you I work in the yard at the Chimneys. I look after the sleds. There's a maintenance sled just come in off servicing. It's parked in the backyard warehouse. I checked it over. No one will stop us. I'm in charge of securing the yard over the holidays."

"I can think of several problems with that. You'd never get halfway to Calypso with one of those. You'd be lucky to get past the Moon. Then you'd die." I shook my head.

"What's a sled?" This quiet question came from Bertha.

"It's a workhorse tug designed to fly heavy equipment up to a high level for rendezvous with a freighter. Barely gets into high orbit." My voice was flatter than a squished frog.

"This is a big Jake Deer Model 8. Built for long runs to service equipment on the Moon and beyond. Hardly ever gets used now." Nick stood. "We gotta go right away. I figured it all out on the plotter ball in the office. Otherwise we'll never make it by Crispness Eve. We have to beat the slavers there or it's all for nothing. Well?"

"Look…" I used my, let's be reasonable about this, voice. "Yes, I could probably pilot the thing, and it might even be able to make it all the way to Calypso, which I seriously doubt, but I'm no navigator. We'd be lost soon as we left visual sighting on the Moon." I could feel my way around a Rudolfo Navigational System on a modern liner, but that is simple programming. The Jake Deer Model 8 would be lucky to have a chart table with a quill and note parchment.

"No problem," Bertha said. "I took navigation at night school."

My eyes, unbidden, rolled into the back of my head. After I sorted them out I turned to my trusty executive secretary and said, in no uncertain terms, "You're not going. That is final."

"And I do have an hour of piloting from a rainy Saturday afternoon session after hours with the cute instructor." She gave me a sweet smile, unusual for her. "So, if you are backing out, I will try flying this thing. How hard can it be?" She rose and turned to Nick. "I'll get my gear."

For the first time since this mad discussion started, even he looked doubtful.

I stood and crossed my arms. "I categorically refuse to allow you to go."

Bertha batted her eyelashes at me. "I quit. I'll send you a postcard." She nodded to the elf. "Shall we?"

I leaned forward on the desk. "I'm too young to die."

She pursed her lips and tried to look thoughtful. "You've led a good life. But if you think you're too old for this expedition, we will understand. Won't we, Nick? Or should I call you Mouse?"

"Mouse will be fine." He looked toward me with eyes that bulged and begged.

"We'll need supplies for a week, maybe two."

"Already on board. Mae sent Toots over with a couple of the waiters from the High Dive. Food and water and other stuff all loaded by now." He bobbed his head and slapped his stocking cap back on.

Why does everyone always take me for granted? Why are they both staring at me? "I have to go home and get my things," I mumbled.

"No time. I can supply clothes and everything we'll need from the company stores." Nick glanced toward Bertha. "That is, if you don't mind wearing coveralls. We have two colors, black and blue."

"That will be lovely." Bertha was scribbling something on a piece of paper. She walked to the front door and hung the sign on the outside glass.

"What does that say?" I checked Bess, my trusty splatter gun, stuffed several additional clips into my pocket then secured her in my shoulder holster. Glass knuckles went in my jacket pocket. Billy stick slipped into place up my sleeve.

"Merry Crispness. Closed for the Holidays. Open after New Seers Day."

"Always the cock-eyed optimist." I sighed and removed the silver flask of Irish from the bottom desk drawer. It still sloshed. The contents might come in handy. For medicinal purposes. Like serious wounds. Or a slow death in space. "Why don't you summon us a sleigh pulled by a team of unicorns? We might as well go out in style if it's our last trip together."

We took a steam cab to the Chimneys. The streets were slippery, and the gaslights just flickered on. Sure it was still morning, but a blizzard had been in the forecast. It may have arrived. The sidewalks were already deserted. Even the shoppers and panhandlers were heading home.

I sat in the back and brooded. This was madness. We'd be lucky to get all the way to Calypso by Crispness Eve. Most likely we'd flame out somewhere around Mars. If we made it to the orphanage, then what? Rescue a pack of ruthless children and avoid rampaging pirates? I don't know which I feared most.

"Do you have any idea how many youngsters there are at this orphanage?"

Nick shook his head.

"What about the staff? I suspect the evil plan is to leave no witnesses to the raid. The slavers will be in an extra foul mood if we manage to snatch the children before they get there. Any idea how many wardens at the orphanage?"

Nick shrugged. "Don't know." He smiled eagerly. "But the sled is pretty roomy. We have lots of supplies. Toots made at least two trips yesterday to load us up."

A headache threatened. The message he delivered indicated there was a pirate contact on Calypso. That meant as soon as we arrived a warning would go out. A sled was sturdy and built for cargo, not speed. The pirates would have a fast sleek vessel. And Captain Rinch was famous for having a short, smoldering fuse.

If we didn't make it to Calypso, that would mean a slow and excruciating death. If we managed to somehow make it safely to Calypso, we had a good chance for a short and painful one.

Not to mention the fact I'm not particularly fond of children, large or small. You may find this difficult to believe, but I was one myself, once. I know what they are like.

I glanced up at Bertha now perched on the edge of a chair beside Nick and sighed.

"Don't worry, Randy." She smiled. "I'll take good care of you.

At least this way you can escape from Mother's cooking." The smiled morphed into a frown. "I guess we probably won't be home in time for New Seers Day Eve celebrations either. Meaghan always throws a great party that night."

"*That* will be the least of our worries." I guessed we'd be lucky if we make it as far as Titan and safety before the sled gives up.

"Oh, I almost forgot. Miss Mae gave me this. I was supposed to hand it to you." Nick fished a folded envelope out of his jacket pocket.

I took the thing from him and held it up to the light. Looked safe enough. I opened the flap cautiously, just in case. Inside were three slips of paper. I drew one out. We had three first class tickets from Titan back to good old Mother Earth. The enclosed note gave off an aroma wild enough to give a strong head illegal dreams but simply read, "Good luck." A lipstick print served as a signature. The print was a shade I was all too familiar with. Mae's.

If Mae had seers in her employ, I hoped they were reliable.

The steam cab turned into the industrial quarter. A few minutes later we rumbled to a stop outside a locked iron gate. Inside, the snow-trimmed brick fingers of three large chimneys pointed skyward. The occasional pale puff drifted upward. Strings of red and green warning lights ran around the brick cylinders twinkling and flickering in the swirling flakes.

Probably faulty wiring. Hopefully, these were the only loose connections we'd encounter in the place.

"We have arrived," Nick said.

"Oh, goody."

Chapter Five

The Chimneys' yard was surrounded by a high wire fence topped by some of the nastiest spells that ever tingled the tips of my slowly freezing fingers. Fortunately, Nick carried the large iron key to the gate. We paid off the steam cab and made tracks through the snow, stalking carefully between the drifts. No one had been in or out today, if a lack of footprints in the white stuff could be believed.

The warehouses were all in darkness. We followed Nick single-file across the yard.

I spoke into the back of Bertha's genuine Arctic faux fur coat. I've never seen a live faux. I hear they're rare. I wondered, briefly, if she was overpaid. "You can still go back, Miss Wildwater. I wouldn't hold it against you. In fact I highly recommend it."

"This is your chance to celebrate Crispness properly," she tossed over her shoulder. "To make up for all those times you went home and slept through the festivities instead of sharing in the spirit."

Given my usual choice of either heading off to the Bear and Gill and listening to Faith and Hope nattering about how successful their big sister Charity is and endless questions about when was I going to visit her in Hogland, or being dragged to the Wildwater residence and smothered by Bertha's brothers, or overfed by her leering mother, hibernating for a week had always seemed the safest festive option.

"All I'm saying," I refuted, "is that you have no idea what real cold feels like until you spend a few days in a battered tin can hurtling toward Calypso. Not to mention the fact you could die out there." *We* could die out there.

"I just replaced the sled's heater last week," Nick said. "It's a brand new Polar North model. Guaranteed to last ten years or they service it for free."

"Check the fine print." I snorted. "I'll bet those service calls are only valid within the official land boundaries of Central City."

"Besides, I could just as easily be run over by a stampeding unicorn or put down by a bout of putrid plumbed pud or undercooked foul fish. Is this our sled?" Bertha stopped beside a warehouse to stare at a towering ring of dull metal that vaguely resembled a rusty donut standing half-buried in a snowdrift.

Nick shook his head. "No, that's scrap. Ours is inside." He struggled with the heavy double wooden doors.

"Had me there for just a minute." She sighed and went to help him move them aside.

I watched. Might as well save my strength for what folly-la-la was to come. The snow followed us inside.

Nick turned on the overhead lights. "Isn't it beautiful? This ship is called the *Hauly,* registered code Bar-E." He disappeared through a door in the rear of the building.

"This is not a ship," I corrected. "It is a scrapyard tugboat. The equivalent of a high-altitude forklift. And it appears to have survived several seasons of hard labor."

The gigantic metal donut stood on its base in the middle of the warehouse floor. The crest just managed to clear the three-story ceiling.

"It looks sturdy enough." Bertha leaned back, hands on hips, and studied our transport. "Do you know I've never been off-world before?"

"Lucky you, at least up until now. I have, and believe me, it's nothing to scribble home about out there, let me tell you. If you think Central City is cold, just wait."

She shook her head. "No place like home, eh boss? I thought you enjoyed your last trip to Venus."

"Home doesn't have fire-breathing dragons and folk-eating hungry swamp plants?"

"You haven't seen our back yard garden." She smiled. "I have invited you over."

"Yes, to one of your mother's famous illicit barbeques. I've seen the glowing reflection against the glowering clouds, heard the sounds of sirens and stampeding unicorns."

"Our family parties are not that bad." She would have continued but stopped cold, mouth ajar and stared.

Nick had turned on the *Hauly*'s exterior lights. He came back into the room carrying a pile of neatly folded heavy-duty clothing.

The sled glowed from the thousand bright warning lights that wreathed it.

"It's beautiful," Bertha breathed. "Looks all ready to celebrate Crispness."

"Change into these," Nick said. "I have to hook up the launch balloons."

"Balloons?" She held up a set of sturdy blue denim bib overalls and frowned. "I'm supposed to wear these?"

Nick was pulling down heavy cables from pulleys located on the ceiling and attaching the clips to four connections on the sides of the sled. "Regulations. The sled won't start unless the crew is wearing official safety gear. Oh, and it may get a bit crowded inside. There's loads of room in storage, but the main cabin is only designed for two."

"Slip them on over your civvies if you're shy," I said to Bertha. "I won't peek." I had noticed she was wearing a dress for a change and garbed like she was planning to go to a Crispness party. Ankle-length like most of her stuff, the hem of the gold gown was decorated with blue and gold candy canes. The neckline was wreathed by gingerbread stick figures.

She gave me a *look*. "I was all dressed up to go shopping after work at that posh new emporium, Masie, Seers, and Doe. I guess now this is another year the office won't get decorated. Hold my coat and turn around. No peeking if you know what's good for you. I'll tell you when I'm ready."

"Nothing there I probably haven't seen before," I grumbled, but then carefully added, "Not of you, of course."

I went around to the other side of the sled and changed. There was the minor problem of distributing my armament, but the overalls had ample tool pockets and hiding places.

"You look very fetching," I said when I returned.

I suspect her garment had been designed to fit a medium-sized ogre or hobgoblin. To say it hung loose would be an insult to exaggeration. She'd rolled up the pant legs and tied the bib around her neck twice. Fortunately, Bertha is on the tall side. Unfortunately, she tends toward seriously slender.

"I don't fetch or carry," she snapped.

"There's room for another in there with you," I continued, the cold making me reckless.

"Only if they want a quick and painful death." She glared down at Nick. "What you staring at, junior?"

He smothered a grin and pressed the hatch release. The access portal at the base of the machine groaned open. "Everyone inside. If you two take your places in the control room I'll handle the launch sequence from the storage compartment."

Nick had attached four large limp canvas bags to the free ends of the cables. They began to inflate, slowly, turning into miniature blimps covered in large patches.

I climbed up a narrow ladder, through a hole and plopped into a thinly padded seat. The two control chairs were set so close together we bumped elbows when Bertha dropped in beside me. The flight deck was the size of a shrunken closet. Cramped, would be an apt description.

"There's usually only one operator on a run," Nick said through the open hatch behind us. "A normal tour is eighteen hours long so there's not much padding."

"I've noticed." I glanced at the primitive controls.

There was a directional red and white cane-shaped stick and an array of cloudy dials. Three of the gauges had cracked crystals and were missing arrows. A large green button was marked "On". An oversized red button beside it was probably marked "Off" but only the "O" remained. Whatever Nick was doing in the depths of the compartment located behind us caused dials and screens to flicker into life. An overhead image showed a view of the warehouse ceiling. A smaller screen gazed out at the doors we entered the building through. There were two foot pedals.

"Left pedal is down, right is up," he announced as he fiddled with release mechanisms.

I frowned. "I don't suppose we need a license from the Committee of Inter-City Travel and Touring before we launch?" Maybe we'd be lucky and not allowed to leave until it was too late. Then Mae couldn't blame me for failing in this mad rescue scheme.

"They're closed for the Crispness Week Break." Nick's head poked through the hatchway. "Besides, The Chimneys fall under the Committee of Terraforming and Planetary Welfare. We have Crispness Card Blanche." He disappeared back into the depths.

"I think I've found us some suitable music." Bertha had been toying with a black box mounted right on the low ceiling above her head. She held a headphone up to one ear.

The sounds of *I'm Scheming for a Bright Crispness* filled the tight cabin.

"I really hate that humbug song," I growled. "Gives me a headache."

"Old grouch." She turned up the volume.

"Here we go, balloons released." Nick's voice echoed from somewhere in the abyss of the storage compartment. "Everyone hang on. The good ship *Hauly* is launched."

"Where are the seat belts?" She fumbled around the worn edges of her chair.

I joined in the search. "I believe they all have been removed, probably to provide the pilots with a fraction more seating room."

"Clever that." She didn't sound pleased. "Where is my navigation table?"

There was a loud whoosh as the cables on either side of us snapped tight. The sled shook violently from side to side. An extended groan echoed as the warehouse roof opened skyward. The balloons went straight up like giant party favors escaping from a stampeding riot of young-uns. With a shudder, we followed, rising rapidly through the gap, rose past The Chimneys, and on toward the heavens. The *Hauly* did manage to sway slightly, adding an uncomfortable sensation to an empty stomach. I suddenly recalled I'd missed first breakfast in my rush to see Bertha tangle with Nick.

"Better start the engine." His head thrust in the narrow gap between us. "The launch balloons will start to deflate rapidly once we reach firing altitude and then we're on our own."

I punched the "On" button. Nothing happened. I pushed down hard. "There is juice in the tank, isn't there?"

We plunged upward through fluffy cotton-candy clouds and into the wild blue just short of yonder. My stomach struggled to stay out of my throat. Bertha's face turned a pleasant shade of green.

"Wave your union card," Nick shouted. "There should be one in your pocket. Hurry!"

Our ascent slowed. The overhead view showed collapsing balloons. They were certainly colorful. Someone had patched them in blue and gold Crispness colors.

My stomach slowly settled back into its proper location. Bertha released her grip on my arm. I think she'd even bruised the upper bones there. I fumbled through the myriad of pockets and secret places in my overalls. "Are you sure there's one in here?"

"Should be."

My stomach decided to shift again, this time rising more gradually upward. The *Hauly* provided us with a distinct impression it had reached its apogee. It slowed. In another moment, the sled would begin to sink.

I pressed the On button again. Nothing.

"Oh, here, take this." Bertha handed me a square orange plastic card with raised lettering. "Or would you like me to drive?"

I clenched my jaw, waved the card across the control board with my right hand while holding down the green button with my left.

The ancient engine began to turn over with a groan and a painful ho, ho, ho. The *Hauly* started its fall back toward the clouds below us.

I pressed down hard on the right foot pedal. The *Hauly* vibrated, coughed, and gasped into some semblance of life. Our descent slowed, and we began to rise again.

"Nothing to it," Nick said from the depths of the cargo hold. "Anybody hungry? I can make sandwiches, have cookies, milk. I cleaned out the company kitchen fridge before we left. Nothing more than a few days past due date."

Chapter Six

"If I take a sighting on the North Polar Star, then go ten degrees to the right, and vector in the *Hauly's* vibrations, we should reach Calypso early on Crispness Eve." Bertha mumbled through a pencil clenched between her teeth as she balanced a clip board on her bony knees and made extended circles with her protractor.

"You did say you took navigation at night school," I asked.

"Yessthh." Her answer was dampened by her clenched jaw. A frown topped the jeweler's eyepiece she was using to peer out the front window.

"Did you pass the course?" I persisted.

The moon was a faint dot far behind us and fading into a vast collection of even fainter specks that included Gaia, old Mother Earth. Ahead lay much more of the same, spots of light, that is.

Bertha reached above her head and turned up the sound. The ear-straining sounds of *Crashing Through the Show* increased in volume.

Another tune from the long list of Great White Way stage productions that deserve a well-earned permanent retirement.

"Would anyone like more milk and cookies?" Nick asked. "I found another package of pineapple and chocolate chip peanut butter cookies. We really should use up the milk. I've skimmed off most of the green stuff floating on top."

"No thanks. I may try to survive on the powdered oatmeal and freeze-dried peanuts." I peered behind me and down into the depths of the storage compartment. Loose bulbs powered by surplus gas from our exhaust cast a red and green glow. Nick was curled up in a pile of dried soup and candy. "I thought you said Mae from the High Dive sent over the supplies. I haven't seen anything yet that looks like it might have come from her classy kitchen. So far all you've passed out to us up here are the table scraps from a busy long weekend."

"Don't forget, if we don't have time to stock up at Calypso while we're rescuing the darling children, we'll have to feed the little dears on the trip to Titan." Bertha had ceased chewing on her pencil. "I figure that trip might take us another twelve days."

"Which is odd," I said, "considering it will only take us seven to get to Calypso, and Titan is in the same neighborhood. Look at your calculations again."

She frowned. "Oops, I slipped a decimal." She spit out the pencil, caught it in midair and started scribbling on her pad. "I have it. With luck, and my brilliant navigating, we should make it from Calypso to Titan in about twelve hours."

"This is twelve hours too long when we will have a much faster pirate ship on our tail and the captain and crew upset because we've stolen their cargo of miniature mining slaves."

"Nothing much we can do about that," Nick offered almost cheerfully.

The trip to Calypso continued in much the same bloodless vein. I began to suspect I was taking root in the pilot's chair.

After three days the air inside the *Hauly* tasted stale. I increased oxygen levels. Nick uncorked a box of slightly used romantic candles from the High Dive tables, stuck them on the walls of the storage compartment and fired them up. When that didn't work, he rinsed the air scrubbers with odor du steak sauce. I suppressed a brief and fleeting urge to ask Bertha to dance. Fortunately there was no room, and sanity prevailed.

On the fourth day our water rations were reduced by half to conserve something for our anticipated passengers. Mae had supplied us with a quantity of Crafty Wines in festive flasks. Probably left over from her New Year's Daze event at the High Dive almost twelve months ago, but three thirsty beggars can't be choosers. Besides, we couldn't leave the bottles of Three Lads and Partridge Pear Juice for the innocent children. Water would have to do them.

Is there such an oxymoron as innocent children? Remembering my own youth… But I digress.

On the fifth day of Crispness week Nick found a slightly used package of leftover humbugs monogramed with the High Dive logo. We finished them off.

I was having third and fifth thoughts about this expedition, but no one else on board seemed to care. Were the humbugs loaded and muddying our thoughts as well as our tongues? Normally I do not like stumbling into situations without at least three plans—a straightforward frontal attack, a back door approach, and a sideways bounce off a wall.

My normally creative mind had shut down. I suspected oxygen deprivation and cranked up the atmosphere. At least we had lots of the stuff, containers left over from a trip to the outer limits. This didn't help. I decided I'd wing it like the rest of my peculiar crew.

Bertha had taken to playing hangman with her navigation pad, when she wasn't composing farewell notes to her mother or poking me with her pencil. Everyone-calls-me-Mouse-but-my-real-name-is-Nicholas, or just plain Nick, had discovered an old ship's manual in the dim and dusty depths of the storage compartment.

"I want to modify the flapjack in the flugel valve located under the rear exhausted vent," he announced. "According to chapter and verse this should increase performance by twelve percent."

"No playing with the delicate equipment," I threatened. "You can fiddle with the sled all you want when you drive it back to The Chimneys after Bertha and I take a cruise ship from Titan."

"We're not leaving Nick behind," she stated in a tone used for questioning my expense reports.

"We have first class tickets," I countered. "I'm not sleeping upright in a narrow chair one more hour than absolutely necessary."

"We'll see about that."

"Don't worry about me," Nick said.

"Hush up!" we chorused.

She turned up the sound, sang along and flooded the cabin and the storage compartment with a hearty version of that old faithful *When They Wash Their Socks* complete with random foot stomping.

Nick joined her in mid refrain. His voice was even worse. I tried to sleep.

Chapter Seven

'Twas early Crispness Eve morn when Calypso finally showed up on the *Hauly's* antiquated crystal ball. Whichever guild of wizards had fine-tuned the flickering device, they were less than careful about finessing the finer details.

Folded like a warped pretzel, I was dozing in my chair. Fortunately, I'd given my co-pilot a crash course in driving our oversized delivery wagon. Only my forehead struck the forward view screen when she braked.

"We're here!" Bertha screamed and threw the release for the anchor as we approached the mass of the minor moon at a velocity guaranteed to loosen teeth and more than a few screws.

With every bolt straining, the *Hauly* dropped from warped speed to something approaching a major train wreck in an amazing amount of time.

The shrieking of the anchor's flukes would have woken me even if the blood streaming into my eyes had not. I saw the mass of Calypso's gray pockmarked surface filling my crimson-shaded view. I heard Nick bouncing off the walls and supply cupboards behind me like some unfortunate loser in one of those cursed vid games. My seat commenced to groan and collapse around me.

"Are we there yet?' I gasped and braced for impact.

For a minute my sleep-depraved mind couldn't remember the proper position for a crash landing. Anyway, we lacked enough room between me and the exterior bulkhead to stuff my aching head between my knees without removing it, my head, not the now important bulwark.

"Everything's under control," she growled. The muscles in her arms strained as she pulled back on the drive cane.

I watched, helpless, as events from my past life streamed across in front of my eyes. Of course, scenes I'd rather forget were prominently displayed in full color and slow motion.

Every joint and panel on the *Hauly* complained. The sled shook and shuddered as we narrowly missed the metal skeletons of the extended docking pier and unloading crane and continued toward the complex of minor buildings on the surface ahead. I must admit, in hindsight, the strings of colored lights along the dock and crane did look festive.

My brain registered that most of the habitations on Calypso would be underground. This far out from home the Committee of Terraforming and Planetary Welfare hadn't even bothered trying to rework the surface to suit their re-imagined ideal moon. Saturn didn't provide enough heat to make the effort worthwhile, and the moon fell into the too-small-to-bother-with, category. So, we had just another crapped-out miniature mining colony ahead. Only, instead of turning this one into a trap for tourists or a home for unwanted seniors, some bored desk-bound clerk marked the place for an orphanage.

With a final groan, the *Hauly* eased to a stop and into the arms of the heavy-duty bumpers built to handle large ore carriers. The equipment might have been old and long unused, but our sled was a feather boa compared with what those iron girders were designed to wrestle. We scraped to a halt and suddenly silence reigned everywhere. The dust settled.

"I think the dead duck has landed." I sounded hoarse.

Bertha sat motionless staring ahead, her bloodless fingers clutching the directional cane to her chest, left foot still pressing the pedal to the floor. Her clenched jaw protruded beneath wide bulging eyeballs.

I leaned over and punched the Off button. "We're here," I whispered.

"I think I'm going to be sick," came a small voice from the storage locker. "I think I was sick."

The short-range radio, which had been turned off during our voyage, crackled into life. "Identify yourselves. This is the head of security. Identify yourselves."

Before I could open my mouth Nick crawled in between us then snatched the mic from its cradle. "This is a special supply shuttle from Chimneys with a load of presents for the staff and children. Recognition code for the week is SUGARPLUMS. We request a docking sleeve and access so we can unload."

My vague impressions of just plain Nick, aka Nicholas, or Mouse, went up at least two notches. I should have been the clever one to formally announce our arrival in a way to allay suspicions. After all, if I remembered his sad tale correctly, the dreaded pirate, Capt'n Rinch, had an agent on board the Calypso facility.

"We have no record of a delivery expected today," came the response. "The docks are closed for the holidays. There's no one here to unload your ship. You will have to come back next week."

A pause while we all looked at each other and frowned.

The crackly voice continued, "I suggest you spend the next week on Titan and return after New Seer's Daze. Calypso, out."

"No wait!" It was Nick again. "We have presents for the children, and for you too. They have to be delivered today, before Crispness Eve. It's in our contract."

I grabbed the mic from him. "Besides, some of the presents will expire if we have to wait a week. They're set to go off at midnight tonight."

Bertha pried the mic from my hand. "This is the captain. We don't have enough fuel to get to Titan. We have to unload then refuel."

"Since when did you get promoted?" I grumbled.

"Since I did most of the work getting us here while you slept."

"I was tired. It's been a long year."

"The usual length, Boss, you're just getting old." She went back to the mic. "Do you let us dock and refuel *now,* SUGARPLUMS, or do I put through a call to the Com P.S. detachment on Titan and have them send a squad of nasties over here to clear up this little misunderstanding? They'll be in great humor, what with you disturbing their holidays. I have a fistful of legal documents here in my hand. I know my rights."

"Well played," I muttered reluctantly.

"I'm not just another pair of pretty ankles." She almost swallowed the mike with a loud, "*Well*?"

I could feel the reluctance seeping through the airwaves. "Docking access granted. You'll have to go to the restricted quarantine dock beside the custom dome. Unfortunately. it's a long way to the hatch leading inside. You'll have quite a walk to unload. Security, out."

She turned to me. "Do you know how to park this thing?"

"Leave that to me," Nick said. "One of you move out of the way and let me take over the controls."

I motioned for her to join me in the storage compartment. "Are we really low on fuel?"

She shrugged. "According to my calculations, which I have triple-checked, and the mis-named *Guide to the Galaxy*, which I discovered stuffed under my seat, we would run out of juice about an hour after arriving at Titan, if the trip takes twelve hours."

"I'm not fond of those odds." Normally, all we needed was enough to get us started in the right direction, and sufficient for braking and some maneuvering, and the rest we could do by drifting with just the environmentals on and cooking.

It was the thought of maneuvering that made me nervous. If we ended up trying to avoid a pirate craft we could be in for a touch of serious difficulty. Help might be hard to come by quickly. All the security and rescue patrols would be comfortably snug in their berths in dry dock, their crews already in party mode.

"Well," I said, "as we really don't have anything to unload, and a passel of children to pack on board, we had better get out there and get started. I saw an old work suit in one of the lockers. I'll go out and hook us up to the hatch so the rest of you and our passengers can go suitless, if they hurry. I don't imagine the docking connection has much in the way of heating, and it will be sub-subzero out there."

Of course Nick insisted on doing that work.

What'sa matter? Did he think I was too old and feeble? Who cares? He knew what he was doing. We watched his struggles through the forward view screen as he hooked us up to the tunnel and plugged us in to recharge our batteries.

"Nick's waving at us. Let's go outside and rescue some orphans." Bertha actually beamed at the thought.

"Sure," I said. "What can go wrong with this picture?"

Chapter Eight

The flexible access tunnel to the first dome was barely survivable even with the system turned up to high. Pink frost streamers coated the walls. The soft light cast by Saturn gave the alien icicles a sickly warm glow. Nick had turned on the atmosphere pumps and heating, but we still wore breathers and hurried to get inside before we froze. I had all my weaponry secured about my person. Bertha carried a length of iron pipe. He brought up the rear, balancing a large soft duffel bag like a sack over one shoulder.

"Well, we told them we were bringing presents. They'd be suspicious otherwise," he explained.

"What about the agent the pirates are supposed to have located here? Any idea just who that might be?" I glanced at him over my shoulder.

He shook his head. "Nary a clue. That sort of knowledge is way above my pay grade. I searched the office files. Couldn't find the names of any of the staff on Calypso. Guess we didn't need to know that information to ferry them up supplies and stuff."

We paused in front of the large round metal hatch leading down and inside.

"How do you want to play this, Boss?" Bertha asked. She swung her pipe in a wide circle. "I feel light-headed and fleet-footed. What's the gravity of the situation here?"

"About fifty-percent of Mother Earth and artificial, like the atmosphere, and be careful with that pipe. You could injure someone, mainly me."

"Relax, Randy, I played defense for the all-ghoul's street hockey team at night school. They called me a crack shot, because I broke the mask of the goalie on the other team, last game we played."

The door rolled to one side with a sound like a herd of tiny stampeding hoof prints, followed by a last gasp of stale air, leaving the entrance open. A tall cadaverous hobgoblin stood barring the way. "I'm Little Dick Enns, head of Security on Calypso. What do you have for us?" Hands on bony hips, he leaned down and peered at me. "Are you sure I don't know you?" His voice dropped to a dry whisper. "Are you one of them, you know, the ones coming to, to take the children to a better place?"

"You guess it, Little Dick, that's us." One way to get his cooperation and avoid a brawl, convince him the pirates sent us.

He frowned. Eyebrows like a pair of trained wooly caterpillars scurried up his forehead. "What are you doing arriving in that piece of junk? I expected the full sonata with the Capt'n hisself arriving on the *Stalking Moon* with his crew of cutthroats. I want my share *now*. That's the deal." He held out his large hand.

"First, can we step inside, we're freezing out here." Behind me I heard Bertha shuffling around, probably taking a stance and ready for a swing.

Little Dick Enns stepped aside and let us in. The door hissed shut behind us. "How do I know you is who you say you are?"

"How would we know about the plan to kidnap the children if we weren't who we claim to be?" I sounded reasonable.

He frowned again. "I want my share now, before we move the children." He shook his head. "Is the *Stalking Moon* on the way? You'll never get them all on board that little thing you brought. Where's Capt'n Rinch?"

"He had to make a detour. Someone tipped off the Com P.S. and they sent out a couple of patrol ships packed with wild wizards. He'll meet us off Enceladus in two days."

"I want my share *now*."

He was certainly single-minded. Not just half a brain but all cells firing on the subject of his payout. "Well I don't have your just reward. You'll have to take that up with Rinch."

"Then I'm coming with you. Make sure I get what's comin' ta me."

"There's no room, you said so yourself."

"I don't care." He frowned. "We'll, I mean you'll, have to kill the headmistress, Mistress Holly Knight. She won't let the little monsters leave here without a fight. She's already suspicious of why I'm the only staff left on Calypso for the holidays. Right burned up about it, she is too. She'll be foaming at the mouth wondering what we're talking about out here. Told her I'd bring you right straight to her. I'd recommend you do her in quick, and I'll dispose of the body. They won't need the recycler for a while till they get this place back up and running again. That could take years. Follow me."

We started down the corridor.

"Let me talk with this headmistress first. Maybe I can reason with her. Use some of my undeniable charm."

Little D snorted. So did Bertha. If there had been a water clock in the neighbourhood I would have glanced at it. The longer this exercise took, the more likely we were going to stumble into a nasty band of child-slaving pirates.

We entered what appeared to be a large dining hall, with bleachers set all around against the polished rock walls. The gallery was crowded with young goblins and gremlins of every size and shape, from those just hatched and wet behind their floppy ears, to larger, red-eyed, and toothy. A tall, willowy elf stood in the middle, hands on hips, staring at us. A frilly white apron hid most of a floor-length black gown. Shoulder-length brilliant ebony hair swept back beneath a black peaked cap. She pointed at us with a wooden spoon the length of Bertha's piece of pipe.

"We've just finished our lunch, and it is now nap time. What is the meaning of this unscheduled interruption?" Her icy gaze swept across me, tripped over Nick, and locked on Bertha. "Well?" She ignored Little Dick Enns.

Bloody Zeus and all his misbegotten, misshapen relatives, if this is already mid-day Sol Standard it's later than I think, and we've just about run out of luck and time. Have to get a move on, double-quick.

Bertha stepped forward. "We have been ordered to aid in the evacuation of Calypso. A rogue asteroid has been reported in the neighbourhood, and we've been sent to take you and the children to Titan."

"And *you* are?"

"Bertha Meaghan Wildwater, of Wildwater and Associates. This is my senior partner, Randolf C. Aloysius. We were chartered by the Committee for Obfuscation and Procrastination acting at the request of the Committee of Wealth and Healthfare. It was a rush job due to the urgency of the situation. The *Hauly* was the only ship available on such short notice." She paused for breath. "We came here from Titan as fast as we could."

Of course, if we were at Titan, why didn't they send a patrol craft instead of a forklift? Hopefully, Mistress Holly Knight doesn't know the difference.

She stared at Bertha. "Interesting. And you expect us just to pack up and leave with you? You will have to allow me to confirm this nonsense with our office on Titan. In the meanwhile, would you like some green tea? We could have that served in my chambers."

The interplanetary intercom failed to generate anything but static.

Fortunately, I'd instructed Nick to disconnect the communications array linking Calypso to the outside world while he was hooking up the access tunnel. They were cut off.

"We have to leave immediately," Bertha said.

"No time for even a small cup? It will take us several hours to pack. Would you like to freshen up in my room while you wait?" Miss Knight appeared disappointed.

"You tell her, Little D." I turned to the Head of Security on Calypso. "We don't have any time to spare. They will have to leave here with just the clothes on their backs."

"True enough, Mistress Knight, no time to waste." He stared at the floor. "Should get going right now."

She gave him an icy stare guaranteed to freeze a Medusa in her tracks. "You follow this nonsense? You have confirmed it? Stand up straight, Mr. Enns!" The finger she pointed at his face seemed to grow longer. The nail gleamed crimson. "You agree this is a legitimate crisis? You take full responsibility for us abandoning our posts in the face of this oncoming annoyance? Well?"

"Yes mam?" Came out as a hoarse whisper.

The wooden spoon waved above her head. "Classes, youngest first, march in triple file to the access tunnel entrance. Packs on your backs. No pushing, biting, or gouging. No fighting of any kind allowed. March!" She turned to Bertha and smiled. "I, of course, expect I will have quarters suitable for a matron and headmistress in my position. I prefer a private cabin, but certainly, given these desperate circumstances, I will be quite willing to share yours. March! That's it, everyone keep in step. And no talking!"

A minor horde of small and medium-sized creatures came down from their bleachers and fell into three ragged lines. At least half of them stared up at me. Unblinking yellow and red eyes gave me the once or twice over. A couple licked their lips. A few smiled. One blew me a kiss.

Did I mention I don't like children?

Chapter Nine

If I said the *Hauly* was crowded I'd be accused of gross exaggeration. We were packed to the girders even after borrowing an old lifeboat from the depths of the school warehouse to take the student overflow. The teaching assistant, a wide-eyed and nervous young goblin senior student name of Lee Touh was placed in charge of that crowd. She certainly had my sympathy but no offer to change places. We linked the *Ivy* to our craft, connected and fired up life support, and prepared to tow. Of course this set-up meant the fuel situation was close to critical.

On board the *Hauly* there was barely room to breathe the rapidly fouling atmosphere. Goblins hung from the ceiling without care. Gremlins swung from the walls. Miniature mongrels like me made up a quarter of our passengers. Little Dick Enns clung to my side and looked greener than usual.

Even though Mistress Knight had instructed her charges not to say a word until we reached Titan, there was an overwhelming almost silent bubbling background chatter, like excited ghosts at a family picnic.

Beside us Nick was submerged beneath a living carpet of kids. He did poke his head up for a minute once in the midst of story-telling to gasp, "A good thing we don't have too far to go. I don't think the air in here will last until we get to Titan."

"Something to look forward to," I said, peeling a small gremlin off my head.

Did I fail to mention Bertha, my trusty executive secretary? She was up in the control room, or modified broom cupboard if you prefer, tucked in beside Mistress Holly Knight. The Headmistress had insisted on riding in one of the only two seats on our trusty craft. She refused to allow me up there instead of Bertha with some feeble reasoning about the fact she was a respectable single female, and we would be in close quarters for far too long. Besides, she needed to travel with a window to prevent her from coming down with a case of the vapors.

Bertha told me not to worry. She could easily handle both piloting and navigating. Actually told me to relax. The pair of them made me mad enough to spit. I would have, too, if there was any room.

I had visions of the *Ivy* crashing into us as Bertha attempted to dock when we reached Titan. Would she bother to ask for my expert assistance? Probably not.

"Have you come to take me away from all this?"

I opened one weary eye. A goblin, probably in her last year at the orphanage before aging out, hung from the ceiling on a rope made out of someone's clothing.

"Sorry, no room to adopt a pet. I live alone." I had to duck as she drifted close overhead.

"I was thinking more like the brave prince rescuing the beautiful princess from the ogre," she said, swinging by and knocking at least three other students aside as she dropped into the heap of bodies.

"Bella, stop speaking to that common creature immediately." The voice of Mistress Knight bounced through the storage compartment, causing the dull hush of conversation to drop a degree. "He is far too old-worldly for you. I said you will be going to a finishing school on Titan to learn to become a headmistress."

"Hello." A smiling gremlin balanced by my elbow. She drooled, "Hello, again," and blinked. "Pretty." She clutched my glass knuckles in her tiny paws.

The gremlin was quick, I was faster. "Not to be played with, young thing."

Bella scooped up the gremlin. "Reath, behave yourself, I saw him first." She gave me a lopsided smile. "I'm a senior monitor and TA in training."

"What about the heater in the holster under your left arm?" Long fingers raced over my jacket. One goblin attempted to distract me while another reached for Bess.

I swatted prying hands away.

"I almost wish I'd stayed on Calypso," Little Dick Enns moaned in my ear. "You could have mailed me my share."

A drop of perspiration trickled down the back of my neck. The thick air was warmer. We couldn't turn anything down or we'd suffocate.

"I think you owe me double," Little D continued. A small

gremlin rolled up in a ball, dropped on his head and bounced. He swatted at it and missed. "In fact I insist on a just reward."

"Serves you right for getting caught up in this silly scheme. What made you think it was a good idea to steal a herd of children and sell them to the mines?"

Bella was running her long thin fingers through my hair. "You are *really* old."

"I'm just involved in getting them from Calypso to the transport. Nothing to do with the sales. What rank are you anyway? Are you Capt'n Rinch's second-in-command?"

Before I could answer either tormenter there was an announcement from the control room.

"Randy, can you come up here right away? I think we have company coming." The sound of Bertha's tense voice drifted into the maw of the chaos surrounding me.

"By Belial's Tangled Tail, if that news is what I think it is our goose is stuffed and probably roasted." I pushed bodies aside and clambered toward the forward hatch.

"What's going on?" Little D went down, submerged beneath a warm pile of squirming arms and legs. "Is it the *Stalking Moon?"*

"I'll find out." I thrust my head, elbow level, into the narrow space between Mistress Holly Knight and Bertha. "What do you have?"

"A craft on the opposite course has turned around and is tracking us and closing fast." Bertha had somehow managed to get the dash-mounted crystal ball working again and pointed. "See there."

"Does this mean Titan has sent out a proper rescue vessel, and we will soon have suitable accommodation and a hot shower?" Holly Knight asked.

I squinted. The ship was headed straight for us, the gap narrowing rapidly. I palmed the glowing ball to get a clearer image. Sleek, black, and almost upon us. "I don't suppose we can go any faster?"

"Nick told me we are at the safe max with this overload. Any more speed and we do a slow meltdown." Bertha reached overhead and turned down the volume. The suggestive notes of *Jiggly Belles* faded away.

"What's the problem?" Holly Knight turned to Bertha. "Simply hail them and request assistance. Let me speak to their captain, and we will straighten this matter out immediately."

"We may not have explained the entire situation to you completely correctly." Bertha's fingers tapped a tune on the dash.

The audio crackled as an incoming announcement overrode

everything else. "Prepare to be boarded. This is the dreaded pirate Captain Grimm Rinch speaking. You cannot escape me. Stand down and prepare to be boarded." There followed a static-filled interlude where Holly Knight and Bertha exchanged glances, and then both turned to stare down at me. "Surrender immediately, and your miserable lives will be spared. Resist and you will walk alone in space. Your choice. Your ships are mine, your cargo is mine, and *you* are mine. Boarding has commenced. We have the hooks into both your craft. Shut down your engine, *now*."

I stretched up and pressed the Off button and got my hand slapped, hard.

"What have you done? You have given us into the clutches of these fiends. You should be prepared to die defending our honor." Headmistress Holly Knight's index finger battered my nose. "We have two shiploads of defenseless women and children."

There is an oxymoron in there, I think, based on a certain amount of previous accumulated experiences.

"If we behave ourselves we may just survive this experience," I muttered. At the moment I couldn't think of a way out of this situation, but surrender seemed like a good place to start.

A loud clang echoed through the *Hauly,* like the jangle of a large bell. A sound I recognized as heavy clamps rang against our outer wall.

"I don't think they intend to use the door," I advised the control room.

A glowing wreath of fire appeared on one wall.

"Cutting through." I stuck my head back into the storage room and shouted, "Everyone stay calm. Stay away from the wall that's steaming."

Of course the little orphans ignored me. They crowded around like spectators at a pre-game entertainment.

"Now you're in for it," Little D shouted, waving his fist in the air.

Or at least he tried to shout. He was half-buried beneath a roving tidal wave of small and medium-sized giggling folk.

A large section of the middle of one outer wall collapsed and crumpled outward. There was some confusion while the pieces were wrestled away. A rush of fresher air swept inside pursued by a hint of stale tobacco, perspiration, and a heavy dark beverage I was familiar with from my misspent middle years.

A large flexible tube illuminated with colorful lights connected us to a larger vessel.

When the last of the debris was cleared away a tall cadaverous individual with a skeletal face and body stood in our latest doorway. He had the look of a half elf, other half unknown. He carried a rather tall scythe in one hand. I gave him points for his outfit. Rinch wore elbow-length blue rubber gloves and a red silk suit topped by a floppy gold hat trimmed with a large purple feather. A black cape pinned with a gold broach in the shape of a hand and knee-high black rubber boots with gilded spurs completed the ensemble. I must admit the effect was striking.

He leaned forward on his scythe. "Well, Mister Whook, what have we here? Do you suspect we have found our missing cargo? What say you, my dastardly First Mate?"

First Mate Whook was definitely more a Mistress than Mister. A bloated vampire, with heavy lips and bulging red eyes, she stared right at me and drooled. Her fashion sense came from the same school of Proper Pirating her captain did. She wore a purple crushed velvet jacket and matching pantaloons. A violet cape clasped around her throat was held in place by a silver broach shaped like a bare foot. A bright blood-red bandanna circled a mass of thick black hair escaping halfway down her broad back. When she licked her lips, her canines shone white.

I think she had a forked tongue.

A polished bone handle protruded from the crimson sash wrapped around her waist. This might have been the finger end from one of those ancient dueling pistols, or it could have been attached to a long sharp blade. The wrap hid more than a few secrets.

She cracked her knuckles. "Looks like a real fine haul, Capt'n Rinch. Some tasty morsels to share out. And a lively pack of young miners eager to spend the rest of their lives deep underground on the outer asteroids."

Her red eyes kept wandering back toward me, like a shopper studying a cut of fresh meat, or a choice tomato. She winked.

From behind them, a crowd of bloodthirsty gremlins peered out between their officer's legs. Most of them wore little but dirty loincloths. Their teeth were filed into points. They carried wooden clubs. A murmur of, "Keel them," bubbled. "Keel them all!"

"Settle down," Capt'n Rinch said. "That wouldn't be nice."

"And wasteful," added his first mate.

Little Dick Enns raised his hand from deep in a pile of bodies and called out, "I expect to be paid double what I was promised for having to travel in this indignity."

Capt'n Rinch turned to his companion. "Do you know this

personage?"

"Never seen him before in my life," said the mate.

He glanced down at his eager crew then pointed. "Take him to the brig."

A swarm of gremlins poured into the *Hauly*, dug out Little D, and dragged him away, protesting loudly, until they stuffed a pair of dirty loincloths in his mouth. Someone tapped him on the back of his skull with a club to cap the job.

I knew things had been too quiet.

Mistress Holly Knight lowered herself through the hatch and into the room. The shifting tide of children parted. "What is the meaning of this? Do you know who I am? I will have you all drawn and quartered. These are the students from the Calypso School of Higher Learning and Fine Arts. We are chartered by the Committee of Edification and Enlightenment under the authority of the United Gremlin and Goblin Minor Miners Association of Titan. These are their precious children. Dare touch one hair of their darling heads, and you will have to answer to me."

Capt'n Rinch turned and gazed at his first mate. "Do you know who she is?"

Mister Whook shook her head. "Never set eyes on her before. All this talk of drawing means she plans to paint our portraits, I reckon."

"Remove her from my sight." He waved his hand. "To the brig with her."

A squad of gremlins moved forward. There was a low murmur from the storage room.

Mistress Knight held up her hand. "Stay." She smiled at the roving bands of children and quietly followed her guards across to the *Stalking Moon*.

Far too calmly if you ask me. A handful of small tykes trailed after her. They were ignored by our captors.

Capt'n Rinch gazed around at the seething collection, gave me a quick glance, and rested his gaze on Bertha hanging down in the hatchway of our control room. "We seem to have two more surplus adults. They're far too large to be of any use in the mines. They are a complete waste of air." He stroked his chin, frowned and pursed his lips. "The lady appears to have some interesting qualities. Leave her undamaged." His glance returned to me. "As for this miserable mongrel creature, I leave it to you to recruit or dispose of as you see fit." He stepped back into the connecting tube, a guard of gremlins swirling about his feet. "The stench from this place is unbearable—hose them down. I will be in my cabin resting. Have some chamomile tea and lemon cakes sent up. See to the second vessel." The jingle of his spurs faded down the corridor.

Mister Whook's grin broadened. "Yes Capt'n." She clapped her rather large, meaty hands.

A squad of gremlins appeared carrying a firehose, unreeling it from somewhere deep in the depths of the *Stalking Moon*. They grinned fiendishly.

"Everyone hang on," I called out.

Icy cold water blasted into the storage room on the *Hauly*. Small gremlin and goblin children went flying in all directions, giggling and cheering. Miniature mongrels did belly-flips from the ceiling. Bertha slipped, and I caught her arm or she would have been swept way into the deep pool forming at the bottom of our chamber.

They must have picked up all this surplus water from an ice asteroid.

"This is ridiculous," she sputtered. "Do something."

"Now is not a good time." Bess, my trusty splatter gun, carried eleven penetrol bullets in her chamber. They could knock out but would only temporarily disable some more powerful creatures, like vampires. The rest of my clips were in the ship's locker.

We were badly outnumbered. I'd prefer to start something when the odds were more in my favor. So far, they hadn't attempted to disarm me. Probably didn't think they needed to search me.

"Go away, he's mine." Staring at Bertha, Bella struggled out of the water, Reath clinging to her back and her arms filled with squirming juveniles.

"You can have him." Bertha snorted. "Now what?"

"Let me explain things to you, dearies," Mister Whook announced, leering. With a casual wave she shooed a gleeful troop of gremlins and their firehose back down the tunnel toward the bowels of their ship.

"You two will come with me to the brig." She pointed at Bertha. "You are most fortunate, sweetie, as the capt'n seems to have taken an interest in you. He likes to see what makes things tick and talk. Capt'n Rinch will certainly want to thoroughly examine you. He has an excellent operating room next to his suite complete with the most charming table, collection of carving tools, and sedatives. I can assure you the experience will be brief and almost painless."

First Mate Whook turned her bloodshot eyes on me. "You may have a choice. How well this goes depends on what happens when you come up to see me. Seize them both and take them to the brig." She sighed, stared around the room, and motioned to the remainder of her horde of gremlins. “We’re already short of room on board. Leave the rest of our nasty cargo loose in here and on the trailing craft. No need to unload them until we get to our destination, the Miners’ Market on Enceladus. Follow me.”

I didn’t like the sound of any of this but decided I could wait a brief while before attempting action. Besides, our elf Nick seemed to be missing, probably submerged somewhere in the middle of the pool filled with small folk down at the bottom of the storage compartment.

Chapter Ten

The *Stalking Moon's* brig consisted of a number of small cells located deep inside the dimly lit bowels of the pirate ship. Imitation torches flickered along the walls casting barely enough light to see by, all very retro. Bertha and I were placed together in one cell, Mistress Holly Knight and Little Dick Enns resided in another directly across the hall from us. Well, *she* resided, he was still unconscious. The piratical crew left us alone down there, and wandered off, giggling, probably to celebrate their latest victory. The place carried the faint aroma of used engine oil blended with vomit.

"Now what?" Bertha leaned over and growled in my ear. "I will be seriously disappointed if you don't have a plan."

"I'm working on it."

Across the corridor Headmistress Knight was leaning down talking to a tiny pair of her gremlin charges who had appeared out of the shadows. A juvenile goblin stood watch. They eventually scampered off, and she straightened and stared across at me. "Bertha has told me some ridiculous stories about you. How long will it take for you to free us?"

"Oh, about five minutes," I said, feeling modest. "Maybe less." The locks didn't look all that difficult.

"Give me a half an hour then break us out of here."

There came the sound of the tramp of heavier than usual feet. A large hobgoblin shuffled down the corridor toward us surrounded by a squad of the pointy-toothed club-carrying gremlins. The hobgoblin wore a bright red jacket and a pink bandana. Moth-eaten trousers fell to above his knees displaying large, hairy bare feet.

He stopped at our cell, frowned, and peered in through the bars. "Which of you is the one Mister Whook wants to see?"

"Who's asking?" I smiled. "You are?"

"Second Mate Jay Marilee," he mumbled. "Second mate o' the *Moon*."

"You wouldn't happen to know a Faster Fredericka do you? I'm a very close friend of hers."

"No. Stop stalling. Who in here does Mister Whook want to see?" He frowned at a scrap of parchment clutched in one hand.

"Her." I pointed at Bertha.

"Him." She fingered me.

"Or maybe it's him." I indicated Little Dick Enns, just now stirring from his crumpled position on the floor of the cell across the way.

"Unless of course, it might be her." Bertha thrust an arm through the bars and waved in the direction of Mistress Knight.

Mistress Holly Knight waved back.

"Can you read?" Second Mate Marilee glared at me. He thrust the piece of parchment between the bars and swatted me across the nose with it. "I bring him the wrong prisoner and things goes bad for both of us. Probably seals us in barrels of molasses and jettison us into the void."

"Now we can't have that. Here give your message to me." I snatched the scrap from him and held it up.

The handwriting consisted of less than fine penmanship, and the scrawled letters were written in thick black ink. At least it wasn't dried blood. I had to hold the note at several different angles to catch enough light to decipher the inscription located thereon. "To the shortish, but sort of cute, prisoner. Why don't you come up and see me sometime? Like right now. PS this is not a request if you knows what's good for you."

I sighed and kept reading.

"PPS There may be refreshments."

I turned the note over. There was another gaggle of wavy lines of poor writing on the reverse. "PPPS Recruitment comes with certain benefits, I'm certain. Failure to comply with this request, which is really a command, will result in several painful deaths. At least one. Also certain."

I shook my head and handed the scrap back to the second mate. "Maybe I'd better go and see what she wants."

He looked concerned. "Are you sure it's *you* he wants to see?"

"Highly probable." I pasted on a cheerful smile. "But first you'll have to release me."

He unlocked the cell door, grabbed me by my collar then yanked me off my feet and out into the hall. "Stay!" he barked at Bertha.

"I'll be back," I called to her.

Second Mate Jay Marilee grunted and said, "I wouldn't count on it," giving me a shove.

We fell into some sort of disorganized line of prisoner and guards and marched away. The procession wound through narrow corridors, up winding stairs, past groups of nasty diminutive gremlins, and the occasional wee child wandering freely about. The children all smiled and waved. The pirates snarled and growled at me most professionally. The second mate and my honor guard remained silent.

Our little parade came to a halt in front of a red metal door. A festive wreath made of hair, and teeth, and the odd ear hung above the frame.

Second Mate Jay Marilee knocked on the door, stepped back right smartly, and pushed me forward.

"Who is there?" came a grating voice from inside.

I recognized the first mate's tones.

"It's me, your honorable worship, Second Mate Mister Marilee." My warden leaned forward and whispered in my ear, "The first mate insists on being given his proper titles. All of them. If you knows what's good for you. Mind you, I don't expect you'll be in there too long."

"Did you bring me my surprise?" First Mate Whook called out.

"Well, Mister Whook. Seeing as how you requested the prisoner, don't think it'll be much of a surprise." He glared at me, heavy hand on the door's handle. "Unless you're not the one he wanted to see. Are you sure about this?"

"Guess we're about to find out."

"Bring him in, I'm waiting."

The second mate opened the door and gave me a hard shove. "Here he is then, Mister Whook." The door slammed behind me followed by the scrambly sounds his feet made in the hall as he fled.

I stumbled into the room and almost fell over First Mate Whook sprawled on a divan covered by an imitation leopard skin. I knew it wasn't real the minute I noticed the angelic wings. She'd tossed her purple jacket and violet cape on the floor and now wore a frilly yellow blouse that was at least three sizes too large. One long thin hand grasped a tall drinking glass holding a shiny metal straw. Her sharp nails were painted alternating red and green. The glass was empty.

The suggestive words and notes of *Good Rest There, Marie* wafted down from a speaker hidden somewhere in the ceiling.

"That's quite an entrance," she gurgled. "Are you always so dramatic?" Her eyes oozed crimson. Red droplets trickled down cheeks covered in splotches of white paint.

I maintained my stance and glanced around for possible exits. "Not always."

Fat, melting black candles s

moked from wall mounts shaped like small, inverted pine trees. The aroma, mixed with a cone of spiced incense smoldering on a shiny gold-trimmed table, lent a dim and shifting atmosphere to the chamber. A warning tingle danced up my spine, as though I really needed that.

She sat up, slowly, and patted the divan. "Come sit beside me, dearie, while we discuss your prospects." The long, forked tongue flicked across her lips.

"If you don't mind, I'd rather stand." This could be summed up as a delicate situation. I wondered what Mistress Knight's plan was and how fast I could get out of here.

"I do mind, my shifty friend. Let me make some things perfectly clear." She was doing one of those vampire tricky things, rising up on her knees gracefully as though made out of smoke. Only in her case it was more like a bad image, all flickering and jumpy. "Pay attention now, lovie, I'm only going to say this once." Her voice reminded me of a tired workman dumping a load of dry gravel from a wheelbarrow.

I've heard better attempts at hypnotism from the black cat who has been known to haunt the narrow alley behind my apartment.

She slithered off the divan. I backed up, trying to avoid tripping over a statue of a tiny demon perched on a skull and staring into an open book.

"When I say come up and visit me some time, I mean *right away*. It also means I'm hungry. If you wish to be a favored member of my crew, you'd better be prepared for a little giving now and then." She was smiling, canines extending.

She held up her glass and removed the straw. "You may call me Dhora when we're alone, if you wish."

I glanced around. Dhora Whook was attempting to back me into a corner. She held the straw up in one hand like a dagger. "I might even make you third mate, if you allow me just a drop or three of refreshment once in a while."

She stabbed with the straw in the direction of my neck. I dodged aside and skipped to the other side of the room.

"We can play games later, after I've had a wee sip," she cooed.

"I'd really rather not," I said. My fingers itched to pull Bess out and shoot the first mate. I knew she was toying with me. Vampires can move surprisingly quickly. It would take at least two shots to stop her. She'd probably be on me before I got off the second shot.

Dhora paused in the middle of the room and shook her head. "Here's the thing, hon. You have only two choices. Join our crew and allow me the pleasure of the occasional romantic evening snack or refuse me. In that case I will have you for the main course and throw what's left of you to those disgusting gremlins down in engineering."

Her smile widened. "If you're thinking of trying to save your lady friend, forget it. Second Mate Marilee's next duty after leaving here is to gather up your scrawny girlfriend and deliver her to Capt'n Rinch's operating room. He's probably cutting her wide open as we stand here chatting. Our capt'n does love to experiment. He's very curious to compare how the various types are assembled. You can almost hear…"

I shot her between the eyes and placed the second cartridge in exactly the same spot. Dropped her faster than you could say Jack's Being Nimble. She started to move forward as the first shell struck her. Ran right into the second. Pretty good shooting if I do say so myself.

"Afraid I must leave you," I said. Considered firing again to keep her unconscious for an extra hour or two, decided not to waste my remaining ammunition. I also thought about tying her up with some of the room's frilly decorations. Probably shouldn't spare the time.

The hall outside her quarters was empty, except for Bella with a small drooling child in hand. "What kept you?" she asked. "Come on, we have to rescue our pilot."

"Lead the way," I said, shaking my head. "If you know the way."

"Already scouted out. Come on." Bella led me down a corridor, past grinning groups of children. "This is the door to the cap'n's quarters. You have to go rescue her *now*."

I frowned, peering around. "Doesn't he have any guards?"

"He did. They're all tied up in that closet." She pointed across the hall. "Our debating team got to them before I arrived. Go!"

I pushed open the door and stepped inside.

Chapter Eleven

Bess at the ready, I found myself in what appeared to be a reception room with three overstuffed red velvet chairs and a highly polished coffee table. The table contained dueling pistols mounted beneath a clear glass window set in the top. An elaborate three-seater matching couch with feet that might have been carved, or real and preserved in clear marbled plastic, occupied one wall. Gas lights set in the ceiling gave out a harsh industrial illumination. There was a large oil painting mounted above the couch. I decided it might be a family portrait.

The beaming parents, both of whom had flowing black moustaches and beady red eyes peered out from beneath matching floppy gold hats with large purple feathers. The drooling child, seated on his mother's boney knee, leered. His oversized hat threatened to slip and cover him completely. I pegged the mother as mainly elf by her ears and hair. The father was something else entirely. I did not have time to stop and contemplate Capt'n Rinch's parentages.

I was on a rescue mission. A closed door lay just beyond the portrait. I tried the latch and carefully pushed it open a crack. A conversation was going on inside.

"This will only hurt a little." That sounded like Capt'n Rinch's voice. "My instruments are extremely sharp. A bit of carving here and there, and I can take a peek to see what makes you different. I pray I will not be disappointed by what I find. Most—subjects are frustratingly boring when you get right down into them up to your elbows."

"Loosen these straps and your day will not be dull. I promise you." That low, spitting growl definitely came from Bertha.

"You must allow me this little hobby, my dear. The life of a heroic pirate captain can be so tedious, a wee bit of murder now and then, some petty thievery, a minor kidnapping or two. You have no idea how lackluster a life I lead. Are you still comfortable?"

"No, I'm not. Let me up, lend me one of your sharp toys, and you'll have more excitement than you can handle."

I did recall Bertha mentioning once that she had majored in wood carving at night school. I believe she keeps a large knife in her desk drawer.

"Oh no, my dear, these instruments are precious, far too exquisite and sharp to be used for anything but the most delicate of operations. Have you had a chance to examine the specimens I have mounted on the far wall? No? A pity. When I'm finished, I think I will stuff you with scented wood chips and colorful cotton balls. Do you have a preference?"

There was a tug at my shoulder.

"What are you waiting for?" Bella whispered in my ear. "Get in there, *now*." She leaned down and wiped the runny nose on the wee gremlin she held in tow.

"Oh, all right." I pushed the door open wider and, picking the largest target, fired at his chest. Nothing happened.

"Hello?" Capt'n Rinch turned around. He wore a full length, red-hooded surgical gown, his blue rubber gloves, and held a carving set in his hands, a long sharp knife and lengthy fork. "*This* is a private affair, sir."

Bertha lay stretched out on an operating table. Narrow brown leather straps bound her wrists and ankles to a white tablecloth. A broad black band with silver bells secured her waist.

"This is most inconsiderate of you," Rinch commented, frowning. He shook his head.

I ducked and fired again.

The carving knife buried itself halfway to the hilt into the wall beside my right ear. The fork whistled past me on the other side.

"He's wearing a fancy protective vest of some kind underneath his gown," Bertha cried. "Aim for his head."

"No fair, you're cheating." Capt'n Rinch charged like an angry bull, short bright blades appearing in both gloved hands.

I stepped aside, gracefully I might add, with a move a bull-leaper would envy, and shot him on the bare forehead. He staggered and turned back toward me. The next shot took him between his narrow beady eyes. Rinch stumbled and dropped, sprawling flat on his face. Cutlery went spinning in graceful arcs across the floor.

"Let me up and I'll finish him off," she shouted, straining to sit.

Bella rushed to her side and began wrestling with the buckles on the straps.

"No unnecessary murders on this cruise," I said. "We'll turn him in to the authorities on Titan."

"We have to get there safely first." Bertha sat up and glared fiery daggers in the direction of the body sprawled on the floor beside her table.

I turned to Bella. "What's the status of the rest of the ship?"

"Headmistress Knight should have the *Stalking Moon* secured by now." She grinned and nodded toward our sleeping captain. "I'll gift wrap him for you." Bella produced a cheerful length of red braided rope. "Took this fancy bit off a wall hanging."

Bertha was already dragging the limp captain toward her former table. "I know where this turkey goes. Give me a hand, and we'll hoist him up."

We strapped Capt'n Rinch in place. Bella's expression registered disappointment.

"Don't worry," I said to the girl. "You can practice tying your knots on the next prisoner." The hopefully still unconscious First Mate Dhora Whook immediately came to mind. "In fact, we have one lying around and waiting for us at our last stop. Why don't you take the infant back down the hall with you and go wrap her up?"

"Is it safe sending two innocent children all alone out into the corridor?" Bertha stared around the operating room. "I'd like to start a crackling good fire and burn this place down. It needs a serious cleansing."

The room's décor was best described as modern creepy, what with samples of the good captain's peculiar hobby hung with care on all four walls.

"Explosions and flames are not a good idea while we're still floating out in space somewhere halfway between hither and yon. As for the children, I doubt they can cause too much damage. Besides, Bella isn't all that little. I'm also not so certain about innocent." My tired mind wandered. As far as goblins go, and they probably do… If I were a century or two younger…

I shook my head. It didn't rattle.

Bertha paused to stuff a rubber ball the size of a baked apple into Capt'n Rinch's mouth. "There, that should do it."

Bella and her squirming charge appeared in the doorway. "First Mate's gone. Done a runner. She's loose somewhere on board."

"Oh, bother," I said.

Bertha yanked the long carving knife loose from the wall and pried the matching fork free. "Well, I guess we should go do something about her. How many shots do you have left?"

"Five," I muttered, examining the clip. "Either the penetrol has gone stale or it's a bad batch. She should have stayed down far longer than this."

"Maybe your latest girlfriend has built up some immunity? She did strike me as a bit off." Bertha glanced at Bella and friend. "You two stay right here where you'll be safe. You can watch Capt'n Rinch struggle if he wakes up."

"Of course," Bella said.

They followed us out into the corridor instead.

Chapter Twelve

The first mate's fancy cabin was deserted, but the music played on.

"Where could she have gone?" Bertha held up a long, brilliant yellow feather boa and waved it overhead. She stopped and stared at me, eyes narrowing. "Just what were you two up to in this den of obvious indecency before all the shooting started?"

"Never seen anything like that before in my life," I swore.

I did have a vague recall of witnessing something very similar used to great effect to amuse some tired troops on leave at a disreputable bar located in a dim back lane on Iapetus. There was this long-legged Hobgoblin, who could twist herself into the most eye-boggling positions—but I digress.

I headed out the door. "Bella, any idea where the action is?"

The goblin nodded and started down the hallway at a trot. Her small charge bounced along behind her. "I think Headmistress Knight plans to make a stand in the ship's galley. Lots of supplies, limited access, central location."

We followed. I had this sinking feeling I should be out in front with Bess prominently displayed to dissuade any attempts to ambush us on route. On the other hand, we could just as easily be subject to attack from the rear, and Bertha seemed eager to take the lead. She had already caught up with Bella.

"How did the headmistress know where the galley was located?" I asked.

Bella glanced over her shoulder. "We're a school for the offspring of folk who work out beyond the asteroid belt. Our parents also operate the ships that travel in-between. When we graduate, we have two choices: look for employment on the outer moons or serve on the crappy craft that operate between them. One of our main classes is

Ship Recognition and Detail. The *Stalking Moon* is a retired Com P.S. cutter, standard layout. Everyone knows that."

"Of course," I said. "Just checking to see if you knew."

We crept toward the galley located somewhere toward the ship's stern and not too far from where we were originally held prisoner. When we arrived at the dining hall a minor riot was in full progress, only considered *minor* because of the size of the main combatants.

Holly Knight had barricaded the entrance to the galley with an overturned kitchen table ripped from its moorings. She could be heard from somewhere in the background urging her charges on and beating out a martial tune on a metal pan. A band of small gremlins and goblins sheltering behind the table, and armed with stirring spoons, were launching an assortment of dented cans and old vegetables into a crowd of screaming club-wielding gremlins.

The children were using their long serving spoons like atlatl, to gain power and range. The result was a scramble of bloodied gremlins in the center of the room. Another detachment of children armed with mops and brooms kept the open serving window clear. They appeared to be enjoying themselves as they flailed and poked at anyone who dared approach.

Second Mate Jay Marilee stood well out of range of the flying kitchen utensils and supplies at the rear of his chattering troops, urging them on. His once bright red jacket was covered in assorted soups and stews. His pink bandanna kept slipping over one eye as he raged.

There was no sign of First Mate Dhora Whook in all this mayhem.

Before I could give out some strategic advice, Bertha charged, and Bella followed, babe in tow. The sight of tall lean Bertha Wildwater, long dark hair and bright full skirts flying, and waving a lengthy carving knife and matching twin-pronged fork, was enough to send the bravest club-wielding gremlin scampering. Second Mate Jay Marilee turned to witness her approach and roared out a challenge.

I did the only thing I could under the circumstances, and the fact I was several steps behind. I shot him twice, and he dropped like a stunned mastodon. Bertha hardly missed a beat, skipping over him on her way to the relief of the forces holding down the galley. I was down to three cartridges left in Bess's clip. Goblins carrying garbage can lids for shields stepped aside. We scrambled over the barricade.

Holly Knight met us by the gas stove. She held a black iron frying pan and a steel rolling pin. "What kept you?"

"I had to rescue a fair maiden." I nodded toward Bertha.

The headmistress ignored me. "Are you all right?" She directed this toward my wayward assistant. "They didn't hurt you?"

"Fine, just slightly annoyed and a wee bit riled." Bertha glared around the galley. "What's our status?"

Holly Knight smiled at her. "Master Nicolas has taken the grade eight mixed football squad to attempt to seize the engine room. The forward cabin blast doors are sealed so we can't reach the flight deck. Once we take complete control of the ship we will commence negotiations. Bella, please set up a hospital in the pantry. We haven't had any casualties yet, at least on our side, but we must be prepared for eventualities."

"Yes, Miss Knight."

She nodded to Bertha. "While I check on our defenses you can take an inventory of our available missiles. I believe there is a cupboard in the back we haven't emptied yet."

"On it, Holly."

"So, everything is well under control," I muttered, staring out through the serving window into the dining hall.

The buccaneer gremlin crew was milling about the wreckage of uprooted tables and chairs, obviously waiting for instructions from Mister Marilee. He should be unconscious for at least another hour.

"Of course not, fool," Holly Knight snapped. "We are drifting in a pirate vessel in the middle of nowhere towing a maintenance sled full of defenseless children with your useless craft flimsily attached to our outside. It is a recipe for an unmitigated disaster. Why don't you do something useful and go speed up Master Nicholas and his team? Take control of this ship, send a message for help, and seize the day."

"Yes, Captain." I stared around the galley and hesitated. It had been several years since I served on a Com P.S. cutter. When I did, my duties didn't include the kitchen area. Now, was there a way to the engine room without going back through the mob milling about in the dining hall?

Holly Knight sighed, rolled her eyes then pointed toward the ceiling. "Climb up through that vent, take the exhaust system for ten meters to a wide junction box. You will be facing a large metal fan. Remove the fan and follow through that ventilation system to a grate in the floor. The grate will bring you into the ceiling of the engine room. You will have to dispose of any occupants." She shook her head. "I can't do that for you."

"Found a supply of small round tins," Bertha announced cheerfully. "They should fit in your launchers quite nicely. The pirates must have raided a pet store."

"Excellent." Holly Knight turned back to stare at me. "Well, what are you waiting for—Crispness?"

Well, that is tomorrow.

She frowned. "And stay clear of the steam pipes."

"I'm going, I'm going." I climbed up on a counter, pushed open a grate then hoisted myself inside.

"Be careful," Bella called from somewhere below me.

I hadn't done any tight and nasty climbing of this off-grid nature since grade school when I made a late night trip to visit a young lady of my recent acquaintance. My suspension only lasted two weeks so it was well worth it, but I digress.

The vent was warm but not as hot as expected. I found the junction box, dismantled the fan with a small tool removed from my shoe heel then reached the engine room grate. I could hear pounding below and peered down.

Six nervous gremlins armed with wooden clubs stood facing a door where the noise emanated from. Obviously, Nicholas and his crew were still trying to break in. Probably a blast door, if I remembered rightly. Mouse and his miniature minions could pound away merrily until next week. He still wouldn't get anywhere useful without explosives. Blowing a hole in the side of the *Stalking Moon* was not a good idea.

Bess remained in my shoulder holster. Those last three shells might come in handy later. I slipped one hand into my glass knuckles and gripped my Billy club in my teeth. Hoisting the grate aside I dropped through, into the middle of the unsuspecting gremlins.

I caught them by surprise, and we went down in a sprawling scrambling heap. I came up swinging. At least I had a fighting chance. The top of their heads just came to my belt buckle. Their clubs could reach my skull, though, if they connected. Fortunately three had dropped their weapons as I tumbled into them. Unfortunately, they all still had their sharp pointy teeth and extended fingernails and made a serious effort to use them.

Chapter Thirteen

Managing to break free long enough to reach the blasted blast doors and pull down on the handle, I went under flailing away beneath a flood of piratical gremlins. Before they could turn me into a piñata the door burst open, and Nickolas bounced into my red-hazed view followed by a swarm of small gremlin and goblin children. A tide of busy fingers and feet engulfed us. I decided I could breathe again.

When Nicholas, aka Mouse, helped me sit I stared around. My assailants were wrapped up neater than presents at a wizard's birthday fest. Strands of bright ribbon and wool yarn wove a tight pattern about pirate arms and legs. The children from Calypso were busy in the process of gagging them to cut down on the fowl language and other nasty bird calls emanating from our prisoners.

"Your companions seem to be making efficient use of knots instead of their usual naughty language," I commented, dusting myself off and checking my limbs for signs of any puncture wounds or other serious injuries.

"Oh, they're really all good children," Nick said. "I commandeered the entire senior knitting and wool-gathering weaving class. They'll have your assailants wrapped up like stored hammocks before you can say Bob's your maiden aunt."

Nickolas took a deep breath, gazed around and turned to me. "We've secured the engine room. Now what do we do? Do we shut her down or try to steer from here?"

I checked the gauges. The steam pressure seemed on the low side. I tapped the glass. "Just keep an eye on these dials. If the needle sinks into the red zone, shovel some of those blocks of compressed seaweed into the furnace."

He grunted. "I know the drill."

"Next we call for help. I'll see if I can break into the communications system and contact the Com P.S. We still have gremlins on the loose, a second mate who may wake up at any time, and a missing first mate."

"Not to mention a large number of helpless children and defenseless females." Nick nodded and licked his lips.

"Yeah, right." I figured the headmistress and my wayward secretary were secure enough inside their galley fortress as long as they didn't attempt to sally forth and seize the day.

The crowd on the *Ivy,* being towed behind us, should be safe enough, although I should contact them to make certain. I found a cable box, inserted one of my special heel tools, and placed the short range call to the young teaching assistant left in charge on board.

A very juvenile-sounding voice answered on the third ring. "Hello, we'd like to order a dozen pizzas with extra cheese and a sprinkling of cinnamon and peppermint candy."

"Can I speak to Miss Touh, please?" I shook my head. Obviously, the situation was not too bad over on our auxiliary transport.

"Only if we can get two dozen Crispness pizzas and a couple of gallons of red and green apple cider."

"You sound too young to drink. Are there any pirates on board your ship? Please put Miss Lee Touh on the com. I have to speak with her."

"There were a few bad pirates, but they were rude and misbehaving so we stuffed them in a sock locker. Can we have some pizza? All we've had for lunch today is warm water and those sticky chewy rations from the emergency box."

"Where is the teaching assistant, Miss Touh?"

"I think some members of the grade two class tied her up. They were playing a silly game."

"I'll see you can have all the pizza you want when we get to port. Just untie Miss Touh and let me speak with her. *That* is an order!" I made the firmest and angriest principal sounds I could. I did have some early experience with the receiving end of the proper menacing tone.

"Yessir." The com went dead except for background static and someone playing *The Joy of the Whirled,* a tune I long loathed from those days back at the school gym and the awkward dancing lessons they forced upon us.

There was a long pause amid the rumble of background confusion. Mouse paced around in circles behind me releasing nervous energy. I made frantic motions for him to keep his juvenile charges away from the delicate machinery in the engine room. If they disconnected anything serious we'd need a maintenance wizard to get the *Stalking Moon* going again. Being cold and dead in the water, so to speak, out in the depths of the distant void was a situation best to be avoided. Right now we were drifting. The pirate ship had not powered up and gotten underway since stopping to seize the *Hauly* and the *Ivy*.

Moments later I heard a faint quaver. "Hello, this is Miss Lee Touh."

"This is Randolf Aloysius, Captain of the *Hauly*." Might as well give her a sense of confidence. "We're in the process of seizing the pirate ship and getting the situation back to normal. Are you all right over there?"

"Oh, it's a bit chilly. I think we're running low on fuel."

"Are the children behaving?" A silly question.

"I think so. As well as can be expected. They've eaten most of the supplies."

"I'm going try and to reel the *Ivy* in to resupply you. I'll send Mr. Nickolas over to fix the heating problem. Try to keep calm. I'll sign off now and get right on it."

"That would be nice." She sounded faint, with just a hint of tremor in her voice.

"Hang in there, kid." As if she could do anything else. "Mouse, I have a job for you. Round up a tool kit and as soon as I have attached the *Ivy* to a starboard access port, get on over there before they all freeze to death. Just don't take too long."

"Aye, aye, Captain."

This exercise took us a few minutes. Fortunately, Com P.S, cutters come rigged for varied emergencies and the pirates had left these intact for use when boarding captured vessels. I had to break into the towing line controls, and we reeled our wayward lifeboat in toward a docking lock and clamped them on. Then I searched for anything remotely edible.

Nick suited up and made his way across the outer hull with a backpack filled with stale peanut butter and strawberry jam sandwiches from an engine room locker, a few chipped chocolate cookies, and a large container of butter tarts decorated with cranberries and mint leaves. He dragged along a small fuel container to top off our auxiliary vessel.

"That should keep the little monsters quiet for a while," I muttered, watching Nick until he was safely on board the *Ivy*. "Those tarts look like leftovers from last Crispness Eve. They should be chewy enough to hold their tiny jaws closed until we get to Titan. Now, to try and reach the sticky fingers of the law on Titan."

Before First Mate Mistress Dhora Whook managed to rally the crew and retake the ship, or some other such disaster, where innocent people, including me, got hurt.

We were at the extreme range for a ship-to-shore call.

"Wednesday, Wednesday, we are on board the pirate vessel, *Stalking Moon.* We were captured by pirates while on route to Titan. We were ferrying a load of school children from the Calypso Orphanage. We have managed an escape and have barricaded ourselves, but most of the buccaneer crew are still running loose on board. This is the vessel, *Stalking Moon,* under the piratic command of Captain Grimm Rinch." *Who is hopefully still indisposed and well secured.*

I took a deep breath. "Wednesday, Wednesday, we require an immediate rescue. My name is Randolf Aloysius. I am unable to operate the ship in our present state but have cut off access by the forward control room, so we are deadlocked, for now. I will leave this channel open. Follow the signal to our location. Please acknowledge."

Nothing but static echoed from the speakers. Even the jarring ear-shredding notes and commercial words of *I'm Scheming for a Bright Crispness,* would have been appreciated right about now.

"Make certain the engine room blast door is latched," I said to my motley crew of wobbling weavers. "We don't need any unexpected guests barging in."

Faint words crackled into the air overhead. "This is the Com P.S. cutter *Comet Dancer* en route to Titan, First Officer HoHo Gung speaking. What is your emergency? I repeat, what is your emergency? And this had better be good and deadly serious because I'm supposed to be on Crispness leave as soon as I make the dock at Titan. Your transmission was too faint to receive in full. Please repeat your Wednesday."

So I did, in full, quite loudly, and very slowly.

We waited. The lengthening seconds ticked by.

"Acknowledged. *Comet Dancer* changing course to intercept. Titan operations base advised. Estimated time of arrival—three standard hours. Can you hold out for that?"

"We'll do our best, just hurry, Aloysius out." I supposed now I should venture back into the dangerous curved halls of the *Stalking Moon* and check on how Mistress Holly Knight and Bertha Wildwater were doing in their makeshift sanctuary.

Chapter Fourteen

I made my cautious way toward where I thought the galley should be located. There was no sign of any gremlin activity in the corridors, but it was only First Mate Whook I was really worried about. If she had developed some immunity to penetrol cartridges, then I needed to save all of my remaining three for her. Pirate crew would have to be dispatched by hand. Based on several previous experiences, free-ranging angry vampires were not to be trifled with.

I heard the general buzz and a knocking sound coming from the direction of the dining hall. Peeking around the corner I made out Second Mate Jay Marilee still sprawled on the floor, unconscious. Large groups of gremlins milled about tapping anything within reach with their wooden clubs. Leaderless, the crew tended toward indecision.

At least the commanders on our side, Holly Knight and Bertha Wildwater, hadn't ventured out to do battle. They were visible, peering through from the other side of the galley serving window.

I stepped forward and into the open. "Attention to the crew of the *Stalking Moon*. A Com P. S. cutter will be here shortly. We have seized the engine room. You cannot control the ship. Your capture is only a matter of minutes away."

Well, hours, actually.

I took a deep breath. I still held their attention. "I wish to offer you a once in a lifetime opportunity for a reduced sentence. You are aware that these are often available during Crispness Week. I will so recommend in your cases if you lay down your arms immediately and return to your quarters now. Save yourselves while you can. Your officers will be tried separately and judged far more harshly. You have five minutes to take advantage of my very generous offer." I smiled, fingering the glass knuckles in my pocket and shifting my Billy Club into easy reach.

The gremlins stared around the dining hall. They gazed at the limp form of Mister Marilee. They gawked in the direction of the galley where armed children stared over the barricades at them. The pirates frowned at me. I smiled again and nodded. The first one threw down his club and the rest stampeded to follow. I stepped aside as they rushed out the door toward their quarters.

"Well done, gentlemen." I nodded approvingly.

Now all I had to do was check on the captain to make certain he was still lashed to his table, track down and secure Mistress Dhora Whook, and keep the *Stalking Moon* operating smoothly so we wouldn't freeze before help arrived. This all sounded quite simple if you didn't think too much about it. First, I touched base with Fortress Galley.

"Are you ladies and charges all right?" I glanced in through the serving window.

"Of course." Mistress Holly Knight frowned. "Why wouldn't we be? Have you secured the ship? Have you contacted the authorities? When will we be arriving at Titan? Don't just stand there with your mouth open, speak."

When you pause for breath. Elves can be a pain at times, especially when they're awake.

I smothered a sigh. "Everything is under control. I recommend you stay in the galley though, until the Com P.S. arrives. I'll scout around after I tie up the great lump over there. Do you have any strong wire or chain?" I gestured toward the inert form of Mister Marilee.

"You look as though you've been wrestling inside a bag stuffed with annoyed cats and lost." Bertha snorted, hands on hips. "Your face is a mess, and your clothes are in even worse condition than usual. You have a tear in your jacket, and one pant leg is missing. You should be in care."

"My face is normally a mess." I grunted and shook my head. "Now, about something to make knots with…"

"Just let me tear out a few yards of wiring." She retreated inside the galley. "I think I noticed some in the ceiling."

"Be careful." I waved both hands.

"Oh, don't be such a worried weasel. Last year I graduated with honors from a weekend class in electrical engineering at night school." There was a brilliant flash from inside the galley, followed by a loud, "Oh!" and some smoke and colorful sparks. The lights went out.

"Give me a minute." Bertha's strained voice. Teeth may have been clenched.

"Are you all right?" Miss Holly Knight.

"Oh, Good Gilgamesh." Bertha again. "Got it. Is this enough?"

The gaslights flickered on. A length of bare arm and long thin fingers reached out through the galley opening clutching a roll of coated wire. A sprinkle of ash and soot coated the back of her hand.

"Just right," I agreed, taking the wire. It would have to do. The last thing we needed was Bertha dismantling any more of the ship. I glanced at the dining hall ceiling. The lights seemed to have taken on a tendency to twinkle. Very festive, as long as the situation wasn't life-threatening.

I wrapped up the still-unconscious second officer, Jay Marilee, tighter than one of those gag gifts at a Crispness Eve office party I used to detest. Now, off to check on Captain Grimm.

"Stay put," I warned the ladies.

"Not very likely," Bertha said. "We do tend to wander if unsupervised, but we'll try to restrain ourselves to the dining hall and the galley, for the moment."

I suppressed a growl and headed toward the captain's cabin. I found Capt'n Grimm Rinch still securely lashed to the operating table. He was wide-eyed awake and staring, making strange angry noises. The rubber ball stuffed in his mouth may have impeded any attempt at intelligent speech.

I squinted down at him. "Glad to see your first mate hasn't attempted to rescue you." I cupped an ear. "What's that you say? Sorry, I can't make out what it is you want."

His face was slowly turning color, giving the good captain rosy cheeks and a red nose. A curl of smoke drifted from both pointy ears.

"Do you have any idea where Miss Whook could have gone?" I leaned over and listened to him struggle. "No? Well, I guess I'll have to leave you there, all trussed up like dinner, and go see if I can track her down. Hope you don't mind."

I pause in the doorway. "Not very loyal of Miss Whook, going off on her own and abandoning you like that. If I were you, I'd consider hiring a new first mate."

If glares could fry, I would have been roasted right there on the spot. Smiling, I headed toward the control room, moving cautiously, Bess drawn. The door was open. The piloting and navigating chairs stood empty. The place lay deserted. Closing and latching the door behind me I sat and studied the dash.

A very long time ago I knew how to drive one of these things, or at the least, an earlier model. "Now, let me see, I think this little switch turns the machinery on."

It did. Lights and dials and knobs and buttons twinkled into life. Needles wavered and glowing numbers flashed. From somewhere deep inside the instrument panel the sad notes of *Hurry on, Carole,* drifted into the crackling air. That's when I first noticed the chill. Then the wrap-around wall only inches from my face turned transparent.

Frost coated the inside of the massive window, drawing delicate, suggestive patterns of whitish gold against the harsh velvet black of the void. A small dial indicating falling temperature began to flash red. A larger gauge registering atmospheric pressure blinked anxiously. The steam-pressure gauge glowed orange.

"Please re-set the environment," a scratchy mechanical-sounding voice announced from deep inside the workings. "You have approximately thirty minutes before complete system failure, depending on the crew complement. Please reset and input necessary data."

I scrambled to find the ship's communicator, fiddled with the dials, and sent out a broad short-range call. "Mouse, Nicholas, come in, we have a minor emergency. You are going to have to suit up and get back over here, ASAP. Mouse, Nickolas, Nick, can you hear me? Nick, come in. Randy, over."

All I could hear inside the control room was the pleading words from the heavy breathing lover begging Carole to come home to him. I couldn't even figure out how to turn him off.

Then the audio crackled. "Nick here. Sorry, we have a situation over here. I can't leave. Impossible. Nick out."

"Wait!"

Nothing but dead air.

What's so important…?

I closed my eyes, leaned back, and tried to dredge up a spell that might help to recall anything I knew about the operation of a Com P.S. cutter. Did we even have an apprentice wizard on board?

The words to *Hurry on, Carole* faded away and were replaced by the all-too familiar strains of *Good Rest There, Marie*.

"Hello, dearies, yes it's me, First Mate Mistress Dhora Whook. Love that song. Don't bother to search for me. I know this ship like me own underarm pit. You'll never find me in your short lifetime. But don't worry about me, I'm quite safe. Have enough heat and oxygen to last a century or two in here. But then, in case you didn't know, vampires don't really need too much of either to survive. Getting a bit hungry, though. Just a touch.

"But enough about me. I've set the *Stalking Moon* to self-destruct in one hour from now. I suggest you all get into the lifeboats.

Oops, I forgot. I locked them and buggered up the locks. You can't use them. Well, your only solution is to gather yourselves in the main water tank. It's empty, and just wait in there for me. Oh yes, and if you've locked up the crew, release them first. Don't really care what you do with Capt'n Grimm. That's about all. If you follow my orders, I'll be out in an hour to take over. If you don't, you'll all be dead, so it won't matter. Would be a pity though, I like my Crispness dinners warm and kicking.

"This message will repeat now in case you weren't listening. Cheery-oh."

Chapter Fifteen

I tried Nick again, no response. I attempted to shut down the control board, no luck. Launching a feeble curse learned in the school yard had no effect. I headed back toward the galley at top speed.

"You did, *what?*" Mistress Holly Knight stared out the kitchen pass-through and seemed ready to launch herself at me through the narrow opening.

"It wasn't my fault. She booby-trapped the thing."

"You are referring to First Mate Mister Dhora Whook. Use proper names when you are speaking. *She* might be a cat." Miss Knight sighed and shook her head. "Also, the ship's environmental system is not a *thing*."

It's not just the environment we have to worry about.

I chewed on my tongue. "Yes Mam. Do you have any experience with counter-spells?" I added, "Miss Knight," for good measure.

"I could try to override it." Bertha glanced up from beside the sink where she was washing the few remaining unbroken dishes.

Not that I don't trust my fateful assistant, but I've seen the occasional test results from night school. Preventative magic was not one of her better subjects.

Holly Knight frowned. "We do have an enchanting kindergarten class. Miss Bella Rhingrr, the senior school class president, is in charge of that diabolical group. I'll see what they can do to save the situation."

My current favorite goblin appeared from the pantry with a small child attached to each arm. She smiled at me and winked. "Yes, Miss Knight?"

"Mister Aloysius has made a horrible mess of things. The first mate has taken over control of the ship. We need your group to dispel any witchery or fascination she may have placed on the operation of the *Stalking Moon*."

"I'll go to the engine room and see what I can do from there," I said.

A long arm and red-nailed finger attached to Miss Knight swiveled in my direction. "You. Do not move from *that* spot. You stay right here ready to defend us."

I felt a sudden chill in the air. Hopefully, it was just my imagination. "Yes, Mam."

"Would anyone like some tea?" Bertha called out. "I have the kettle bubbling on this steam vent."

Oh, why not?

We gathered around the galley kitchen-pass-through, sipping chamomile tea and asteroid honey, while Bella herded a covey of a dozen or so small, mixed-breed children into the center of the dining hall. "Everyone hold hands. Rowsea Cheequs, stand in the middle of the room. Now class, form a ring around Rowsea and everyone close their eyes and concentrate. We are going to banish bad thoughts and dampen nasty vibrations away from this lovely ship."

Bella glanced over her shoulder and gave me a very suggestive slow wink. "Everyone think pleasant thoughts, and now push, push hard."

I almost choked on my tea. Almost.

"I'll bet on innocence over evil intent every time." Headmistress Knight smiled. "You just watch."

"Not if you'd seen some of the things I have," I muttered beneath my breath.

Bella leaned back and led her class in a low, sing-songy chant. I couldn't make out the words, although to my untrained ears they sounded much like, "Abstract Peanut Butter." I think little Rowsea, standing eyes closed in the middle of the crowd, was singing, "And jelly," or something sounding very much like that, over and over again in a high-pitched voice.

"I think it's working," Miss Knight whispered. "You can feel it."

Maybe the temperature inside the ship had stopped dropping. I expelled the pent-up breath I'd been saving for emergencies. Hopefully, First Mate Dhora Whook's threat had been an idol one in an effort to frighten us into submission. I'd never put much faith in idols. Didn't notice any in my hurried visits to her quarters.

"I think you have everything under control here." I gave Miss Holly Knight my best heart-warming smile. There was no sign of a thaw. "I should go back to the engine room and check on things there. If the system has stabilized that's one less threat. I'll try and hurry up the Com P.S. before Mister Whook gets suspicious and tries something physical."

"I'd like to see her try." Bertha glared over the rim of the measuring cup she was drinking from. "I finished third in our night school kick-boxing tournament a week ago."

"I thought you told me there were only three contestants entered," I offered to the conversation. Not that I'd ever consider entering my chin up against those long legs and multi-colored painted toes.

Bertha turned her icy glare in my direction. "This was the Crispness Boxing week finals. There were entrants entered for the entire twelve days, I had a match a day."

"I'm certain you were marvelous." Holly Knight slapped her palm with a metal ruler she materialized from somewhere hidden. "I always have this as a last resort. If it makes him feel better, I guess we can allow Mister Aloysius to go off and comfort himself by checking over the engine room." She pointed the ruler in my direction. "After that, I expect you to track down First Mate Whook and see that she is properly secured. Loose, she is a danger to the smaller children."

And to us grownups.

I fled. The small gang of children left by Nick to keep an eye on the situation inside the engine compartment were perched on a boiler playing an illegal game of Broken Bones. I suspect they'd lifted the game pieces from the loin cloths of our six battered prisoners who remained securely tied to the steam pipes.

"Everything under control here?" I asked.

The dealer, a lean young goblin wearing an oily rag as a bandanna eyeshade, peered down at me. "Want us to cut you into the game?"

"No thanks." Last time I rattled the carved bones in the back room of the High Dive I was lucky to leave there with my shirt.

I checked the gauges. The pressure seemed to have equalized but it was still on the low end of the spectrum. The drop in temperature had slowed, but it would be on the chill side in the *Stalking Moon* by the time the Com P.S. cutter arrived.

Bess in hand, I began a careful room-by-room search for the missing vampire. The ship wasn't all that large, and most of the rooms were stuffed with groups of giggling children or pirates intent on draining the vessel's considerable store of nog. The students seemed to be sorting themselves and arranging into their classroom groups. The gremlin crews were rushing toward sedation. No place for First Mate Whook to hide in among either of them.

When I finally returned to the dining hall Bella was still leading her calming circle. Bertha had joined the ring and was holding hands with the senior school class president and her class. Their low chant was a mind-numbing hum.

"I see they're still at it."

"Of course." Headmistress Knight frowned and shook her head as though I was deficient in gray matter. "If they stop now the spell that shut down the system will return in full. They can't defeat the sorcery completely, only suppress or slow the enchantment. What else would you expect from a kindergarten class?"

Drool?

Miss Knight granted me her full attention. "The temperature is growing cooler in here. Have you tracked down Miss Whook yet? What have you been doing, lolly-gagging? This is not a large vessel. Yours was a simple task, while the rest of us do all of the heavy lifting."

I noticed she was on her second cup of tea. "We may have to wait for the Com P.S. cutter to arrive and leave her to their gentle hands."

"Typical." She turned back to watching the enchanting circle.

Some of the smaller students seemed to be swaying. Bertha was holding the one beside her up in place. We couldn't wait for rescue. I chewed my lower lip. What was Nick doing? Why hadn't he returned? I wonder…

"I think I'll take a walk across to the *Ivy* and check in on them. I sent Nicolas across to fix their heating. He hasn't returned, and he isn't answering my calls."

"If anything happens to Miss Lee Touh and her students I shall have your head removed, bronzed, and will keep it on my desk to remind me of your ineptitude." Headmistress Knight strode across the dining room floor and joined the chanting circle on Bella's other side.

"Good to know," I said. I had always wondered if anyone would remember me after I departed. I started for a locker I'd spotted in the adjacent corridor and hurried from the room, calling over my shoulder, "You can always use me as a source of inspiration for the students."

Holly Knight paused in her chanting long enough to call after me. "I will use you as a paperweight, to hold the exams from those students I intend to fail."

Chapter Sixteen

The survival gear in the hall lockers I checked was gremlin-sized and too small to fit me, so I found a more suitable suit in Capt'n Rinch's quarters. Gave me another opportunity to check in on him and gloat. His walkabout was a bit large for me. I almost had enough room for a second passenger inside the suit with me.

Slipping out the forward airlock I stepped onto the outside of the hull. Two thirds of the way toward the stern rested the *Ivy*. The *Hauly* was attached to the *Stalking Moon* somewhere out of my sight on the other side of the hull. Using the suit's magnetic boots I stomped my way slowly toward the shapeless lump of the life craft from Calypso.

"I hope you do realize that Bess is safely secured inside a pocket of your flight suit and you won't be able to reach her until you strip out of the survival gear." The words echoed inside my helmet.

I don't usually talk to myself out loud, but it is sort of lonely and deathly quiet strolling across the outer hull of a space-going vessel surrounded by a vast view of inky cold nothingness a long way from the sun. The stars were strings of tiny decorative lights strung out a long way off.

"Do you even remember the airlock situation on the *Ivy*? Can you seal the access door from the inside while you strip out of all this gear?" Probably not. It would make no sense to be able to lock the door from the inside of the entrance access. Any locking would normally happen from the interior of the lifeboat.

"But then in the case of a crash or emergency landing, wouldn't the rescue team have to be able to break into the inside?"

I stood beside the *Ivy* and stared up at the large gray and dusty shapeless mass. The words, *Calypso School of Higher Learning and Fine Arts,* were painted across the hull in chipped gold lettering. No exterior windows. They would have some sort of ability to view what was going on outside them. Therefore the folks inside probably already knew I was standing out here. There was a ladder built into the hull leading topside to the main hatch.

"This is one little mystery that won't sort out by itself, Randy, me lad. Either you go up and crawl inside and find Mister Whook waiting, or you won't. In any case, you will discover why Master Nicholas isn't answering your calls."

I went up the ladder, hand over hand, found the access wheel and cranked it. The hatch opened with a sigh.

"Anyone at home?" I asked. The words echoed inside my helmet. I launched through the gap and floated to the floor.

The empty airlock was large enough for six average-sized folks to exit or enter at a time. I guess in emergencies there might be a need to hurry. I closed the outer hatch behind me and a dim ceiling light flickered into existence. At least they still had power. Oxygen hissed into the chamber. I knocked on the interior metal door with my heavy gloved hand. The sound echoed. No answer.

"If they didn't know you were coming before, they do now," I grumbled. The airlock continued to pressurize. After counting a slow ten plus two for good luck I gave the inner handle a crank. The door disappeared into the wall.

Nick stood facing me. "You shouldn't have come."

Quiet rows of children sat around the interior, facing us. The *quiet* gave me good reason to pause. "Allow me a couple of minutes to extract myself from all this gear," I said cheerfully, "and I'll be right with you."

"You should go," he said. "Now."

"A bit chilly in here, isn't it? Where is the apprentice schoolmarm, Miss Lee Touh? Did she leave you in charge while she went for a stroll?" I stepped out of the suit and fingered Bess.

The rows of children were all staring at me. They were strangely motionless, even the tiniest gremlin scamp. The *Ivy* was a standard issue lifeboat. One large main chamber for storage or passengers, a small engine compartment the size of a cramped closet in the stern, and a forward cabin where the crew, if there was any on board, could have some private time to figure out where they were going and how to get there.

"Mind if I go forward?" I started toward the crews' cabin door.

"She said she'd kill her if we interfered. Promised not to harm her if we behaved." Nick blocked my way. His face was pale as a snowman's caught in a blizzard. "She just wants to escape."

"And you believed her." I pointed Bess at the elf. "Step aside."

He did, chewing on his lower lip. "I jimmied the controls so she couldn't detach the *Ivy* from the *Stalking Moon*'s hull or start the engine. Not enough fuel to go anywhere anyway. She's trapped in here until we're rescued."

"So is little Miss Lee Touh." I sighed.

The door to the cabin could be locked from the inside. I had enough experience on detention as a monitor to know where the override lever was. I handed him a large wrench from the wall toolkit. "If she gets past me, use this." I yanked hard on the handle, and we both stepped back. The door swung open. There was blood splattered everywhere.

First Mate Dhora Whook lounged in the pilot's chair cradling Miss Touh across her knee. Bright crimson rivulets of blood dribbled down Mistress Whook's chin. Red stains covered the front of her frilly yellow blouse. She raised her face from the assistant's neck, licked her lips, and smiled. Bulging eyes drank me in.

Miss Touh appeared unconscious.

"I do apologize, dearie," Dhora gurgled. "I must look a right mess. I forgot to grab a straw when I departed my quarters in a rush. Not the most graceful of exits." She stroked Miss Touh's cheek with her sharp red and green nails. Thin streaks oozed where she touched the goblin's skin. The forked tongue danced between white and red fangs.

"Let her go." I aimed Bess at the vampire's forehead.

"What's the hurry, hon?" She held her victim close. "It's been a while since I tasted someone quite so fresh. Although if you'd like to volunteer to replace her, that would make me really happy. You do want to keep me happy, now, don't you, lovie?"

"I'm going to count to three." Which also happened to be the number of shells in the clip.

"Oh, if you are going to be like that." She rolled Miss Touh off her lap, tumbling the limp assistant to the floor, and slowly uncoiled to full height, reaching behind her and coming up with a handful of violet cape. "I do need a cover-up of sorts what with all this mess."

"Back away slowly from the kid."

First Mate Dhora Whook smiled and stepped over her limp victim. "Did I happen to mention that shooting me with your pop-gun simply added strength to my natural immunity to the nasty stuff? I'll be willing to bet, sweetie, that it would take a full clip to stop me now. Do you have a full clip?"

She flung the cape at me at the same time as she lunged.

I dodged to one side and fired. The shell hit the cape. I swung the Billy Club with my left hand as she landed and pinned me to the floor, clawing for the gun. The club glanced off her right arm. Her left grasped for my wrist. I fired again. This time the shot buried into her mass of thick black hair. That might take a while to do any good. She squeezed. My wrist cracked, and Bess dropped from my fingers.

"I do so love a good tussle." Straddling me she leaned down, smiling. "Sure you don't want to join my crew?" Canines extended. Forked tongue flicked. "Well, if you insist, I don't mind doing things the hard way."

Nickolas rang the heavy wrench off the side of her skull, then swung back again for a repeat blow. The grip on my wrist released. I scooped up Bess from the floor, stuck the muzzle into Mistress Whook's gaping red mouth, and fired the last shell. She collapsed on top of me like a highway bridge built of bricks. Bess went spinning across the floor.

"Now what? the elf asked.

"First, get this great lump off me, and then see to the teaching assistant. She'll need first aid."

So will I, eventually. I thought my wrist was broken.

Nicholas, with the aid of a squad of eighth grade goblins, dragged the first mate off me, and I tried unsuccessfully to sit up.

"You'd better find something to secure the prisoner with," I told the ceiling. "I have no idea how long she'll be out."

A herd of mongrels and gremlins carried Lee Touh out of the forward cabin and laid her on a pile of mattresses. "She's alive but bleeding," a tousled-headed youngster in a plaid skirt announced. "We need antiseptic and bandages."

Children scattered to search the cupboards and lockers on the *Ivy*.

"She'll need more than that," I said. "Probably a quiet vacation on a pleasure planetoid away from children and vamps. Nick, how are you coming with the mate?"

He struggled into view with a section of thick pliable cable he dragged from somewhere, hopefully not connected to anything important. "Don't worry about me. I'm used to securing heavy loads for lift by the *Hauly*. She won't get loose in this century unless she has help."

I took a deep breath, sat up and crawled across to where a small gremlin examined Bess. "I'll take that back, thank you." Now what?

I noticed the room seemed chill and the air getting a bit thin. *Oh goody.*

Chapter Seventeen

It took some doing, but I finally pried Nicholas away from the side of the unconscious form of Miss Lee Touh sprawled on a pull-down bunk and turned his concentration toward the potentially life-preserving connections between the *Ivy* and the *Stalking Moon.*

A squad of gremlins from the third grade were attending to her. They cheerfully slapped red emergency steam suppression bandages and bright yellow hull repair patches on any portion of the young teaching assistant's pale green skin still oozing fluid. Their leader, obviously having passed the Crisis Management Basic Aid course, was keeping up morale and rallying the little dears with a chorus of, *Crispness is coming, and dinner's going flat.*

"Listen Nick, the young lady will be fine, she's just down a pint or two of blood. The kids can look after her until we can import an adult. I need you to figure out why things are cooling down in here and it's getting a bit difficult to breathe."

Our Elf spent all of five minutes checking over things inside the *Ivy* before announcing, "The problem isn't in here—must be over at the pirate ship." He licked his lips. "I think we have about fifteen to twenty minutes before everyone in here is unconscious."

"As tempting as that might be," I said, "we have no time to waste." I stuffed both of us into walkabout suits and launched us back across the hull to the main airlock. We arrived with five minutes to spare and made for the control room. I attempted to power things up.

Miss Holly Knight's frowning face floated across the main screen in front of us. I made my brief report. Nickolas crawled under the dash-about board searching for a way to set the systems right.

The lips on the viewer flapped. "Well, if the first mate laid on the curse, and she is now unconscious, then Rowsea's magic calming circle should bring things back to normal. Are the drive controls working?"

How did the headmistress get inside the communications system? "I'll check." Lights came on across the panel. "Everything seems to be working now. No, cancel that. I can get heat and air back to normal inside the ship but still can't start the main engine."

The frosty image on the screen frowned. "Do I have to think of everything? Send that nice Mister Nickolas down to the engine room. I'm sure he can correct whatever is wrong. Report back to me in the galley when this disgusting craft is back underway. And make certain I have plenty of hot water in my cabin."

You have a cabin? "Yes Admiral." I disconnected. Nick was already on his way into the depths of the ship. I leaned back in the captain's chair and closed my eyes. Peace and quiet lasted all of a minute.

Communication hiccupped. A faint voice burbled out between rustling waves of static. "This is Com P.S. cutter *Comet Dancer* en route to pirate vessel *Stalking Moon*, First Officer HoHo Gung in command. We are thirty minutes out. What is your status?"

"This is acting Captain Randolf C. Aloysius. Pirates suppressed and under control. We are barely comfortable and still drifting. When you get here I suggest you come onboard with a large armed party and arrest the pirate crew."

"There are just two of us, myself and my second on board the *Comet Dancer*. We have been instructed to tow you to Titan and secure you in the nearest Com P.S. lock-up. You will have to be held in quarantine until we can ascertain the truth of your claims. Wizards will be in attendance for that purpose."

Prepare to be interrogated. "Message understood." Miss Holly Knight will be some upset.

A pause. "Just to let you know, everyone back at HQ is right annoyed at having to work on Crispness Eve. So be on your best behavior."

"Copy that," I acknowledged.

The atmosphere in the control room freshened, and a hint of warm air seeped from the vents. Nickolas must have stoked the steam engine for the climate controls.

"So, what are your plans for Crispness?" HoHo again.

"Don't have any." I suspected I'd be lucky to be home by New Seers Day at the rate current events were unfolding.

"Know anyone on Titan?" was my translation of the incoming chatter.

"Not that I'm aware of."

"I have an empty crash couch at my pad, in almost new condition. It's off a Phoenician cruise ship that crashed on Tethys during its maiden flight. I was part of the salvage operation."

I thought that sounded like a female voice. She must be desperate. Correction, things must be desperate on Titan. Either that or everyone else has somewhere to go. Or, were all the hostels full for Crispness? *Be polite to the rescue party, Randy.* "Thanks, but I'm sure I can find a place to stay instead of inconveniencing you. Don't know how long we'll be stuck on Titan. Hate to impose. Do you always invite strangers over? I might be an open-mouthed cereal eater."

"I requested and read your file. Contact in five minutes. Standby. We will attach a tow line and drag you in. HoHo Gung out." Static faded into heavy silence.

I frowned and scratched my chin. Just what would be in my file? Which file? My Com P.S. file? Nothing I can do about that now. Better get ready for sudden movement. "This is Randy in the control room. The Com P.S. cutter *Comet Dancer* will be attaching a cable to us in the next few minutes, so I suggest everyone find a seat or bunk and secure themselves. Things may be a bit bumpy until we get going. I have no idea how long the trip to Titan will take so I recommend minimal moving about the ship while we're underway."

"This is most irregular." Miss Holly Knight's gravelly growl burst into the control room. "Do they know who they're dealing with? I know the governor of Titan's second maiden aunt. I need to be presentable. The showers are not working. The galley down here is a mess. My change of fresh clothes is on the *Hauly.* I will not be wearing any of the disgusting garments I've found in the closets here. Mister Aloysius, are you there? MISTER ALOYSIUS!"

I reached for the off switch. Decided the *Comet Dancer* might require communications and sighing, turned the volume way down.

I heard Bertha's faint voice say, "Randy, it's almost Crispness Eve. What will we do? Do they celebrate Crispness on Titan? Will we be home in time for New Seers Day? Mother will be preparing a feast. Two feasts. I told her you'd come over for both Crispness and New Seers. Randy, are you there?"

I leaned back in the pilot's chair and closed my eyes. Couldn't help smiling. There was no way we'd make it home in time for New Seers, never mind Crispness. The *Stalking Moon* lurched suddenly then settled into a calm rhythmic sway. The cutter had connected with us gentle as falling out of bed. Hat's off to HoHo Gung if she was doing the piloting. "Couldn't have linked us up any better myself, if I do say so."

The forward screen showed a league long cable clamped to the nose of our craft and tightening. Increased magnification brought the view of the stern of a late model Com P.S. Cutter. They held the reins. We were underway.

Someone on the cutter was piping music through the com. The sounds of that old familiar foot-tapping party tune *Good Kinda Wastefulness* rocked through the control room. That brought back forgotten memories of a long-lost misplaced youth. My smile widened. The second verse revved up with the line, *I lucked out, still on my feets uneven.*

I sank deep into the chair, strapped myself in and hummed along. The worst was over. We were going to survive the recent madness intact, and I'd managed to avoid the dreaded week-long celebrations. They'd be over by the time we secured passage back to home in Central City. Titan would be a picnic.

Chapter Eighteen

"Approaching Com P.S. Lockdown Station Eight Tiny on a bearing mark twenty-five. All passengers aboard *Stalking Moon* and its sundry auxiliary ornaments should be secured and holding on for dear life." The voice of HoHo Gung woke me from a chilling dream where I was being chased by a horde of small children flinging frozen sugared plums at my top hat.

I do not ever wear a top hat. Ever.

I sat up, shook, muttered, "Acknowledged," and gripped the arms of my chair. The *Stalking Moon* swayed violently from side to side until I feared the *Hauly* and the *Ivy* would be torn loose from their positions on the outer hull. The shaking ended with a sudden and loud *bang*!

The *Stalking Moon* came to rest in the grip of two gigantic inflatable orange gloves that reached out to catch us and draw us gradually into the bosom of the station. Batteries of gas lights on either side flickered into life like welcoming hearths. A transfer gate glowed. White face, opaque red windows, and the outline of a main transit door, the gate reminded me of one of those banned clown images.

We have arrived.

I was struggling to unfasten the straps securing me when Bertha broke in over the airwaves. "Randy, what's going on? Randy, are you there? I've been trying to reach you for half an hour. Randy? Boss?"

"I'm here in the control room. We've just arrived at Titan. Try to keep everyone calm. I expect we'll be boarded shortly by a squad of CPS wizards wanting to interrogate us. Get everyone's stories straight and try to keep the children in line. We don't need any unnecessary naughty tales that will land us in trouble with the authorities."

"*Mister* Aloysius, I will have you know the children of the Calypso School of Higher Learning and Fine Arts always tell the truth." The familiar sound of the headmistress's voice filled the cabin.

"I would expect nothing less," came out as I shut down the ship and headed toward the sound of a connection being made against our main hatch.

The station's hanger doors clanged shut outside us, and the airlock dials in front of me showed the atmosphere around our ship being pressurized and the temperature rising toward reasonable levels. Such luxury was unknown back in my day. No wonder taxes were so high.

The waiting stretched out for half an hour. Of course I was joined beside the airlock doors by Bertha, Holly Knight, and Nick, who quickly excused himself to get over to the *Ivy* to discover how Miss Lee Touh was doing after her recent ordeal. He took a pair of senior students with him who claimed to have some knowledge of multiple anatomies and emergency repairs. All three carried med bags, and the party looked quite official, for one scrawny elf and two gremlins half his size.

The main doors finally opened, and the official Committee of Public Safety party exited led by a figure I took to be First Officer HoHo Gung. She was my height but half again as wide, and even without the twin throwing axes at her belt, recognizable as pure dwarf.

Pigtails decorated with red and green ribbons stuck out sideways from beneath a metal cap which didn't look regulation. She wore a knee length chain shirt and thick gauntlets that reached to her elbows. A bright red cape and black leather boots completed the ensemble. Bright blue eyes looked me over from a broad, clean-shaven face.

Behind her trooped three standard local Committee of Public Safety wizards, probably the lowest on the totem pole available for the holiday season, and a squad of hulking hobgoblins looking eager to exercise their collection of heavy weaponry. The wizards still owned salt and pepper beards, a sure sign they had barely escaped apprenticeship. Instead of the usual menacing black-robed guards, the hobgoblins appeared fresh out of a recruitment pool in their civvies.

HoHo grinned. "You've aged since your last official picture."

"Mortality happens," I said. "We have the pirate captain and his two mates neatly wrapped up and the rest of the crew in storage in their quarters. There's another one of the villains in this caper name of Dick Enns locked below in a cell."

She snapped her fingers and four hobgoblins stepped out from the crowd behind the trio of wizards. "Round 'em up boys. No need to be gentle."

"I'm Headmistress Holly Knight from the Calypso School and Orphanage. I demand to see your superior immediately." She pushed around me.

That effort earned her a glance-over from the dwarf. "Okay, you go to the end of the line. Randy here and I are going for a chat while he tells me the story." She gave me a *look*. "The *whole* story."

"But I demand…"

HoHo nodded toward Mistress Knight and indicated a wizard. "You, interrogate that one first. I expect a full report."

Miss Knight opened her mouth to protest, the wizard pointed, silence reigned. They departed, followed by a pair of lumbering hobgoblins.

"Take your time," HoHo called after them.

Ah, this first officer may be higher up the food chain than I originally guessed.

"What about me?" Bertha asked, leaning forward, hands on hips. The look she gave HoHo was halfway to hostile. "I'm his senior partner."

"Well?" The first officer turned to me.

"You can trust her. Completely reliable. She works for me."

"I work *with* him. When he works, which isn't often. And the lady's name is Bertha, Bertha Wildwater."

Before I could step in or step back we were joined from the depths of the *Comet Dancer* by a walking beanstalk topped by a mass of escaping red hair. I don't think I've ever seen a goblin that tall. Correction, a goblin blended with some extra height genes, possibly hobgoblin, or something else further removed. He wore a mail shirt, polished metal cap with a pair of tiny horns that almost hid two bright sapphire eyes and featured the wisp of a blond beard. His broad black leather belt contained the largest assortment of personal artillery I've seen gathered in one place.

"*Comet Dancer* all secured, Boss." He grinned at HoHo, nodded to me, and slowly considered Bertha from the disorderly bangs of her runaway hair to the tips of her twinkling painted toes.

"This is my ancillary, Tim Sel, the other half of our crack crew." HoHo turned thoughtful. "Okay Bertha, you take Short Tim, show him where everything is, and grab a dozen of these raw but eager lads. Gather up the piratical prisoners and have them transferred to a holding cell that is being floated over to the cargo bay."

"We also need a med team to the *Ivy,*" I said. "There's a vampire and her latest snack on board."

"Do it." HoHo turned to one of the remaining wizards. "Go." She gestured to his partner. "*You* can start by doing quick scans on the senior students. I want a complete report before the witchy hour turns into tomorrow." She winked at me. "Might as well try and have all of this mess wrapped up by the time the cuckoo belts out *They Came Upon a Midnight Beer,* so we'll have our Crispness free."

"Where will you be when I'm finished?" Bertha, unmoving, stared at our host. "And where will *he* be?"

"You can find us both at the Follies LaLaLa, a bar located just inside the transit door leading into the interior of the station." HoHo's grin broadened. "Don't worry, Bert, he'll be safe with me. The place is closed for the festivities."

She led me away. I could feel Bertha's glare burning into my back and hear her parting words, "The name is Miss Wildwater, to you. Mister Sel, follow me."

"You can call me Short if you like," he said, falling in beside her.

Her words, "I don't," faded away as they stalked back into the depths of the pirate vessel.

"You seem to have a lot of inexperienced staff on duty tonight." HoHo's collection of hobgoblins and wizards was less than first rate. I had to step lively to keep up with her. "I guess everyone with any rank is already out celebrating."

She smiled. "That's one way to look at it. Or, maybe I simply prefer to work only with local folks fresh out of the academy. That way I know their work ethic hasn't had the time to be corrupted."

We crossed through the squeaky-clean interior of the *Comet Dancer* and out onto the main platform leading into the interior of Lockdown Station Eight Tiny. There was an official-looking welcoming party waiting for us inside the entrance.

Out front of this group stood a large, well-fed troll decked out in a full dress crimson CPS uniform and hung with enough gold braid to serve as stage curtain pulls for half the theaters in Central City. Behind him towered a full white-bearded wizard with a floor-length mauve gown and wearing a pointy hat covered in silver stars and half-moons that exceeded regulation height by half. A dozen well-dressed hobgoblin guards in immaculate shiny black suits were arranged in two perfect ranks behind them.

The troll looked us over, sniffed, and shook his head. He cleared his throat. "I am Eban Eazier, Senior Potentate of Titan and the Guardian and Keeper of Laws and Orders."

He smiled and licked his purple lips. "As the commandant of the garrison at Titan City and the ranking Committee of Public Safety officer in this jurisdiction, I will be taking over this investigation. All of the prisoners, including that disreputable-looking one standing beside you, will be turned over to me for safekeeping and questioning." His narrowed eyes shifted sideways to his companion.

"The *Stalking Moon* and its attached auxiliary contents will be held in quarantine, probably for at least a month." The wizard sounded bored. "They are to be transferred to the Dangerous Goods Containment Dock immediately." He raised his left hand and uncurled a forefinger.

"I don't think so," HoHo Gung said.

Chapter Nineteen

The silence in the hall became heavy as extra helpings of a fatted plumbed pudding after an extended Crispness feast. The hush drifted into a squinty-eyed staring contest between HoHo Gung and Eban Eazier. The wizard beside him concentrated on the ceiling curves. Someone finally cleared their dusty throat, and the Guardian and Keeper of Laws and Orders broke the strained eyeball contact.

"I must apologize," Eban Eazier announced through clenched teeth, the words spitting out reluctantly. "Let us begin again. I realize you are new to this detachment and may be unaware of the proper established protocols in this jurisdiction. You report to me. *I* am your commander. *You* are a patrol officer. Your beat is the void anywhere from the atmosphere of Saturn out to the outermost moon. My responsibility is anything that happens on one of Saturn's moons. As the *Stalking Moon* and its contents, cargo *and* passengers, are now firmly attached to Titan I must take full responsibility for them."

He forced what might have passed either for a smile or serious indigestion. "I will forgive you this once, but any further transgressions will be reported to the High Command. Now step aside and allow us to proceed."

The double rank of hobgoblin guards took a smart step forward in foot-stomping unison.

HoHo removed a gauntlet, reached inside the sleeve of her mail shirt, and withdrew a small scroll tied with a neat black ribbon. She extended the document. "I believe you will find this in order. It is signed by a certain Miss Vickky, or Victrini, if you prefer, of the Central City home office. I believe you know of her?"

I certainly did. Her associates have been known to refer to her as Queen Victoria. She has been known to rain on several parades. I've tangled with her before, and normally prefer a large safe distance between us. However, in this case…

I've never seen a troll turn pale as Eban Eazier did. "What does it say?" he croaked.

HoHo smiled angelically. She tucked her gauntlets under one arm, removed the ribbon and unrolled the scroll. She began to read, "To whom it may concern, depending on whether or not it is any of your bloody business. This is a special authorization for First Officer HoHo Gung to conduct a deep investigation on behalf of the Com P.S. into certain suspicious carryings on in the vicinity of Titan, but with broad authority to look into any irregularities in the outer systems beyond the orbit of Mars."

She gazed from Eban Eazier to the wizard who appeared to be studying the curly tips of his pointy shoes. HoHo slowly scrutinized the ranks of hobgoblin guards. They stared straight ahead. She continued with her reading. "You will give her every cooperation and assistance. She has my full authority to requisition any required assets."

She stared at the double row of guards. "That means you folks, unless you wish to find yourselves assigned to night watch duties at the incinerators on Pan."

"Yes *sir*, whatever you say, *sir*." Twenty-four oversized regulation black boots hit the floor and twelve large thumbs gave a salute.

Eban Eazier bowed. "In that case, we will naturally withdraw our claims and leave you in charge of this mess. If you require me I shall be at my official residence looking after my important guests. This is Crispness Eve after all. I bid you good day."

He turned on his heel and scurried away, the wizard bobbing in his wake.

HoHo nodded to her new squad of hobgoblins. "My associate, Tim Sel, is somewhere on the *Stalking Moon*. Track him down and assist in the operation. Follow his instructions."

We watched them stomp away.

"Don't trust 'em," she said. "Have to take whatever help I can get." HoHo crooked a finger. "*You,* follow me. I want the full story. From the beginning. Leave nothing out."

We trailed into the depths of Lockdown Station Eight Tiny, and she unlatched a heavy door that was constructed of imitation oak planks. The flickering sign above the entrance announced the Follies LaLaLa in bright, transparent green and blue letters.

Hidden red and green gas lamps illuminated the translucent walls. Round glass tables set with little twinkling plastic trees took up most of the room except for a cleared area representing a dance floor. Fingers of frost decorated an extension of an exterior dome set into the ceiling. The soft sounds of that late night favorite *Gad, Rest Thee Merry-Lyn* wafted from hidden speakers in the ceiling.

The bartender, a yawning youngish goblin in a soiled apron and hugging a broom looked up from his sweeping. "Sorry folks, we're closed."

"Not anymore." HoHo glanced around the garish room. "I'm commandeering this place for my temporary headquarters. I'll have a hot chocolate and Irish, my friend here would enjoy a La Bat's Breath."

I raised an eyebrow.

"It's in your file. Now, begin at the beginning. How did you get here? Why are you here? And leave nothing out." She waved at the bartender. "Do you have a name, junior? I'm going to deputize you."

"Bub Scratchitt."

"Okay Bub, raise your right hand. Your other right hand. That's it. Solemnly swear. Any old curse will do. Good. You are now a member of the Committee of Public Safety Auxiliary Forces. After you've served us our refreshments pour yourself a tall one." HoHo paused for breath and shook her head. "And please play a different tune. That one will put us to sleep faster than you can say Bob's your maiden auntie."

HoHo sighed, removed her helmet then sat it in front of her on the table. She shook her pigtails loose, smiled and gave me a wink. "We have no time for useless frivolities—for now."

The lively notes of *Deck the Trolls* bounced down from somewhere high above as our drinks arrived. A platter of peppermint fingers and chocolate-dipped cookies followed.

"Okay, Randy me fine lad, start talking."

So I did.

Chapter Twenty

"Supposedly, this nonsense all started back at The Chimneys in Central City. And you say there was a pirate contact working there in the yard. Do you have a name for me?" HoHo frowned and sipped her hot chocolate. Green steam wafted into the air.

"Yes." I racked my tired brain and unrolled my mental rolodex. Seems to take longer these days to access the immense volume of generally useless information stored up there. "He was the foreman at The Chimneys, a Mister Rooge, a goblin, a Simon Rooge I believe." I blinked. "He told the pirates he'd meet them on Titan this week."

"Then where do we go to find this Simon Rooge?" She chewed on her lower lip and licked up a daub of green goo attempting to escape.

"Eban Eazier's Crispness Party," we both said in unison.

"You go first." HoHo drained her mug and put on her helmet. "How do you figure?"

I gazed at my fingers and disconnected them from my frosty mug.

"One, the infamous pirate, Grimm Rinch, has had a free collection of cutlery carving around in this section of the universe for several years. He's conducted raids from the outskirts of Mars all the way out to Ultima Thule. No one seems to have been able to catch him in the act or track him down afterward."

I nodded thanks to Bub for the plate of roasted chestnuts he set on the table before us. "Two, the local High Potentate, Eban Eazier, is the character in charge of the Saturn sector, which happens to be more-or-less slap dab in the middle of this area of piratical activity."

I raised another finger. "Three, the target this time was an orphanage filled with children who few folks of any consequence would miss in the big picture. The local area is filled with minerals and mines that have serious problems getting workers. At least workers of the right size to toil for low wages in ridiculously small, tight places. Shipping machinery out here that could do the job is even more expensive than shanghaiing some disposable slaves. I'll bet if you check the official records, you'll find Eban Eazier owns a good chunk of some of these mining operations."

HoHo helped herself to a handful of chestnuts. "Already have, and he does."

"Four, Master Eazier appeared to be in some great hurry to recover the *Stalking Moon* and its cargo and crew. I'll bet if you turned everything over to him you'd find things disappearing, or showing up indisposed and safely dead."

"But I need someone to spill a tune the villains can dance to." HoHo held up her mug for a refill.

"We have Little Dick Enns locked up on board the Moon. He was point man for the pirates on Calisto. I'll bet he'd sing a pretty song without too much hard work on your part."

"I find threatening to shove someone out an airlock naked works wonders during interrogation." HoHo smiled sweetly. "And if we add this Simon Rooge to the mix…" She glanced at the wall clock. "We'd have a convicting canary-voiced duo."

The timepiece on the bar wall, a carved wooden image of Mother Crispness in a full and severely stained baking apron with a large spoon acting for the hour hand of the clock in one hand and a rolling pin in the other, beamed down at us. The piece looked positively ghastly in the glow of the flickering red and green flames mounted on either side.

"We have less than four hours before the official local midnight hour comes stumbling in and Eban Eazier's party breaks up." She stood.

"And sixth, I simply don't like the look or the sound of this Eban Eazier character. Don't trust him any further than I could throw him, and he appears to be pretty heavy. Makes my professional and highly trained private eye instincts tingle." I rose to my feet and checked to make certain I still carried most of my weaponry.

"That was only five," she said.

"I'm certain I slipped an extra one in there somewhere."

HoHo pointed toward young Bub Scratchitt. "*You* are in charge of this facility until we return. I'm declaring the Follies LaLaLa and its excellent staff as seconded to the Committee of Public Safety until further notice." She flicked a finger at me. "That goes for you too."

"Do I get a proper title and a uniform with gold braid? How about a pension for life?"

"If you behave yourself and do good work I may fix you breakfast." HoHo turned on her communicator. "Calling for Tim Sel and Bertha Wildwater. Once you have all the villains from the *Stalking Moon* securely secured in the lock up go over to the Follies LaLaLa and wait there for us. Leave the prisoners well-guarded; we don't want any slipping away or being rescued. We shouldn't be long. Just send a squad of a dozen or so hobgoblins after us. We'll be at the Eban Eazier estate."

"Shouldn't we wait for the reinforcements?" I accepted the penetrol cartridge clips she handed me for Bess. They came out of a small chainmail purse at her belt.

A collapsible baton appeared from somewhere inside her sleeve. HoHo grinned evilly and gave the baton a shake. The shiny metal clicked into a nasty length half her height. "What would be the fun in that? Let's go. Everything is close by in Titan City. We'll walk."

HoHo paused beneath the glowing Exit sign. "We need to depart stage door right with some suitable martial music. Heats the blood and gets it flowing. "Give us another stirring round of *Deck the Trolls*. Replay it for me. Play it again, Bub."

Chapter Twenty-One

Everything civilized in Titan City was located underground except for a few iced-up observation domes, some exhausted out-of-date vents, and a scattering of poorly-weathered communications antennae. Shaped like a wheel, with the main business route running in a wide circular loop through the tunnels, the city focused secondary corridors toward the hub where the administration and beating heart of the complex lay buried deep beneath the surface and reasonably safe from any stray radiation or wandering comets. We traveled along one of these spokes to the residential quarter. This compound included the Eban Eazier estate. *Estate* was a bit of a misnomer.

Eazier's residence was reached by a mock brick arched bridge built across a dry moat. The ditch held large steam pipes instead of water. Some artist fresh out of elementary art school had carved the stone wall beyond into the shape of half a castle tower that ran from street level to the tunnel's ceiling. The iron gates were cranked up into the structure and the imitation wooden gates lay propped wide open. Two hobgoblins dressed in suits of bright red plastic armor stood on either side holding tall, fake battleaxes. The sounds of music filtered out from inside.

I recognized a popular dance tune from my secondary school daze. *Holly's in the poison ivy,* throbbed out into the passageway. Resisting foot-tapping was futile.

"No admittance without an invite," one of the gaudy guards announced.

I glanced at HoHo. "This is your party, your move, boss."

She stomped over to the guards and glared up at the tallest of the pair. "I am about to launch a serious raid on this tawdry affair. You have one short minute to stand aside and let us enter, or you will spend the next ten years in hard labor on the surface of Enceladus mining frozen methane and working off the exorbitant fine I will levy."

The larger guard glanced at his partner. "She looks serious. He doesn't pay us enough for this."

"Last time he stiffed us out of half of what was promised."

They propped their toy battleaxes against the wall. "It's all yours. If you want to question us later, we'll be in the Blitzen Haus getting ready for Crispness. Better do it before midnight if you want any straight answers."

"After you." I gestured toward the open door.

HoHo drew a megaphone out of her sleeve then headed inside. I followed.

The Crispness Eve party was in full swing. Bags of candy, fruit, and nuts hung from the ceiling. Strings of red and green colored lights decorated the walls. Full-sized cutouts of Mother Crispness in her soiled apron leaned against pillars and hung on doors. A steam powered beverage and snack bar manned by a goblin wearing a yellow-feathered pointed cap and a black eye patch slowly chugged through the crowd handing out samples. The bartender was assisted by a pair of trained parrots patrolling the polished service surface. The hired band, a sextet of gremlins in long red frock coats were fronted by a chanteuse towering over them who struck me immediately as a younger and improved version of First Mate Dhora Whook.

Beneath a heavy mass of thick black hair that seemed intent on escaping down her back she was wrapped in a purple, painted-on gown shielded by a violet cape. A vampire, with heavy crimson lips and slightly bulging eyes, she glanced my way and waved. She certainly could belt out that song strong enough to make me ignore the fangs. I almost missed the zombie quartet back-up group swaying on the stage behind the band.

"Holly's in the poison ivy, an' Mary's on her way…"

The packed crowd of guests swayed to the beat.

"Randy, Focus!" HoHo's voice cut through the artificial fog clogging my skull. She held the megaphone above her head and pulled the trigger. "Now hear this," boomed across the room loud enough to cause the quaking gas chandeliers to sway and spit smoke.

"Good, now that I have your attention, I am looking for two people, a Simon Rooge, and your genial host, Eban Eazier. If they would present themselves, they are now under arrest. Any delay means I will have to charge everyone in this room with impediment of the Committee of Public Safety in the course of its lawful and ordained duty." She leered around and licked her lips.

Oh sure, the two of us are going to round up a hundred or so of the most senior of the locals and march them quietly through the corridors.

The crowd ground to a halt like a giant sprawling ameba. The swaying ceased.

A character garbed with an imitation apron and a white Mother Crispness wig staggered forward. "Do you know who I am?"

A typical know-everything elf, probably a lawyer.

"Not if you're lucky." HoHo stared around the room. "Well, I'm waiting." Her glare raised the temperature in the room by several fractions of degrees.

The previous speaker faded into a cluster of associates garbed as assorted shrubbery.

Probably law students.

The singer blew me a kiss and waved as the band ceased playing. The zombie backup dance group kept on swaying.

The assembly pushed Eban Eazier forward, his Mother Crispness costume obviously new and never spilled on. "Now see here young lady, you are overstepping your authority. I refuse to go with you anywhere."

The crowd surged forward around him murmuring protectively. A half a baker's dozen of thuggish-looking goblins moved out, fingers reaching beneath their costumes.

"Randy, do your duty." HoHo pointed her megaphone at Eban.

"Are you the Randy from the *Stalking Moon*? Mother told me all about you when she called. She was right. You do look delicious." This squeal came from the singer in purple.

I fingered Bess, drew her out of my pocket then took off the safety.

The goblins spread out across the dance floor. HoHo headed directly for Eban, megaphone in one hand, throwing ax in the other.

I took aim at Eban, and the sound of heavy feet thundered in from close behind me. I turned around. Two dozen hobgoblins in official black came parading through the entrance door, carrying short regulation clubs and following a full-badged Com P.S. wizard.

The wizard doffed his pointy hat and nodded to officer HoHo Gung. "Reporting as ordered, sir."

"Simon Rooge is hiding in the pantry," Eban Easier screamed as they marched him away, fuzzy slippered feet slipping on the polished tiles. "I'm not going to take the fall for this mess on my own."

HoHo glanced at me. "You didn't think we were doing this bust all by ourselves, did you?"

"No, of course not."

The vampire slithered off the stage and drifted across the floor toward us.

"A friend of yours?" HoHo frowned as she re-belted her ax.

"Never seen her before in my life."

The songstress slipped to a pause before me. "Mother called from her ship when she captured you. Said she had a new recruit. Would let me have a sample." Drool dripped from her lips. "My name is Minnie, but you can call me Fish, everyone else does. Are you free tonight?"

"No, he's horribly expensive," HoHo said. "If you don't want to spend the next century being examined in a Com P.S. lab, drift away little girl, quickly." The top of HoHo's helmet just came to the bottom of the vampire's chin.

Minnie frowned. "I don't think you're very nice."

"I've been told that before and proud of it. Well?"

She sniffed, took a step back then drifted back across the floor toward the band.

"I did enjoy your singing," I called after her.

"Thanks," was a fading husky whisper.

"I suppose you're upset I derailed that little adventure." HoHo grinned.

"Not at all. What now, boss, we spend the night writing up detailed reports in quadruplicate?"

"Sorry to disappoint you, Randolf my lad, but that is what minions are for. I have a squad of locked-down teenage elves in training for administration posts. I have other plans for this Crispness Eve."

Chapter Twenty-Two

The timepiece on the wall had Mother Crispness pointing her spoon and rolling pin toward midnight while the face of the clock captured the expression of an exhausted baker who had been dipping into the spiced icing with great gusto. Her skin reflected a ghastly green glow, enhanced by the fact the red gas light on the other side had snuffed out.

The Follies LaLaLa was crowded with staff called back for emergency duty and enjoying the overtime immensely although they did seem a bit unruly.

Bub Scratchitt, the goblin bartender, stood on top of the bar swaying gently and crooning into the handle of his broom. His apron had become a cape. The backup singers consisted of a trio of gremlin waitresses in oversized Mother Crispness masks and wigs and little else, whose moves behind him might have caused earthquakes if attempted by anyone larger. They were all lip-syncing and foot-stomping to the familiar tune blasting forth from the room's sound system.

"Green Brew is all we serve..."

My left foot insisted on attempting to follow after the mangled melody. Suitable for our current location, I suppose.

I was sitting at a round table with HoHo Gung and watching Bertha and HoHo's ancillary officer, Tim Sel, doing something on the dance floor that reminded me of a pair of barefoot grape stompers standing in a frigid vat of berries and juice either trying to keep their feet warm or avoid something deadly in the bottom. I knew Bertha Wildwater had taken classical jigging at night school, but I had never seen her in action. 'Twas a sight that would probably follow me to my early grave.

Bella Rhingrr, senior monitor, TA-in-training, senior school class president, and general pest, made one attempt to drag me out onto the floor. I demurred, HoHo glared, and Bella eventually gave up and went elsewhere in search of easier prey.

Why isn't she back at the barracks supervising the younger-uns? But then, it was not my problem. Detectives may be naturally inquisitive, but I was now off the cuckoo clock.

The elf Nicholas, aka Mouse, sat at a table for two in a dim corner of the room with Miss Lee Touh the senior student who had apparently survived supervising the children on the *Ivy* and being the snack of a hungry vampire. Miss Touh looked pale, for a goblin. He appeared hypnotized.

"He's a goner," HoHo commented.

I shook my head. "Just the usual brief mark of a short-hauler Crispness affair. He'll be over her by the time he wakes up at noon tomorrow."

"How much you want to place a little wager on that?"

"I don't gamble." Not since…

HoHo squinted over at the pair. "If he stays behind on Titan and cashes in his ticket home before you leave, you owe me a breakfast."

"You haven't tasted my cooking. That would be a serious penalty for you."

"I'll take my chances." She reached over and just about crushed my hand. "Good, it's a deal, then."

The number of underage school children in the room seemed to be growing. They had been billeted in the attached barracks and half-empty warehouse. They drifted in and out of the shadows and slithered along the walls. Some were attempting to copy some of Bertha's more drastic moves. I suspected there would be a plethora of tired muscles and bruised bones the next day. All-in-all there appeared to be a serious lack of grown-up supervision going on around us, given the adult-style venue.

I glanced about our table and changed the subject. "Where did Miss Holly Knight go? I didn't see her leave us."

"How very observant of you. She packed it in about half an hour ago."

"I thought the decibel level had dropped in here." I glanced up at the clock. "Almost midnight."

The double kitchen doors beside the bar burst open followed by a blinding flash of light, a puff of purple smoke, and an apparition materialized behind a marching goblin in an outsized cook's cap banging a heavy metal spoon against an iron frying pan.

"It's started," HoHo said.

It took me a minute to sort out the creation that followed the leader then to recognize the face beneath the massive white wig. Holly Knight danced around the bar and into the center of the floor. A quartet of gremlin cook's assistants followed carrying the traditional goodies. There were plates of crisp peanut brittle and crunchy candy skeletons and fried sugar cake and sparklingy frizzled fruits. The last gremlin in the parade hoisted a large platter filled with small overflowing paper cups overflowing with a suspicious green liquid.

I pointed a shaking finger at the last tray and started to rise. "Those beverages are definitely not suitable for small children."

A firm hand rested on my shoulder and held me back down. "I'm certain Miss Knight will take every precaution. She is responsible for the children's welfare." HoHo pushed. I sat.

The growing conga line snaked past our table. Miss Knight leaned over, whispering hoarsely, "Relax. I do this every year. The children love it. The drinks are tame, asparagus juice." She was gone, leading the dance away winding between the bobbing crowd on the floor and those few still seated.

I shook my head. Holly Knight was in full Mother Crispness gear, white wig, soiled apron, hands covered to her elbows in flour and baking materials, and waving a rolling pin and a wooden spoon. Of course, the familiar stains on her apron were escapees from the traditional brittle candies and sugar crisp cakes. I've seen far worse representations of the Goddess of Overindulgence and Mayhem in the Kitchen.

The sounds of screaming children echoed from the steel rafters overhead.

Bertha swept by, paused for breath at our table, and stuffed some marshmallow brittle into her mouth. "Don't you just love Crispness Eve, and better yet, the presents and tomorrow's feast?"

She sighed. "My whole family will gather at our house. Mother will be preparing the Crispness Dinner: roast turnip basted with brittle candy figures, turnip soup, peanut brittle, toasted marshmallow brittle, peppermint brittle squares, and dark chocolate coated in chewy hard candy and served with your favourite cinnamon-flavoured whipped cream. Then the presents come out later in the day after everyone is too full to move from their chair or complain about what they received." She sighed again. "And here we are stuck on Titan in a warehouse district that's closed for the season."

"I suppose your infamous mother will be dressed as Mother Crispness." I couldn't help myself.

"Oh yes, frilly little snow-white apron, scarlet mini skirt, high ruby heels, and the cutest shoulder-length whitish-blonde wig you've ever seen—and definitely no mask." Bertha rolled her eyes.

I had never met the lady but that lithe image burned into my brain.

The band shimmying on the bar picked another tune to mangle, this time live. *Oh, Come on, Alia, what you want for Crispness?* poured out across the floor.

Tim Sel tugged on Bertha's arm. "Come on, the music can't last all night."

I could barely hear him above the noise being made by the celebrating students and instructors from Calypso School of Higher Learning and Fine Arts.

I think they're just warming up.

"If you two promise to behave yourselves, you can come over to my place for dinner tomorrow. Tim knows where I hide out." HoHo Gung raised her glass. A tall toffee stir-stick peered over the rim. "A late dinner; it won't be fancy. Some brittle veggies and crisped up imitation meat. Just don't make it too early in the day. We will be having a late breakfast. Randy needs to practice."

"Practice, what, why, where?"

She patted the back of my hand. "For when after you lose your bet you have to make me a breakfast. Don't worry. I'll give you some lessons, tomorrow afternoon, before the children arrive." She nodded toward Tim and Bertha and made shooing motions. "Go play, I'll keep an eye on the old man."

Bertha giggled as Tim dragged her away.

I stared at the ceiling. Swirling flakes of methane snow danced across the image from the outside dome. "Who's an old man?"

"Well, according to your file, you're much older than me. But I don't mind. Is *everything* in your restricted dossier true?"

The loud wail from the direction of the bar of *Rocking around the Crispness Tea* drowned out my muttered reply.

About the Author

Ron can be found dreaming about sailing on Lake Winnipeg when he's not writing novels or critiquing for an on-line magazine. He won first prize for a Canadian Authors Association short story contest with a ghostly love story, but his preference is for writing longer novella or novel-length works including speculative fiction and medieval-style fantasies.

This latest trilogy is his first venture into a full-blown space opera, something that has nibbled on the edges of his mind for years. He hasn't completely forgotten high fantasy, and you can expect more of the often wild *Housetrap Chronicles*. They help to keep him mildly sane when he has to dispose of an annoying idea.

A member of several writing groups, he is currently on the national executive of the Canadian Authors Association. Writing as R. J. Hore, and supervised by his usually understanding wife and a large demanding cat, most of his writing efforts continue toward fantasy, with occasional lapses into science fiction and horror.

R. J. loves to hear from his readers. You can find and connect with him at the links below.

Website/Blog: http://www.ronaldhore.com
Facebook: https://www.facebook.com/RonaldJHore
Goodreads: https://www.goodreads.com/author/show/5752744.RJHore

~ * ~

We hope you enjoyed this volume of *The Housetrap Chronicles* as much as we did. If you did, please write a review, tell your friends, check out another of R. J.'s books, or go give one of the other terrific offerings at Champagne Book Group a try.

Missed the first six books? Turn the page for a peek into *Housetrap*, book 1, where it all started.

A MISSING BOYFRIEND
AN ELF ON THE RUN
MARTIAN VAMPIRES

TURN THE PAGE
FOR A LOOK INSIDE!

Chapter One

I don't like Elves, never have. I sat tilting back in my chair counting the stains on the ceiling when she walked through the open door of my inner office unannounced—unannounced, because I'd just given Bertha the afternoon off to visit her sick brother. Bertha's half Banshee, thin as a lamppost with long straight dark hair and *big* brown eyes. She's always got a relative down with the Black Death or some obscure curse; I think she has twelve brothers, but I digress.

The Elf arrived in my office wrapped in a full-length gold lamé coat with a large hood covering her head and hiding most of her features, but I could tell she was pure Elf. Those yellow eyes are a dead giveaway even if you can't spot the pointed ears. I'm a student of nature, have to be; the breed often determines character, or motive, or veracity. In my business you have to stay two jumps ahead or you're squashed like a scarab.

I'm a Mongrel myself. You can never tell about Mongrels, and there are more of us around now ever since the Goldilocks affair. Now there was a real witch, not the kind with just a warty nose, but she married that Wolf back in the days before they gave femmes the vote. Then they went overboard and made it all legal in the Intermarriage Act of 1812, and everything has tumbled Jack over Jill downhill ever since.

The Elf glanced about the room nervously, then in a single fluid motion crossed her long legs and slid into the battered chair opposite me like maple syrup poured from a mason jar. I sighed deep inside, rocked forward to rest my elbows on the scratched oak desk, painted a smile across my ugly mug and waited. I had all day; it had been two weeks since my last case.

She fidgeted for a minute and I matched her, stare for stare, until my eyeballs screamed for mercy. The Elf had the kind of face you see perched high on a mantelpiece, thin bone china, pale, delicate, and carved by a master.

She broke first. "I need your help, Mr. Aloysius." Her words vibrated in the air.

That's why creatures usually come to see me—that, or to try and collect on past due bills.

"Why?" I asked, wondering if this would turn out to be the usual bored and missing mate or vagrant lost love. Maybe we'd have some real excitement for a change and I could rack up a full day or two in extra fees, perhaps even slip Bertha some of her back pay. I think I was only three months behind, but...

"Are we alone?" The Elf drew her hood back revealing the usual rich flowing mane and glanced about again, peering into the shadowed corners of my little room.

I don't know what it is about Elves, but they either have long hair draped halfway to their waists or all cropped off short above those ears. My offices are tiny, no nook large enough to hide a teenage Hobgoblin. There may be an inch or two of dust and debris in the corners, but although Bertha doesn't do windows either, she always casts about each morning for listeners and weaves a keep-out spell around the place just in case.

Bertha's been taking Shamanism at that cut-rate night school down the street for the last two years now and already refers to herself as a professional Sha-person. Sometimes I think this liberation stuff has gone a bit too far.

"Yes," I said without blinking.

She slowly moistened her lips. 'Tis true, some Elves have pointed tongues too. This one was, pointed and blood-red.

"This is a dangerous matter, and I have no one else I can turn to."

Her voice dropped down a few octaves and I had to blink and stare at the open doorway behind her. Something made me wish that Bertha sat at her desk, instead of shadows. An icicle formed along my spine. After all, I have some Sidhe blood, on my grandmother's side I think, and when Elves turn on the charm they can be deadly. And they usually only bother to turn on that fatal charm when they want something very badly, or when there is serious trouble.

"Maybe you had better tell me the full story," I croaked, wishing for a cool dark bottle of La Bat's Breath to lubricate my rapidly parching throat.

"You will help me?" she purred, those eyes pure melted honey.

"Of course." I stretched the painted smile until my face almost cracked. "Anything... for the proper fee."

Silently the Elf reached into her sleeve and pulled out a fashionable silk purse shaped like a sow's ear, handing me three gold coins. "Will this be sufficient to retain your services?"

I rolled the coins around in my fingers. They were pure gold, ancient, five wizarey each, and just starting to show signs of wear. The face of some long-deceased and self-important Elf King glared right back at me. Probably brought over in the family chest when her ancestors migrated from Europe. Elves tended to be traditionalists. I could unload these for a bundle of paper at the local counting house.

"That will do for a few days," I stated, "but then, there may be expenses."

Long delicate fingers, careful not to touch me, dropped a fourth gold coin into my damp palm. "Let me know if you need any more."

"I will, sweetheart! Now, what's the problem… and… as you already know my name, maybe you should begin by telling me yours."

She winced at my familiarity, then sighing, spoke so faintly I had to twitch an ear to catch her words. "My name is Rose. I came here from the east four years ago, taking a position as assistant headmistress in a college for quality young ladies. Things were progressing well at school, I found a penthouse apartment overlooking the river, was enjoying my work... and then I met a charming young gentleman from a good family."

I knew it—another loused-up love affair.

She hesitated and glanced around the room again. "Do you have anything in this place to drink? There is enough dust in here to bury a Brownie."

I raised an eyebrow and chewed on the stem of my cold briar pipe.

"I mean spruce tea, chicory coffee, pure spring water...anything wet. And a clean cup, if you have one."

Slowly I pushed back my chair and stood up. Elves are seldom subtle, unless they are up to something, which, now that I think on that, they usually are.

"I can offer you a little pure Irish." I smiled. "In your chicory, of course."

The yellow eyes drank me in, then spit me right back out. "No thank you, straight black coffee will be just fine."

"So continue on with your sad saga," I muttered, knocking the dried grounds out of the earthen urn and into a neat little pyramid on last month's faded issue of *Thyme*. "I'm a trained professional. I can listen and boil water at the same time."

"We quickly fell in love. I gave him my mother's antique wedding ring as a token. We were to be married, you know. This June. At the end of the school year." She dabbed at her eyes with a delicate bit of white lace.

I wished I was close enough to see whether they were real tears. Elves seldom cry, but at that moment I was too busy trying to coax the little stove to light using an old spell I'd learned in the fifth grade. A blue flame finally danced beneath the coffee urn and I turned my full attention back to my guest.

"Go on."

"We were very happy," she sniffed, "and deeply in love. He wore the ring everywhere as a token of our undying affection."

My mind tends to wander during this sort of drivel, away to thoughts of beer and baseball. The sound of a streetcar rattling by penetrated the closed window and I pondered the chances of the Centre City Carp in the upcoming season. The opening game was only a few days away and they had this new pitcher, a Troll, with arms that dragged on the ground. If he could throw…

"Please continue. What is it that you would like me to do for you, Lady Rose?"

My idling brain churned out a list of possibilities. *Get your precious ring back from an unfaithful lover? Find a missing and frightened bridegroom? Search his bedroom closet for fresh skeletons? Perhaps do a background check to see if he has buried as much coin as he claimed?*

The list of options appeared almost endless. Let me guess, a spinsterish young Elf maiden from an ancient and most honorable Eastern house; that would probably have me shaking the young swain's family tree to see if any Hobgoblins, Mongrels, or Humans tumbled from the branches.

She wrung her delicate hands most convincingly while I tapped the dust out of a pair of mugs decorated with scenes of scantily clad Fairies and unsated Satyrs. I poured out the coffee, added a touch of the green Irish to my own cup with a deft sleight of hand and sat back down at the desk.

With a dramatic dab of her handkerchief, Rose carried on with her tale. "Rupert has disappeared, you must find him!"

"Rupert, eh! Ah, well, perhaps he has simply had a change of heart?"

"Never! I fear foul play. If he had deserted me he would not have taken the ring with him. Rupert is far too noble for that."

A missing love and a stolen bauble too, oh well.

"Why do you say that? Why do you suspect something has happened to this Rupert? Perhaps he has simply gone off on a business trip?" Already I was wondering just how long I could stretch this case out before I must uncover the lad cowering beneath some damp limestone slab.

"When Rupert did not show up for a dinner date, I went to his apartment. There were signs that someone had searched his rooms. His clothes were all still there but everything was tossed about. I checked with the shoe store where he worked; they said he had come in early that day, complained of feeling ill and left with his pay check, stating that he was going to visit a neighboring medicine man. That was a week ago. I have tried everywhere, contacted the Committee of Public Safety… nothing, you are my last hope."

I sighed. *Only a common store clerk, missing in action.* Probably fled in fear with just the clothes on his back at the thought of spending the rest of his life wed to this formidable maiden. She remained silent and I gazed at her pale and very lovely face. You can never tell how old an Elf is, that long-life stuff about them is true.

And just when you think you may uncover some of their mysteries, they stare at you with those big unblinking yellow eyes until you feel like a sparrow being served up to a snake. Of course, if the eyes don't sink you, the voice will turn you to crab apple jelly. Not as quickly as a Lorelei or a Siren might, but in the end it doesn't matter, your goose will be stuffed and sputtering on the spit long before you can cry out Jack Sprat.

Unless of course, you are an experienced creature of the world, like Randolf C. Aloysius.

"You will help me find him," she whispered.

I shook off the creeping feeling that someone was sharpening a carving knife and stirring up the gravy.

"If anyone can find him, I will." The words croaked out like the leavings from an old speech by some retiring frog prince.

"I knew I could count on you." Uncoiling, she rose to her feet like a wisp of smoke, slightly taller than I recalled.

"I will need a description of our missing fellow, detail of his employment, residence, anything you can provide."

She dropped a folded square of paper in my palm, her long gilded nails tingling against my skin. "All the information you require is here."

The Elf drifted toward the doorway, then paused and as she raised the hood of her coat, focused back on me once more. "Find my love, Mr. Aloysius, and my mother's ring. That ring has been in my family for centuries. If my heart must be broken, at least you may spare my fragile parent her grief too. Locate Rupert, return him to me at any cost, along with the ring. I will pay double your fee for the return of the ring, for my dear sweet mother's sake."

~ * ~

I stood alone in the office squinting at the bold handwriting on the paper and pondering my visitor. Outside, evening settled around Central City. A gentle rain streaked the windowpane, creating false images and moving pictures that faded and ran. The flickering glow from the dangling yellow bulb overhead cast barely enough light to read the note by. The wizards at the powerhouse were having problems harnessing the tornadoes again tonight... and this still early in the season. At last I took off my glasses. Might as well start now and visit the young gentleman's apartment tonight.

If I were a gambler, I'd wager that Randolf C. Aloysius would have this case wrapped up by dawn. Why hurry, you say? Take your time, stretch out the fee. But then, what else does an old bachelor have to amuse himself on a cool spring evening?

Opening the desk drawer, I pulled out the plastic splatter gun, checked the load for the nine hollow bullets resting snug in their chambers and slipped Bessie into my shoulder holster. Dropping the glass knuckles casually into my jacket pocket, I patted the short, hardened glass billy club hidden in up my coat sleeve. I prefer glass or plastic. Certain folk, like Elves, can usually smell iron a long way off.

This job seemed like a simple domestic case and Central City is a civilized prairie town, not like some of those frontier places out on Saturn's moons, or beyond. Still, you never can tell what you may bump into on a quiet evening stroll. The Committee of Public Safety is usually too busy discussing the next five years' budgets to patrol all the streets after dark. I locked the office door, put a hex on the handle, then headed down the stairs, the collar of my Big Mack turned up against the rain.

Chapter Two

I don't trust most modern conveniences, never will. The row of street lamps barely held back the night, flickering and dancing like a line of drunken Pixies bejeweled by their tiny bright breath of swamp gas. Darkness hovered over the entire city, resting just above the second-story levels, as though ready to sink down at any moment and saturate the cobbled roadway with a hazy blanket of black.

A street car rumbled by, metal wheels clanging on rusted track, the twin rods sparking as the electricity ebbed and flowed. The Committee of Groundside Transportation had ended the local strike two days ago and things were rolling again. Never on time, and never when you wanted them though; some situations never change.

I pulled the brim of my waterproof Tilleerie fedora down and started along the brick sidewalk. It wasn't raining all that hard and the first address on the piece of paper resided only a few blocks away from the office. For an up-and-coming young gentleman, Rose's lost love could have chosen a better neighborhood in which to set up residence.

Few pedestrians were out strolling in the gloom, only stubborn throwbacks like yours truly. A Goblin stood across the street staring in a jewelry store window, probably drawn by the sparkling toys inside. A pair of Fairies flickered toward me, laughing giddily; ahead, a transient Troll leaned against a lamp post, bumming cigarettes from the passers-by. Of course the Troll got nowhere with the Fairies; they simply pretended he didn't exist, so the big blob stepped into the center of the sidewalk and glared down at me with those eyes like ripe watermelons.

Trolls remind me of Bears in general shape, only Trolls usually fall a touch short of a Bruin in the attic baggage department. This one could have had a "rooms for rent" sign hanging from his bulbous nose, the way it took him a minute to get his tongue working while he blocked my path. At last something up there made contact and the words tumbled down from above.

"Hey buddy, can you spare a smoke or two?"

I gazed up at him, half again my height. The water dripping off the brim of my hat now trickled down the back of my neck while I pondered this apparition. "Don't you know the Committee of Wealth and Healthfare has decided that smoking will stunt your natural growth?"

"Huh?"

"Your lungs, all four or five of them, are probably corroding even as we speak. Rotted chock full of holes, I'll wager. Have you consulted a plumber in the last month?"

"A… no…"

"My good man, here is the card of my personal private physician. Tell him I sent you and that I expect he will give you the red carpet treatment. See him immediately! Don't take no for an answer!" I passed up a small square of cardboard into a hairy hand the size of a small footstool. "No, my good fellow, don't bother to thank me. I feel it is my civic duty to assist those less fortunate."

Ducking beneath his elbow I trotted on, mildly curious at how my neighborhood bill collector would enjoy meeting that red-eyed behemoth after dark. Such are the interesting swirls of the fates; however, I had other more pressing fish to scale.

I passed by one of the Spirit Folk hurrying down the street wrapped to his neck in a wet blanket, the feathers on his Mohawk drooping badly. A Human sat hunched in the shadows begging for spare change, then quickly disappeared into an alley when a loud brace of bleary Gnomes rounded the corner, weaving up the sidewalk arm in arm.

The duo crossed over to the other side of the road, all the while loudly singing some rude Scandinavian sea chantey, and in this precarious process, barely missing the hooves and flashing wheels of a unicorn hitched to a carved and fancy gilded carriage. It's a good thing the Irish in their leather curraghs discovered Northern America first. Old Brennan was no saint, but he certainly could navigate! Can you imagine what this country would be like overrun with Norse Gnomes?

I paused outside a three-story structure of weathered graying stone designed in that turn-of-the-century gingerbread style that has fortunately passed on to Valhalla. The high peaks and numerous gables were decorated with carved human heads, now decaying and bare of paint. Mounting the worn steps, I pushed open the portals and went inside. Narrow darkened halls and a staircase wrapped in shadows greeted my eyes. According to the slip of paper, and what few numbers remained on the doors, Rose's vanished varlet dwelt upstairs.

Rupert had such poor taste in apartment buildings, I wondered at his good choice in Elves. Rose was obviously a lady of quality and breeding. Somehow I found it difficult to imagine Rupert escorting the tall Elf up the rickety wooden stairs and into his rooms for a quiet how-do-you-do. Of course, if I were a gambler, I'd wager next week's payroll that friend Rupert never lured fair Rose into these dingy quarters. That romantic pair probably cavorted at the symphony, attended opening night at the theatre, or, if I know Elves, played havoc in the Assistant School Mistresses' quarters after dark. I paused outside his door and knocked. On the other hand, Rose had visited this place and she still remained interested enough in tracking down the missing lover to retain me.

Picking the unprotected lock, I granted myself permission to enter. Either Rupert had nothing to hide or, more likely in this town, someone already disposed of any safety spells. The cramped pair of rooms were a real mess, far worse than my own humble sleeping chambers. Someone turned the place upside down searching for something, or alternatively, a band of rowdy Gremlins on a furlough escorting a vat of rejected communal wine had held a three-day fiesta. Both theories were feasible, but I opted for door number one.

Rose was right about at least one thing, though. All of Rupert's clothes appeared to be heaped high on his closet floor. Unless he owned more outerwear than the average Elf, our prospective bridegroom had fled without bothering to pack anything beyond possibly a tattered toothbrush and a collapsible comb.

I searched every corner of the sparsely furnished two-room suite, turning the sitting chamber upside down, rooted through the sleeping quarters, taking time to finger and sniff each item.

Bertha often claims to wonder how I can cover a scene inch by inch without missing a lost hair, or photograph a passing face across a busy street with the camera of my mind's eye, yet can never seem to find my expense forms in our filing cabinet, recognize one of her brothers, or remember her birthday. I guess it just goes to show I'm all business, when it comes down to solving cases, not the petty details.

The second time I ran my nimble fingers through the scattered pile of newspapers and magazines, I pulled out an empty folder and held it up to the single light bulb.

Chewing on the stem of my cold pipe, I turned the folder over. I'd seen one of these before, usually wrapped around a ticket to someplace far away. So little Rupert had fled the picture, all right. This was going to be case closed, probably accompanied with a request for a refund. By the looks and taste of this folded cardboard, darling Rupert had undoubtedly gone off-world.

Nothing more of interest showed up, although my seven senses told me that lover-boy had abandoned his quarters and bargain basement cardboard-and-pine furniture at least a week ago. Rose was also right. She was not the only one who had entered this place in search of our missing swain.

Tossing some trace dust in the air, I watched for patterns as it wafted through the room. Too long ago to tell who was here. Vestiges of Elf were obvious, more than one, along with slight signs of other, even stranger creatures. I watched the dust motes drift slowly to the floor, suspecting at least one of those other visitors to these chambers preferred to walk the paths of the night rather than face the bright light of day.

Shrugging, I started down the stairs. The landlady met me just before I slipped through the front door and into the safety of the street. She imposed herself between the exit and me. At least I presumed that this shaggy Goblin in a shapeless gray housedress, long thin hands brandishing a formidable dust mop, had an official connection with the building.

"Fine what yoo was lookin' for?" Wavering red eyes stared through me.

"There was no one home."

"I coulda toll yoo that… Anythin' else yood like to know?" The mop waved above her head like a royal banner flying from a castle tower, just missing the solitary light fixture in its wild gyrations.

You can't trust Goblins. They will do or say almost anything. This little charmer had inhaled at least a gallon of used furniture polish, I'd wager, from the heady aroma of her breath. Her yellow teeth were filed to sharp neat points; probably a real looker in her day, if you liked the sort of girl with orange and green hair and a face that would make a herd of woolly mammoth's stampede. Unfortunately, her day had passed by a century or two and the swaying specter facing me currently did not appear to be the calmest of ladies.

"Well buster, doan' just stan' there! Yoo was lookin' aroun' the kid's apartment, without askin' my permission. Yoo have to pay a penalty for that!"

I didn't like the gleam gathering in her one good eyeball. The other eye wandered off to gaze calmly down the hall in another direction as though half her brain had already forgotten my existence. I outweighed her, and seldom struck a lady, except in self-defense or other serious emergencies. The mop hovered closer to my head. On the other hand, this little lovely had probably been involved in more alley scraps than Bertha's mother's old tomcat, Ed. And probably enjoyed them just as much as Ed did.

I didn't want to slip her a gold coin, and I hadn't converted any of my advance into paper yet. Sliding off my oriental watch, I held it out to her. The thing insisted on running backward most of the time, especially just before important meetings. The band threatened to separate at any moment, but the smiling face sparkled with thirteen genuine imitation moon gems.

"If you can give me some information about Master Rupert and his recent visitors, this priceless instrument is yours."

She focused both eyes on the watch, moistened her lipless mouth and sighed. "An' a right beauty that is too." The shaggy head nodded happily, boney fingers wrapping around the timepiece. "Little Rupert's been gone a week, he has. Without payin' the back rent he owes. I'm holdin' all that fine stuff o' his upstairs as collateral."

And worth at least a whole hour's honest wage too, I'll bet. Give a Goblin a bauble and they'll babble every time. "Why did Rupert leave home in such a hurry?"

"Doan know… might guess."

"Would his speedy departure have anything to do with the visitors he's had since?"

The Goblin stared at me until I thought the blood vessels in her bulging eyes would burst, then she smiled, a jagged crimson gash spreading across her pale green cheeks. "Say big fellah, why doan yoo come on down to my cozy apartment? We can split a bottle or two an' chat about little friend Rupert into the wee smalls… What say?"

She gestured with her mop toward a black hole at the end of the dim hallway that I could only assume led down into the damp depths of the basement. I steeled my backbone to offset the chill setting in; the thought of descending into the cellar to sip shoe polish with this dear creature was more than my nerves could stand. The coins Rose slipped me back at the office were not enough to encourage me to place myself at risk.

"My good woman, I would truly love to tarry and talk with you a while, but unfortunately my carriage and driver are waiting for me outside. What can you tell me about Rupert's visitors, the ones who have come calling since he departed in such a rush?"

Sighing, the Goblin rolled her good eye toward the ceiling, parked the mop handle securely between her knobbly feet and thought for several long minutes while I gauged the distance to the front door, wondering if I could reach the sidewalk before the mop discovered my skull. There may be worse fates than slow-dancing in a darkened room with a tipsy Goblin, but at the moment I could not recall any. At last she focused on a spot a hand-span above my hat.

"Yeah, there were a few folks upstairs there lookin' for little Rupert I guess. Not much sneaks in or out o' this place without me seein'. I have trouble sleepin' nights." She leered at me knowingly, then shrugged and licked those thin lips again when I didn't respond. "There were a pair o' old Elves, real bitch hard cases, they came durin' the day… afternoon, I think."

"Together?"

"Nah, at separate times, maybe two days apart, I forget—"

"Who came at night?"

"Ah… them… there was a right handsome fellah, hard to get a clear look at though, probably a Demon... and a tall thin pale guy…"

"The pale one, a Vampire?"

"Yeah, that would be my guess. Couldn't get a real good look at 'em, it were dark, an' I was entertainin'… I make real good chocolate chip cookies." The Goblin's eyes narrowed, her squeaky voice dropped and took on the tone of a mill wheel in full grind. "An' I have a cache o' some o' the finest drinkin' chocolate in the neighborhood. Maybe yoo'd like to take the chill off, just a quick sip or two… an'…" The good eye winked.

She almost tempted me then, rich hot chocolate, smothered in thick cream—we all have our secret vices. Then I considered the steep price I would have to pay, shuddered, and with a little bow kissed her cold boney hand and bounded out through the front portal of the apartment building before you could whisper Jack B. Nimble, leaving the startled Goblin staring dreamily at her long damp knuckles. Keep the enemy off guard, I always say.

Outside, the rain was in full control of the night. Rivulets ran chattering down the gutters, while above, the overcast sky, glowing faintly from the reflection off the dim city lights, clutched at the rooftops shrouded in black. A steam car lumbered by, hissing white vapors, the wooden, iron-rimmed wheels splashing through the puddles along the curb. I stepped aside, cursing wizards and their ilk as the dirty water soaked my last pair of good shoes. Another newfangled device; give me the silent elegance of a beast and carriage any day.

A rumbling above the low clouds grew louder, rose higher, then faded slowly away; the late shuttle heading up to the Northern American Outgoing Terminal. I hate off-world travel: the lineups, the boredom, the bad food, the stomach upsets. Give me firm ground and… a mug of hot chocolate laced with fine green Irish and thick clotted cream.

I thought about heading home to a warm bed and a book, or

perhaps a quiet evening at the Bear and Gill. Good conversation and a pitcher of beverage always raise my spirits and might help sort out the few facts I had gathered so far. Besides, now I could make a payment on my tab and thus expect my normal welcome warmed a bit.

Decision made, I started up the sidewalk toward my usual haunts. The corner of my eye caught a slight movement in the shadows. Glancing back, the scene was one of a dark and empty street and silent buildings. Probably a stray cat or prowling familiar.

If I had not been feeling quite so smug I might have noticed something following me.

Chapter Three

I don't like to face mornings, never have. Probably why a normal evening saw me sitting in the Bear and Gill until the wee smalls, sipping on a cool dark La Bat's Breath, arguing politics with Baygee, the immigrant Orang bartender, or discussing philosophy with the grumpy owner himself.

The Bear and Gill is a comfortable establishment, just off the High Street, dim and heavily scented with steaming breads and sizzling meats and the heady thick aroma of the finest potions served this side of the Rockies. The brass fire grates, stoked up against the power of the night, cast circles of dancing yellow light across the foot-worn planked floor and stout stone walls. The high-peaked ceiling, as usual by this late evening hour, disappeared away into dark shadows and faint clouds of drifting smokes and vapors. Fred, Grizzly's resident familiar, drooped plump and lifeless, snoring astride a hewn oaken beam above the mumbling throng. As was his want, the Cat had probably lapped up one too many in the kitchen.

Tonight the old watering hole was crowded and Baygee had both dexterous paws full with the hoots and chirping requests from the demanding clientele. Because of the chill damp outside, I burrowed into my usual dark corner nursing a large mug of hot chocolate and Irish instead of a tall pitcher of La Bat's Breath, the rich green liquid from across the water making interesting swirls in the whipped cream as it dissolved. Gazing about the room, I noted there seemed to be a fair number of strangers in the establishment tonight; must be the inclement weather.

Munching on a crisp watercress sandwich, I mulled over what few facts I had to go on. There was the folder for an off-world ticket, a number of creatures looking for the lost lover in addition to myself, and the hurried departure of said swain. I could surmise why an Elf or two might be on Rupert's trail—that would tie in with the distressed Rose and her search for her missing bridegroom—but where did a Demon and a Vampire travelling together come in?

I licked the whip cream off my moustache. Let's see, an unpaid gambling debt might be one reason for the dangerous duo to be on his trail. Depending on Rupert's strength of character, that motive alone could be reason enough to abandon sweet Rose. Perhaps he decided Rose's family would soon see through his genteel charade, then the marriage and bridal money falls through, and little Rupert is left at the mercy of his creditors. I've been known to take a sudden vacation for the same reason.

After my third Irish and chocolate my feelings toward little Rupert mellowed somewhat and I ordered a platter of potato chippings. Smoke from two dozen briar pipes curled to the ceiling leaving a cloud of blue haze circling the beams and Fred's orange twitching tail. The large main fireplace crackled heat and dancing light, the patrons muttered and mumbled in a hundred versions of Lingua Frank.

One of Grizzly's three brown-eyed daughters, Faith, padded by, winked at me and wiped the crumbs away with a deft swipe of her soiled cloth. A nice-enough kid, with a decent sense of humor for a Bruin. The warmth and babble of the place lulled my tired brain and I slouched back into the padded leather seat. I noticed the pair whispering together in a nearby booth.

The fellow with his back to me had a fuzzy appearance that required more than six ounces of Irish to attain. His companion, a thin sallow sort with sunken eyes looming out of a pasty pale face, leaned toward him, wrapped in animated conversation. I caught Faith's attention and motioned her over to the table.

"Cold enough outside tonight to curl the tail on a bronze monkey eh kid. Brings in all sorts to get warm I'll bet. Who are that strange pair over in booth number five? I don't think I've ever seen them in here before."

"Who? Oh them! Me too. This is the first time they've been in, I think. Came in right after you did. Creepy sort, eh Randy."

I smiled. "Don't suppose you could happen to clean up a table nearby them and overhear any of their conversation? As a favor for your old Uncle Randolf."

"On a case, eh Randy? What are they, international jewel thieves, mass murderers, industrial wizardry spies? I thought they looked like they were from out of town as soon as I laid my eyes on them." She patted the top of my tousled head. "Just leave everything to me, Randy C. They'll never know I'm around."

A difficult enough feat for any normal three-hundred-pound Bear, let alone a disrespectful teenager with an overactive imagination.

Faith shoved a slumbering patron to a standing position and steered him in the direction of the front door.

Returning, she began to clean off and polish the now-empty table beside booth number five, lingering as long as possible before returning and slipping onto the bench opposite me.

"Well?"

She grinned. "A right nasty pair, Randy C. I do think they're talking about you, dear Unc. Getting bored waiting for you to do something clever. What excitement did you get into now, pinch some virgin's fortune, get caught in bed with a wizard's wife? Are you closing in on another master criminal?"

The child has a high estimate of my rather mundane profession, as well as my appetite for danger. I decided the time came to stumble home, even if the dawn still lay hidden an hour or two away.

"Good night, dear Faith. Tell your father I have come into some funds and shall reimburse him tomorrow for this evening's fare, as well as catch up on my arrears."

"I'll pass the word along to Pop, Randy C. Just watch your cute ass on the way home, eh?"

Faith tongued my ear and moved on, leaving me quite damp. I don't know what some parents think about raising children, but Grizzly's methods leave something to be seriously reviewed by the Committee of Public Knowledge and Enlightenment. A young lady should definitely not be brought up and educated in an all-night snack and beverage emporium. And she should at the least learn to respect her elders. I dragged my tired carcass onto a pair of flat feet and headed for the exit sign.

The rain had stopped but the early morning air remained chill. I often thought things out clearest while strolling during these purple-gray hours before the sun cleared the buildings. My own little rooms were only blocks away. After the first block I knew I was being followed.

The empty street stretched out ahead, a long mist-clad tunnel of dark shadows and faint gaslight. One or two of the street lamps in the next block had already burned out, leaving gaps of pure blackness not yet touched by the yawning whisper of the dawn. There were at least two of them trailing behind me; I could tell a lot by the muffled footsteps. Which two, and why they were not bothering to hide their approach, I could only guess at.

But if I were a gambler, I'd wager Bertha's next pay check they had some connection with our little lost love, dear Rupert. Passing through the pale ring of light on the sidewalk cast by the next lamp, I paused, slipping my left hand into the glass knuckles in my coat pocket, and casually turned around so my followers would be caught in the glow.

"Good evening gentlemen, taking an early morning stroll? I don't believe I've seen you in the neighborhood before."

The Vampire smiled, fixing his sunken black eyes upon me. The more elderly and taller partner of the pair, he stood motionless, long grasping hands dangling out from the sleeves of his greatcoat, thin fingers twitching. The Demon shimmered silently beside him, the light sparkling on his green scales. Shorter and stockier than his cadaverous companion, he licked his lips.

The bloodsucker spoke first, in a voice that echoed as a cross somewhere between coarse sandpaper and an untuned fiddle. "I believe you know a close acquaintance of ours, a young Master Rupert? We are searching for him."

"Don't know the lad, I'm afraid." I recognized the tall Ghoul's accent though.

The Vampire drifted to the nearer edge of the dim circle of light. The Demon faded toward my right and the deserted street. I loosened the splatter gun with a slight move of my shoulder.

"Oh dear, we just want to speak with the boy. What can you tell us of his whereabouts?"

Not only was this parasite on the ripe side of the last century, but he had a set of bad teeth and nasty breath I could smell from ten feet away.

"Sorry, can't help you there gentlemen, must be off now…"

"Get rough with him then." The Demon, dressed in servant's livery, flickered just at the outer edge of my vision.

"So sorry," whispered the Vampire with another insincere smile.

I shot him square in the chest then, and once more for good measure because he was starting to accelerate toward me. I don't like Vampires; something about them ruins my appetite. I knew the Demon would hang back; when there is dirty work to be done they always let a partner jump in first. "Where Demons fear to Tread" covered several acres of unhallowed ground.

I watched the patch of red spread slowly across the Vampire's chest. He stood frozen in his tracks some six feet from me. The penetrol dye had done its job. A single thirty-eight mm hollow shell usually takes only a split second to work on anything that size, but given the thickness of the greatcoat and the speed of the night creature, the second dose made me feel much better. I gestured with Bessie's smoking muzzle in the general direction of the Demon.

"Now it's my turn to ask the questions, boyo. Why are you two charmers looking for little Rudolph…er…Rupert?"

The Demon's yellow orbs stared at me out of the shadows, reflecting the lamp's glow like some witch's hungry familiar. "Rupert, him is, and our boss wants to chat. About something him stole…" Only a pool of still, black shadows across the empty road indicated where the servant beast had been halted a moment before.

I stared at the Vampire, standing motionless on the sidewalk, glaring but silent and sightless, like a storm-blasted pine. The penetrol would hold him for a few minutes. Time for me to hurry off to my warm bed, add a curse—or three—upon the outer stairs and living room, plus lay a firm hex upon my stout oak door. I put up an extra sprig of fresh mistletoe over the entrance to my bedroom before turning back the quilt, just for good measure.

Out Now!

What's next on your reading list?

Champagne Book Group promises to bring to readers fiction at its finest.

Discover your next
fine read!
http://www.champagnebooks.com/

We are delighted to invite you to receive exclusive rewards. Join our Facebook group for VIP savings, bonus content, early access to new ideas we've cooked up, learn about special events for our readers, and sneak peeks at our fabulous titles.

Join now.
https://www.facebook.com/groups/ChampagneBookClub/

Made in the USA
Middletown, DE
27 June 2022

67748268R10116